A TASTE OF SAKE

Books by Heather Heyford

A Taste of Sake

A Taste of Sauvignon

A Taste of Merlot

A Taste of Chardonnay

A TASTE OF SAKE

The Napa Wine Heiresses

Heather Heyford

LYRICAL SHINE
Kensington Publishing Corp.
www.kensingtonbooks.com

LYRICAL SHINE BOOKS are published by

Kensington Publishing Corp.
119 West 40th Street
New York, NY 10018

All Kensington titles, imprints, and distributed lines are available at special quantity discounts for bulk purchases for sales promotion, premiums, fund-raising, educational, or institutional use.

Special book excerpts or customized printings can also be created to fit specific needs. For details, write or phone the office of the Kensington Sales Manager: Kensington Publishing Corp., 119 West 40th Street, New York, NY 10018. Attn. Sales Department. Phone: 1-800-221-2647.

Lyrical Shine and the L logo are trademarks of Kensington Publishing Corp.

First Electronic Edition: October 2015
eISBN-13: 978-1-60183-362-4
eISBN-10: 1-60183-362-8

First Print Edition: October 2015
ISBN-13: 978-1-60183-366-2
ISBN-10: 1-60183-366-0

Printed in the United States of America

My father would have been pleased to know that his relentless insistence on proper grammar at the supper table paid off. Dad, I dedicate this book to your memory.

ACKNOWLEDGMENTS

My gratitude goes first and foremost to my editor, Esi Sogah, who has the talent of immediately zoning in on the flaws in my manuscripts and tactfully advising me what to do about them. I'm fortunate to have all the professionals at Kensington Publishing behind me. And to Sarah E. Younger, shaking her pom-poms on the sidelines. I recommend that everyone get a literary agent—even if you have no intention of ever writing anything!

To Art, thanks for putting up with an absent-minded artist and for being my biggest supporter.

Thanks to Chef Elizabeth Robison at Harrisburg Area Community College for welcoming me into her pastry-making class . . . especially, for sharing the delicious results. To Susie and Lizzie at Ciao! Bakery—where the breads for Bricco, Harrisburg's only DiRoNA, *Wine Spectator*, and *Santé* magazine award-winning restaurant, are baked, too—for the baguettes lesson. Pastry Chef Cassandra Callahan, I appreciate you giving your permission.

I promised my devoted reader and friend, Kim McLain, I'd put her dog in a book. Kim, give Taylor a pat from me.

Last, to my readers, my sincere thanks for your continuing support. Every book you buy, every positive review, is appreciated more than you could possibly know. Stay in touch at HeatherHeyford.com.

Dear Reader:

If you're already familiar with Chardonnay, Merlot, and Sauvignon St. Pierre, you may think you know The Napa Wine Heiresses. But those stories belonged to Char, Meri, and Savvy. The book you're now reading is Sake's tale to tell. Be prepared to be surprised!

I grew up in a series of U.S. military installations both in the States and abroad, which was kind of like living in a revolving door. Picture a jumble of American kids—already diverse, by definition—being taught the rules of American English by Department of Defense teachers during the day, then butchering French verbs after school in an effort to communicate with the locals. The universal desire of kids to simply have a friend to play with took precedence over our differences.

That was the start of my fascination with other cultures.

Researching *A Taste of Sake*, I stuck a toe into the waters of traditional Asian civilization. I learned about kanji, the adopted Chinese characters that are used in the modern Japanese writing system, for Sake's tattoos . . . and fell in love with the gentle mode of expression of Eastern philosophy—for example, "not seeing is a flower." (For the meaning of that enchanting phrase, read on.) I also learned which birthdays are considered especially lucky.

Just as fun, I got to attend a college pastry-making class and visit behind the scenes of a real bakery to watch how baguettes are made, so that I could write accurately about Sake's love of baking!

Just as you embraced her more privileged sisters, I hope that you will accept Sake in all her awesomeness, the way she begged to be written.

All my best,
Heather Heyford

Prologue

"*The farm boy and the heiress.*" That was the phrase whispered among the out-of-towners during the long wait for the wedding ceremony to begin. And that's exactly what it looked like on the surface as Esteban Morales, deltoids threatening to bust out of his shoulder seams, led Sauvignon St. Pierre, the epitome of elegance with her auburn hair pulled back to accent her oval face, down the grassy aisle toward a pergola dripping with wisteria, where they were to pledge their vows.

The reality was a little more complicated. True, the bride had been born into one of California's wealthiest wine families. But when it came to substance . . . character . . . call it what you will—the immigrant Morales truck farmers had it all over the St. Pierre dynasty. Every Napan here knew it, but not one dared utter it out loud.

When Bill Diamond got the phone call inviting him to the Domaine St. Pierre estate on this late June afternoon, he had no idea what this affair was all about. Figured it was one of Xavier St. Pierre's summer galas . . . a high point of the summer social calendar. As sometime real estate agent to Chardonnay and Merlot St. Pierre, Bill was pleasantly surprised to find he'd made the cut.

Then to find out that this was a wedding—of St. Pierre's oldest daughter, no less? Even cooler. Bill didn't even mind the hour-long delay in the start of the ceremony. How could anyone complain, when St. Pierre kept the wine flowing freely? Bill passed the time making new acquaintances. No such thing as a shy successful Realtor.

St. Pierre knew how to throw a party, that's for sure. Star-studded crowd—*was that a Mondavi over there?*—and live music and flowers everywhere you looked. Butlered hors d'oeuvres passed from the moment the first guest arrived. Beneath the pergola, a wine barrel served as a makeshift altar. Then again, what else would you expect but a blatant tribute to Dionysus? The god of wine had been good to Xavier St. Pierre. *Very* good.

Bill was seated in the second row on the bride's side of the aisle. The lady with the big pink hat in a place of honor in the front row must be a close family friend. St. Pierre's wife was long gone, killed years ago in a car accident. Every time Bill heard the barely disguised envy in the valley folks' muttering that the St. Pierre heiresses had it all, it stirred up a rogue urge to rush to their defense. Those people seemed to conveniently forget the SPs had been raised without a mother's loving hand. Given his own, hands-on mom, Bill Diamond couldn't imagine growing up motherless.

The wedding party now in position, the music stopped. Three members of the string quartet tucked their instruments under their arms and the cellist slid his left hand down the neck of his cello, his bow hand coming to rest on his knee.

The priest waited pointedly for the guests to quiet, then put on a practiced smile and said to the couple, "Please hold hands."

Game time. So why wasn't Savvy mooning back at Esteban during this pivotal moment? Why was she peering out into the distance, her smooth brow pinched with concern?

And where was Xavier St. Pierre—father of the bride?

A faint *chug-chug-chug* entered into Bill's consciousness. Damn leaf blowers. He realized he'd filtered the engine sound out until that moment, to focus on the spectacle in front of him. Some of the ritzier neighborhoods were enacting bans on lawn machines on weekends. Bill was all for that.

But that was no leaf blower. This sound was coming from overhead. That's when he saw the chopper, the size of an acorn, coming up from the south.

No big deal. Any second now, its course would take it veering away.

But as the seconds rat-a-tat-tatted by, the helo, instead of veering away, seemed to be making a beeline for the winery. When even the groom glanced around to look, a polite tittering rippled through the crowd.

The racket grew, eclipsing the sermon so that Bill only caught every other word: "... love ... trust ... marriage a sacred oath ..."

The priest projected his voice for all it was worth. "Esteban

Morales, do you take this woman to be your lawful wedded wife, to have and to hold—"

"I do," Esteban broke in, loud and clear. Following another backward glance, Esteban's right foot turned almost imperceptibly in the direction of the sheltering mansion.

Bill Diamond kept a discreet eye on the sky, while, around him, the murmuring swelled into nervous laughter. A head turned here, a chin pointed there. Something about the chopper's trajectory didn't seem right. It wasn't flying in a straight line, or at a consistent altitude. It swung from side to side, rising and falling at random.

"Sauvignon, do you take this man to be your lawfully wedded hus—"

"I do." From where he sat, Bill read her lips.

The helicopter drew closer and closer, larger and larger, a big-eyed bug. The tension grew. Christ, why was it rocking like that—as if the pilot were drunk at the controls? A chill went up Bill's spine. Was he actually going to bring it down here? *Right here, in the middle of the wedding?*

The tall cypress trees surrounding the estate began to sway and pitch. Bill's muscles bunched in anticipation. Glancing skyward, the priest raised his voice as loud as he could without letting panic seep in: "ThenbythepowervestedinmebytheChurchofAlmightyGodandthe StateofCaliforniaIherebypronouceyoumanandwife. *Run!*"

The groom grabbed his bride's arm and tugged her toward the protection of the house, but Savvy's feet were rooted to the ground, her mouth hanging open in horror. Not wasting a second, Esteban swept her up—piece of cake for a man of his size—and took off at a tear.

"Go!" shouted Bill, hand on the back of the man standing next to him. Women screamed and men yelled under the now-deafening machine-gun drone of the chopper.

"He's coming down!"

"Get out of the way!"

Chairs toppled like bowling pins. The heavy woman seated next to Bill was knocked to the ground. He stopped and yanked her up by the arm.

"He's not going to make it!" somebody cried.

"Get up!" yelled Bill to the woman. *"Come on!"*

The woman panted, wincing in pain. *"I can't! My ankle!"*

He hauled her to her feet. "Put your arm around my waist!" Burdening himself with her was going to be the death of him, but he couldn't just run away and leave her to burn up in the imminent fire-ball.

"It's going to crash!" said the lady in a wobbly voice, some perverted fascination making her look back, slowing them up even more.

Bill jerked her onward toward an outbuilding. "Keep going! Don't look back!"

This was happening.

Are planes always this loud? This was Sake St. Pierre's very first flight. A half hour—the time it took to fly from San Francisco to Napa—was hardly enough time to get acclimated to the intense whop-whop-whop of the helicopter engine, even with her earbuds in and her music cranked up.

And if it was loud to her ears, imagine how it felt to poor Taylor, her little wire-haired terrier on her lap, panting like a mad dog.

Sake bent to coo into Taylor's ear. "It's okay, baby cakes."

Taylor licked Sake on the cheek, then resumed panting, looking around nervously while Sake did her best to continue to console her, stroking her under her chin.

She glanced over at the pilot in his bulky headgear, starched white shirt worn open at the neck, and sport coat. Back when she was little, she hadn't noticed Papa's refined style. Now, as a woman, she saw that her father was one of the most sophisticated men she'd ever seen, even for an old guy. But the fact that she was the blood of Xavier St. Pierre wasn't uppermost in her mind right now. There were too many other firsts she was dealing with this weekend. Getting sprung from a jail cell only to fly off the very same day to a fancy wine country wedding. Meeting her glam sisters face-to-face. Her pulse thrummed with a queasy mixture of anticipation and foreboding. Once they landed, her plan was to hover in the background and observe. Shouldn't be hard. All the attention would be on the bride and groom.

Her father's right hand left the control stick to point out ahead. "Can you see the house?" he yelled over the engine. "She is the white one with the pool."

Now that they were getting close, the imminent wedding of her sister was having a calming effect on Papa, thank God. Or at least distracting him from his earlier disgust with the way he'd found Sake, his youngest daughter, after all these years.

She craned her neck. The whole front of the chopper, even under her feet, was glass. Everywhere she looked, the undulating valley was combed with rows of vines, leading out to the low mountain ranges on either side. "Looks like corrugated cardboard." Papa smiled smugly, the master of his domain.

Sake tugged at the hem of her black mini, admiring its shiny sequins yet again. Papa hadn't even blinked at the price. But at a hundred eighty-nine dollars, it was far and away the most expensive thing she had ever owned. Yet another first.

Suddenly the chopper bucked and swayed, leaving her stomach back *there* somewhere. "Whoa!" Her hands left prints on the glass.

"Hang on," said Papa coolly, as if this flying snow globe were no more dangerous than the roller coaster at Six Flags.

But *this*—this was no amusement park ride.

Bill Diamond managed to get the heaving wedding guest around the back of the shed—not much in the way of shelter, but better than nothing—where she melted onto the grass. Ignoring his own advice, he peered around the corner. Directly above the altar, the helicopter's engine sputtered, died, revived, and sputtered again. It shuddered and swung in midair for a surreal moment, like a yoyo that had lost its momentum.

Tucking back, Bill crouched and covered his head with his arms, steeling himself for the impact.

There was a dull thud, a sharp crack. The earth shuddered beneath his feet. Next to him, the woman whimpered. And then there was only the sound of the cypress branches, swooshing softly back into place.

Bill peeked around the shed. The lawn was in a shambles. Chairs upended, a portion of the pergola sagging all the way to the ground, floral arrangements broken apart and scattered. In the middle of it all sat the helicopter, leaning sharply to the right.

The rotors were still. There was no smoke, no fire. No twisted metal.

From somewhere in the distance came a faint sob. From somewhere else, a masculine voice intoned, "Call 911!"

Gradually, the surroundings came back to life. Guests crept tentatively out of the far corners of the winery grounds and buildings, brushing themselves off, retrieving lost hats and heels. Esteban Morales sprinted from the mansion to the crash site, followed by his new wife, who ignored his shouted pleas to stay back.

Merlot dashed out of the building housing the blending lab, into the arms of her relieved boyfriend.

"You okay?" Bill asked the trembling woman next to him. At her nod, he jogged toward the wreckage to see if he could be of assistance.

The chopper's right landing skid lay some distance away, snapped off in the impact, which explained why the cabin was leaning so hard. But wait—there was movement behind the reflective windscreen. The pilot's door cracked open. Out on Dry Creek Road, a siren wailed. And then, out of the chopper climbed Xavier St. Pierre. He ducked beneath the blades and zipped around the front of the chopper.

"Bon après-midi!" he called, waving to Bill and the stunned semicircle of people fast accumulating, as if wrecking a small aircraft in the midst of his daughter's wedding were no big deal.

While Bill watched, St. Pierre gave his passenger's door a yank. The bottom edge of it scraped into the turf, building up a dam of dirt. He yanked again, using both hands this time, but it wouldn't budge.

"C'mon." Bill gestured toward the onlookers. "Give him a hand." He and a couple of the other, younger men managed to push the chopper upright, holding it there until Xavier got the door open.

A female passenger fell face first onto the lawn and landed spread eagle, followed by a graffiti-covered backpack.

"She's clear," called Bill. Carefully, the men set the chopper back down.

The bride and her sisters ventured closer to the victim. Everyone knew St. Pierre was a player. Was this his latest fling? The girl just lay there, unmoving.

Bill knelt next to her, then turned to the rubberneckers. "Is there a doctor here? A nurse?" Now would be a good time for one to step up. But all he saw was a wall of St. Pierre's cronies—vintners, politicians, entertainers—staring back at him. None of them were any better equipped than a Realtor when it came to caring for a helicopter crash victim.

His gaze swung back to the person on the ground.

"Don't touch her," yelled a woman on the fringe, cell phone glued to her ear. "There's an ambulance on its way."

Gently, Bill lifted the girl's hair from her face. "Are you okay?"

Adding to the bizarre scene, a terrier-like object flew out of the helicopter and scrabbled up next to the girl. He bared his teeth and growled, revealing a prominent underbite.

Bill held out the back of his hand for the dog to sniff. "Easy, boy." The dog whined, licked his chops, and panted.

"Hang tight. Help's on the way."

Unceremoniously, St. Pierre reached down between Bill and the passenger and pulled her up by the hand. "She is not hurt."

Once she was on her feet, Bill saw that despite being petite, "she" was no girl. No mistaking that. His eyes traveled the length of her body. Her silhouette went in and out, not straight up and down. The almond-shaped eyes beneath thick dark brows appeared shaken, but she wasn't bleeding and everything looked like it worked. The only visible evidence of her ordeal was a grass stain on her cheek and the yellow rose petals stuck to her dress—if you could call a piece of material that barely covered her butt a dress.

The wiry dog ran a nervous circle around her. St. Pierre slung an arm across her shoulders, then looked up. "Sauvignon? Chardonnay? Merlot?"

Savvy and her sisters gathered around, dumbstruck. Behind them, all was silent as the air before a storm, the only thing stirring the gentle billowing of the bridesmaids' full skirts in a summer breeze that had picked up from out of nowhere. Everyone wanted to be able to say later that they heard the first words out of Xavier St. Pierre's mouth after he crash-landed smack into his eldest daughter's wedding.

"I present to you your half sister, Sake."

Chapter 1

You can't hide money. Sake had heard that often enough. Now she saw the truth of it with her very own eyes. Her cheeks burned as the reverse also became crystal clear: poverty was just as obvious as wealth. Standing before those cohorts of her Napa family, she knew beyond a shadow of a doubt that everyone in the elaborate hats and tailored suits could see right through her too-tight, too-short dress, picked out in a rush that very morning—the dress she'd felt like a million bucks in five minutes ago, aka happier times. The same dress that would have blown away everyone down in the Mission District looked unspeakably vulgar here, at this vast, swanky country club called Napa. Sake felt like everyone could see right through it to Rico's cheap apartment, could smell the stale cooking oil in the hall, hear the metallic ring of footsteps echoing through the grayish stairwell, feel the flimsy hand of the everyday thrift-shop clothes she kept in her old moving box in Rico's bedroom.

The pack encircled Sake like a gang of high-class thugs, penning her in, the downed helicopter at her back preventing her escape. Peering down their noses at her with an air of expectation that paralyzed her.

All her life, Sake had dreamed of someday meeting her upper-crust half sisters, but not like this. Not as the center of attention. Agreeing to let her father bring her here had been a colossal mistake, and not just because he'd managed to crash the damn chopper.

She froze with the terrible burden of the stares of the whole of Napa Valley, willing—no, *demanding*—that she say something, do something. *Speak, so we can hear your wrong-side-of-the-tracks inflection. Say something, anything, so that we can repeat it and post it and tweet it, to prove we were here.* She could play those fools down in the Mission any day, but she couldn't play these people. This was another world.

Shame mingled with stage fright as Sake realized she had nothing to give them, even if she wanted to, which she sure as hell didn't, and she resented their judge-y looks, real or imagined. All she had to her name were her diamond earrings and a fierce sense of self-preservation, and she wasn't giving that up for anyone or anything. Call it swagger— a dogged determination not to be torn down, drowned in the undertow of life. That animal instinct was what Sake ran on, what kept her going. It was the air in her lungs, the gas in her tank. Her very life depended on keeping it topped off. Here, before these people, she could feel it being siphoned out of her.

"How do you do."

Sake's shell-shocked gaze was torn from the sea of nameless faces toward a hand extended toward her. She followed the slender arm back to a soft-eyed, auburn-haired woman with a string of pearls around her neck. The bride. Her own sister, Sauvignon. She looked every bit as classy as her name: Elegant. Serene. Privileged.

Everything Sake wasn't.

A bolt of bile Sake never felt coming jetted up her esophagus and spewed from her mouth, right onto the bride's exquisite white gown.

"Ah!" Sauvignon gasped, looking down at her dress, disgust distorting her pretty features.

The crowd of onlookers gasped, hands flying to their mouths.

Sake's head pounded, her knees went weak. *So much for making a good first impression.*

The girl's eyes rolled back in her head and her legs buckled. Bill caught her under her arms just in time, her head lolling back onto his chest.

"I'm taking her to Queen of the Valley," he announced.

"She is fine," said her father. One of his eyes was beginning to swell up.

"She needs to be seen, and so do you. C'mon. I'll take you both."

"And leave the wedding of my oldest daughter?"

Behind them, a voice said, "Wait for the ambulance."

Why wait, when his car was right here? Besides, his heart ached for the young woman. Already traumatized by the wreck, she must be humiliated beyond words at having blown her cookies right in front of everybody. Who wouldn't be? He took off his suit jacket and draped it around her shoulders, wrapped a supportive arm around her waist, and pushed their way through the ogling crowd toward the winery parking lot.

"You're going to be fine," he told her.

"Taylor . . ." she murmured, looking back. "My dog . . ."

"He's right behind us, see? We'll get you taken care of."

"She," Sake corrected him. "She's a girl."

With her terrier on her lap, they drove off the property as a fire truck, siren wailing, drove onto it. Bill reached behind him for the box of tissues he kept in the back seat to catch the drips from his clients' to-go cups of coffee. He took pride in keeping his vehicle spotless.

Sake pulled out a tissue and wiped her face. "Thanks for getting me out of there."

"Hey, no problem. Aren't you going to put on your seat belt?"

She tucked the used tissue into the change compartment in his car door and drew the belt across her body. "There. Happy?"

Bill nodded curtly. He was kind of a stickler for doing things right. In his business, it served him well.

With dismay, she studied the severed wire of her earbuds, then shoved the useless contraption into her bag.

"Got any tunes in this hooptie?"

"'Scuse me?"

"The radio?"

He selected the right screen. "Pick whatever you like."

She scrolled through, stopping at a pop song.

"Take me to the nearest bus station."

He gave her a perplexed look. "Where do you think you're going?"

"Back where I belong. I took off work for the wedding, but I got a three a.m. shift to get back to Monday morning. Besides, I got pay waiting for me. Yesterday was payday, and I missed it."

Bill snorted. "I'm not taking you to the bus station." Clearly, the girl was in shock.

"I'm not going to the hospital."

"Like heck you're not. Dude, you were just in a plane crash."

"Did you just call me dude? Is that still a thing up here?"

"It is for me." Secretly, a little needle of concern poked him.

When had "dude" gone out of style? That's what came of all work and no play. One day you woke up and you were twenty-nine years old and teenagers were making fun of the way you talked.

"Whatever, you're not taking me to no hospital."

They came upon a blue sign that said QUEEN OF THE VALLEY with an arrow pointing left. Bill turned.

She gripped the edge of her seat. "I can't."

"What, are you afraid of hospitals or something?"

"I got no insurance. And I'm not leaving Taylor."

Bill sniffed. "You were just in a plane crash, for Crissakes! You need medical attention. You can worry about the insurance later. And sorry if it's too personal, but aren't you a daughter of Xavier St. Pierre? Queen of the Valley has a whole wing named after him. The dog can stay in my car. It's cooling off outside, I'll keep the windows cracked. Besides, I saw you holding your head like it hurt."

"My head is fine. I just didn't want to go to that—thing."

Bill frowned. "That *thing* is your sister's wedding."

"You're a genius," she said flatly, turning her head away from him toward the passenger-side window and the undulating landscape.

Obviously she had suffered some sort of brain damage. Who in their right mind would turn down such a fabulous invitation? Even without the crash, everyone would be talking about it tomorrow. It would be plastered all over the media.

"You don't get along with your sisters?"

"I don't even *know* my sisters."

What to say to that? Bill had heard Xavier presenting Sake to his three daughters by Lily D'Amboise, but the significance of it had been lost in the pressing need to get Sake medical help.

"Do you?" asked Sake, less snarky now. She still pretended to scrutinize the scenery while stroking her panting dog.

"Know them? Yeah. Kind of. Well enough to get invited to the wedding."

"Tell me what you know."

Behind the wheel, Bill cocked his head and whistled. Where to start? "There's so much to tell. How 'bout you make it easier by telling me what you know, first?"

Tough again all of a sudden, Sake tsked and rolled her eyes. "Okay, I'll play. Chardonnay's the middle one, the one with blond hair. She started some orphanage or something—"

"Foundation for immigrant kids. Not an orphanage," he corrected her.

"Foundation, orphanage, who cares? Anyway. She's held up like some holier-than-thou Girl Scout philanthropist. Which, how hard can it be when all you have to do with your life is spend your old man's money?"

"She has a policy against using her papa's money."

Sake flashed him a look of genuine surprise.

Bill should know. He'd recently said yes to Char's request that he sit on the board of directors for Chardonnay's Children. He had always been a sucker for the underdog.

"But go on."

Again, Sake recovered her bravado. "Then Merlot's the youngest one who's got herself a line of jewelry you can only get at Harrington's."

"Right."

This girl had a chip like a railroad tie on her shoulder.

"And then there's the lovely bride . . . the hot-shot lawyer." Sake picked a crumpled rose petal off her dress and tossed it on the floor of his car.

In spite of himself, the movement of Sake's hand drew Bill's eyes to her endless expanse of leg. Her black dress rode up so high you could see the little hollow between her thighs where they tapered inward toward her crotch. Bill shifted slightly in his seat.

"Probably going to file against me for damages for that designer gown soon as she gets back from the honeymoon."

"Now you know that's not going to happen."

"I only hope she can scrounge up something else to change into for the reception."

Bill let that slide.

"What about him?"

"Papa?"

"Your father."

"Comes in and out of my life like I'm some kinda train station."

"Sorry." *That must hurt.* Bill's dad was as reliable as clockwork.

"Your turn."

"Ahem. Okay. Xavier St. Pierre. Let's see. Born here in Napa, educated in the best schools in Paris, which explains the accent. Parlayed his family wine business into one of the most successful labels in the world. Married a movie star—" *Whoops*. Bill checked Sake's face for signs of having offended her, but her expression was blank. Oh well. Facts were facts. "Had the three daughters with her. Wife died, girls were sent to boarding schools, then college. Never married again."

Not to say he'd been lonely all these years.

"That much I coulda found on Wikipedia," quipped Sake drily.

Something big was eating Sake, that's for sure. Something deep. She was as defensive as a car alarm with an electrical short, going off at the slightest provocation, and fascinating as hell, materializing out of thin air, with those kanji tattoos running in vertical tracks down her arms. He wondered what they signified.

In contrast, Bill Diamond was just your average, run-of-the-mill guy, nothing special. He was the opposite of fascinating. He knew it; everyone did. But then, you didn't want to entrust your commercial property, likely your most valuable possession, with fascinating. You wanted safe. You wanted steady. You wanted trustworthy.

Sake closed her eyes and sank back into her hospital pillow, trying not to obsess about Taylor. She'd sent Bill Diamond on his way back to the wedding with a Styrofoam cup of water and the baggie holding a weekend's worth of dog chow from her backpack, after making him swear to take good care of her dog.

She tried to force her tense muscles, always ready for fight or flight, to relax. Being coddled—first by Bill Diamond, who had taken the initiative to drive her here and even filled out the admissions paperwork for her, then by the matronly nurse who had fluffed her pillow and asked her if she wanted something for the bump the doctor had found on her head where she'd hit the windscreen in the hard landing—confused her. Sake wasn't used to being pampered.

Just as the sky outside her hospital room window faded to black and the pill Florence Nightingale had given her was taking effect, she heard an ominously cheerful clamor out in the hallway. Her eyes flew open to the rustle of golden-yellow skirts swooshing through the door.

"Sake?" The bride had changed into a knee-length party dress, only slightly less fancy than her wedding gown.

As Sauvignon and her sisters glided forward, surrounding the bed, Sake braced her hands at her sides and backed deeper into her pillow.

"Are you okay?" asked Merlot from where she stood at Sake's feet, stacks of bracelets jingling on her arms.

"We came to check on you," said the blonde at Sake's left. Chardonnay was even more terrifyingly beautiful in person than in her pictures. But then, so was the view of the Pacific down the Peninsula, but once it lured you in, its cold water stung you like a Taser. And what about Rico, with his Roman nose, his rakish gait, his natural-born trout pout? Rico, who'd got off scot-free while he watched Sake get cuffed and stuffed into the back seat of the cruiser fewer than thirty-six hours ago? He was beautiful, too.

"I'm fine."

Chardonnay lowered herself gracefully onto the foot of the mattress, and Sake flinched involuntarily, at the same time unable to tear her eyes off her golden-haired sister.

Sauvignon sat down on the other side. "Are you sure? What did the doctors say?"

Cornered by her achingly cool sisters, Sake's heart picked up speed. "I said I'm *fine*," she repeated, pulling the institutional blanket up to her chin.

Her sisters exchanged innocent-looking expressions, but they didn't fool her.

"You came, you saw. How many times can I say it?"

Now all three frowned down at her. As if they truly didn't get why she should reject them, after they'd so soundly rejected *her* all these years.

Sauvignon stood then. "It's okay. You've had quite a shock. You're tired."

Blondie followed her lead. "We'll let you rest now. We just wanted to see for ourselves that you were all right, let you know we were thinking about you."

With a flutter of dainty waves from manicured fingertips they bid her good night, and then they were gone, three gilded birds flitting away to their opulent nest.

When she heard the doors slide closed down the hall and she knew it was safe, Sake got up and padded to the bathroom mirror.

Talk about stuffing a ten-pound day into a five-pound bag. The faded hospital gown did nothing for her sallow skin tone. Her undereyes were smeared with mascara, her hair hung in a tangle over her shoulders. If anyone back at the wedding reception started throwing shade—and they would—the truth was that St. Pierre's Japanese-American bastard was nothing like his other angelic offspring. She was a freakin' train wreck.

Papa—weird calling a man she barely knew anymore by that endearment, but the name had stuck from back in her childhood, when she'd seen him fairly regularly—discovered just how low Sake had sunk the day before the wedding, when he'd been contacted by his lawyer. He was just waiting until after the festivities were over to decide what should be done with her.

Chapter 2

Sunday morning, Bill Diamond thought he heard a whine. He opened one eye to see a long pink tongue hanging out of a shaggy white face. He thought of his fawn-colored pug, his constant companion back when he was a kid. Mollie was her name. Good old Mol—

Taylor barked.

"You need to go out, girl?"

Bill stretched, pulled on a pair of sweatpants, and found a length of twine to tie onto Taylor's collar. He shuddered at the fur that would fly if he had to tell the most tempestuous daughter of Xavier St. Pierre that he'd lost her dog. But more than dreading Sake's ire, he had a sneaking suspicion that Taylor was Sake's most prized possession. He didn't want to be responsible for piling another disappointment on top of what he suspected was already a sky-high mound.

While he and Taylor circled the block, his phone rang.

Without preamble, Sake said, "I'm free to go."

"You've been discharged? That's great. Er, are you calling because you need a ride, or do you want me to deliver Taylor to you at your father's house later today?"

"She's okay?" Sake's anxiety was palpable through the phone.

"Why wouldn't she be?" he assured her, bending down to pat Taylor. "We're going for a walk as we speak, aren't we, girl?"

Taylor wriggled her butt and arched toward Bill, licking her chops.

"Then, yeah, you can come get me?"

"We'll see you in three shakes."

"What's up with your mistress?" Bill asked Taylor after he hung up. He ruffled the dog's fur, enduring her wet kisses.

The wiry face looked up at him and barked again.

* * *

Taylor pawed frantically at Bill's car window when she caught sight of Sake walking across the macadam of the hospital lot toward her.

"Here I am," cooed Sake, jogging the last few yards to the car. The dog flew into her arms as soon as she opened the door. "Here's Mama."

Bill watched Sake bury her face in Taylor's fur as he got in. "She's been fed, watered, and walked."

Sake didn't bother to thank him.

"Does your family know you're on your way?"

Sake tucked Taylor into the crook of her arm. "I'm not going to their place. I'm going back to the city."

"San Francisco?"

"*Word.* Just take me to the bus station. I'll figure it out from there."

For a moment Bill was speechless.

"Have you spoken to any of them since the crash?"

"My sisters came to see me last night."

"That's cool. Did you have a good visit?"

"Peachy. Now, just get me out of here. The sooner, the better." She lowered her plastic, leopard-printed shades—all the better to shut him out—and sat there in his car, spectacularly impassive.

Bill pulled up to the hospital lot's exit. "Did you discuss your plans with them? Do you even know the bus schedule?" he asked, buying time as he considered his options, his route.

"I said I'll figure it out."

Bill took a right instead of the left that led into downtown, hoping his passenger wouldn't be any the wiser.

"So, are you out of school?" Maybe he could distract her with conversation.

She granted him a nod.

"What do you do in San Francisco?"

"I work in a bakery."

"Sweet. What kind of bakery? A shop or a restaurant?"

"Place called Bunz." She smiled fleetingly, and he was struck by how approachable she looked when she dropped that defensive mask.

"You go to college for that?"

She shook her head. "Learning on the job."

"I remember what it was like, trying to get my footing when I first got my real estate license. Took me a while to earn people's trust, build up my reputation."

"That what all that stuff's for?"

His cup holders held pens and multicolored Post-it notes, the center compartment neatly coiled chargers and extra business cards and other odds and ends. Every office supply he'd ever need was there, at the ready.

"My car's my office. I spend more time here than behind my desk, what with walk-throughs, site inspections, and showings.

"I started out selling houses a few years ago, till I found out I had a thing for commercial. Nothing outrageous... I like small towns, small business people. Learning how their operations work, putting them in the best possible locations."

"Did you have to go to school for that?"

"Real estate courses, then a humdinger of a test. Plus, continuing ed every year. I'm working toward an advanced designation." A puff of pride swelled in Bill, surprising him. Why should he care what this little waif thought of him?

He turned onto an elm-lined street.

"This doesn't look like where no bus station would be," said Sake.

"It's not. I just want to drive by a certain property. It'll only take a minute."

She gave him a leery look, but he was already slowing to a crawl so he could check out the house coming up on the right.

There it was, the restored 1935 cottage. He knew the data sheet by heart: *three bedrooms, two baths, hardwood floors throughout, detached garage and garden.* Bill strained to get yet another look through the windshield at the property.

"Someone you know?" asked Sake.

"Naw. Just checking to see if it's still on the market. Every time I'm in the area, it calls to me. I can't keep from driving by." Now that they were past it, he sped up again, returning his attention to the road.

His phone rang, and through the speaker on his hands-free system he recognized the voice of Russ Cross, a potential client whose listing he'd been trying to get for weeks.

Today was Sunday. Not Bill's Sabbath, but still. Did people think he was available to them twenty-four-seven? In a word, *yes.* It was part and parcel of being a Realtor. His mind shifted immediately into work mode. "Got your comps right here, Russ." Bill wanted to do business with Russ Cross, *bad.* Getting a signed listing on his strip mall would be a giant leap forward for his career.

"Hold on." He turned to scope out the back seat. "They're in my briefcase." He could see it where he'd stuck it to keep it safe from the dog, on the ledge close to the rear window.

"Here," he said to Sake. "Take the wheel a sec." Without thinking, he let go, twisting his whole body back through the seats.

But Sake just sat there like she suddenly didn't understand English.

"Take it. Take the wheel!" he said, still turned around. Was that too much to ask, after all he'd done for her?

"I-I can't."

Bill whipped around just in time to see her clutching her dog to her breast, bracing herself, eyes glued straight ahead to the curb now rushing up to meet them at thirty-five miles per hour.

"What the—?" He grabbed the wheel just in time.

"Got 'em," he said into the phone, giving Sake the side eye between righting the car and yanking his bulky briefcase through the gap in the front seats.

He pulled over to the curb, forcing calm into his voice. He couldn't let Russ Cross guess that while he advised him on what price his property should be marketed at, he'd seen his whole life flash before his eyes.

When he hung up five minutes later, he glowered at Sake. "What's wrong with you? Did you grow up around power lines?"

She sat there, quietly obstinate, not meeting his eyes.

"Do you freaking *enjoy* drama?" Bill gestured wildly with his arms. "I practically live out of my car. This is my traveling office, and you almost put me out of commission!"

"I don't drive," she said, eyes still averted.

"You mean you don't have your license?"

"I never learned, okay?" she shot back in self-defense.

A Californian who doesn't know how to drive?

Not driving didn't make you a bad person. Just kind of . . . unusual. How'd she ever get anywhere?

Bill pulled away from the curb, mentally shaking his head. He'd be smart to wash his hands of her, once he delivered her to the winery. Those arcane tats? That pent-up resentment? Sake St. Pierre was nothing like her sophisticated sisters. She was unpredictable. A wild card.

The terrain hugging Highway 29 grew more and more rugged, until there was nothing but the raised seams of vines rolling endlessly out from both sides of the road.

"Wait. I recognize this," she scowled. "You're taking me back to *them*, aren't you?"

"You just got out of the hospital with a head injury. Your family would never forgive me if I took you to the bus station."

She turned on him. "You lied to me! What business is it of yours what I do, where I go?"

"It's not. But like I said, I don't think your family would want you going off on your own yet, without even saying good-bye."

Plus, Bill didn't want the responsibility of explaining to St. Pierre that his injured daughter was alone on a Greyhound hurtling southward . . . even if Xavier hadn't stepped up to the bat to take her to the hospital himself yesterday. Depositing Sake safely in her father's hands was the right thing to do. And Bill Diamond always did the right thing. The expected thing.

Bill heard the force of her angry exhalation as he pulled in at the sign that said DOMAINE ST. PIERRE, saw her chest rising and falling from his peripheral vision. But as the mansion loomed into view, Sake looked more deer-in-the-headlights than mad. Maybe he'd just usher her into the house, as a buffer. The St. Pierres could be pretty intimidating. Despite all her tough talk, she looked so young, so vulnerable.

And there was no denying it, she'd inherited the SP gene for looks.

Chapter 3

That shady-ass Bill Diamond! Tricking her like that—letting on he was taking her to the bus station and then delivering her on a silver platter to the enemy.

Once Sake had made up her mind she wasn't staying in Napa, she quit worrying about Papa judging her for the way he'd found her the day before the wedding. Back at booking and release, there'd been no time for big decisions. He'd given her a quick ass-chewing for getting arrested and her "abominable" lifestyle, waited in his big black Range Rover outside Rico's place for her to grab her toothbrush and a clean set of underwear and Taylor, and instructed her to pick out something presentable to wear to her sister's wedding at a shop on the way to the airport. She was surprised he hadn't asked for his card back yet. Folks didn't go around just handing out their credit cards. At least, no one she knew did.

But once she'd hit the ground, seen the epic snobbery up here— the clothes! the houses!—she had no intention of hanging around. She knew how to watch out for herself on the dicey Mission streets. But up here, where getting stabbed in the back was only a metaphor for crushed feelings, she was lost.

Bill Diamond drove slowly up the white gravel drive, like some tour guide trying to give her her dollars' worth. But he was only making things worse. Sake had seen the property from the air and had a brief glimpse of the back of it following the crash, but now the magnitude of the estate as seen from its main entrance enveloped her, making her feel even smaller and more insignificant. Domaine St. Pierre wasn't just a house; it was like some grand Russian Hill hotel. A tower of water tumbled down from a fountain that formed a broad traffic circle. On the other side of that rose the white stucco mansion with the red tile roof, three tall arches in the center, flanked on either side by three shorter ones. The lawns surrounding the house were smooth as carpet. Here and there, gardeners bent over beds of yellow and red flowers.

The closer she got to the house, the smaller Sake felt. "I ain't about this bougie life. Like Disney Land for rich people."

Without commenting, Bill pulled the car to a stop before a twin set of curving stairs that flanked the front doors.

Grabbing her backpack and her nerve, Sake stepped out of the car, followed by Taylor. While her head was tipped backward to gaze up at the mansion, she heard Bill's door open and close.

"You all in this together?" she asked suspiciously as he came around to her. "They know we're coming?"

"No."

"Then how come—?"

"I thought I'd walk you in." When he offered her his elbow, her instinct was to scoff, but truth was, she could use something solid to hold on to. She took it and together they climbed the stairs to a pair of carved wooden doors with polished brass knobs.

"This is it, your family seat." Bill dropped his arm and eyed her expectantly.

She was at a loss as to what to do. Even if it was her "family seat," she didn't have the right to enter without knocking, did she?

At her hesitancy, he rang the bell for them both.

A uniformed housekeeper opened the door.

"May I help you?"

"Is Mr. St. Pierre at home?"

"May I tell him who is calling?"

"Bill Diamond."

"Good morning, Mr. Diamond." Next, her gaze travelled up and down Sake. "And . . . ?"

Sake was back in her real clothes today, her favorite Sal Val dress with the high-low hemline that showed off her decent knees, suede booties and her trademark leopard sunners with the exaggerated kitten ears covering her eyebrows.

"His thug child," she snapped.

The woman lifted a brow, then caught sight of Taylor and twitched her nose, as if in her opinion, the dog needed a good bath. Which, granted, she did.

"I forgot, the dog," said Bill, stepping up yet again for Sake.

"Oh la la," said the woman doubtfully. "Madame Jeanne, she does not like the dogs. . . ."

Madame Jeanne?

"It is not my place to say," the woman concluded with a shrug. She stepped back to let all three of them in, then disappeared to find Papa.

"Why don't you put her in my car?" Bill suggested. "Just until we find out what's what?"

It didn't feel right, shutting Taylor away in the car, but Sake felt relieved that someone else was making the decision, now that her world had just blown up.

"Come on," she called to Taylor.

When Sake returned to the foyer, Bill asked out the side of his mouth, "Why'd you call yourself his 'thug child'?"

"That's who I am, isn't it? That's what they all think."

"You're not doing yourself any favors, you know . . . being so contentious."

"Sure," she spat, "lemme take advice on getting along from someone who just kidnapped me into coming out here."

Bill snorted. "How come a girl who looks like you, who has this lovely, lilting voice that's clear as a bell, talks like a . . . a gangster or something?"

She gave him a righteous look. "Now you get it. Maybe that's 'cause what you see on the outside ain't what I look like on the inside."

"Ah, hello, hello." Xavier St. Pierre glided into the foyer on an air of expensive cologne and tobacco. Papa kissed Sake's cheeks, then subjected Bill to the same ritual.

"Thank you for bringing my daughter safely home." He turned to his daughter. *"Ça va?* You have the clean check of health?"

Sake drew a blank.

Bill coughed into his hand. "I think he means, 'bill of health.'"

"I'm good," she said. Hella better than he was, from the looks of that shiner.

"Bien." He turned back to Bill. "I will not forget your kindness. But now, if you will excuse us, my daughter and I have important matters to discuss."

"No problem, sir. I'm off to my mother's for Sunday brunch, anyway . . ."

"Of course you are," Sake muttered, covering up a stab of envy.
"... and then to hit some balls at the driving range." He held up a
hand in farewell. "I'll see myself out."

"Wait! What about Taylor?"

Bill whirled back around.

"My dog."

Papa asked, "Where is he?"

"She's a girl, and she's out in Bill's car."

"Your housekeeper seemed a little hesitant to let Taylor in," explained Bill.

"That is because, sadly, Madame Jeanne is afraid of the dogs. An
unfortunate incident when she was a child." He added, "Madame
Jeanne is my cook. More than that, she is indispensable to the management of the house."

Sake's eyes flickered to Bill's. Hoping he'd help, at the same time
hating her reliance on him—on anyone. After all, if you couldn't trust
your own mother, who could you trust? But she didn't have many options up here, where she felt like an outlander.

"Look, why don't I take him with me? Mom won't mind."

"But—"

"That is a marvelous suggestion," said Papa. "Until we think of
something better."

Like reverse origami, all the possible bad outcomes started un-
folding in Sake's head. What if she couldn't trust Bill Diamond?
What if he forgot to let Taylor out to go to the bathroom and she had
an accident and he got mad, or even got rid of her ... dumped her at
the pound or something? Maybe Papa and Bill were part of the same
crew. . . . Maybe this Madame Jeanne wasn't really afraid of dogs.
This could be part of a bigger a plan. Bill had already played her into
thinking he was taking her to the bus station, then brought her here.
Fool me once, shame on you . . .

Sake had to admit, though, Bill Diamond had had her back at the
hospital. And Taylor had survived the night. She had Bill's number,
knew where he lived. If he tried to pull something, she'd track him
down. Besides, her back was against the wall.

Bill said, "No problem. I like having a dog around. I'll stop and
get some more of her brand of dog chow on my way to brunch, then
call you tonight and we'll go from there."

Chapter 4

Papa led Sake, still craning her neck after Bill, out of the foyer. Without Taylor scampering along beside her, she felt like she was missing a limb. Now, inexplicably, she realized that she didn't want to lose sight of Bill Diamond, either.

Sake had always wondered what her father's house looked like inside, and now, here she was. She peered up at the three magnificent arches, then circled the panoramic view of wall niches with sculptures and gold-framed paintings, narrowing her gaze down to a huge bowl of fresh-cut roses on a brass and glass table. The closest thing she had to compare it with was the lobby of the Palace Hotel, where Haha had once pulled her to escape a sudden downpour. Haha hadn't been intimidated by the porter looking down his nose at them. But then again, Sake's mom thrived on the new, the untried. She used men as casually as Sake chewed gum, discarding them as soon as they lost their flavor.

Come to think of it, regular change was the most consistent thing about Sake's early life.

Papa motioned for her to take a seat. "So," he said, settling into a corner of the plush couch across from her chair, crossing his legs. He had the kind of sharp-nosed face that always seemed to be trying to uncover what you'd done wrong. "I see you still have your earrings."

Without thinking, Sake's hand reached up to reassure herself that yes, they were still there. Since Papa had given them to her when she'd turned sixteen, they'd rarely been out of her ears.

"Now. Where were we?"

Sake had been dreading this. But that was the deal she'd made with Papa last Friday: his lawyer would make her PC 240 simple assault beef go away in return for Sake agreeing to fly up to her sister's wedding on the spur of the moment. Aside from having to call off work, it had seemed like a bargain at the time. Now the helicopter was busted and Bill Diamond had refused to take her to the bus station. Her only hope at getting out of here and back to the city was to hear Papa out.

"*Ma chérie*, I must tell you again how relieved I am to be finding you. My lawyer has searched high and low for you and your mother. Every time he got a lead, you disappeared again. Why hasn't one of you called me? After all these years, I feared there was only one possibility: your mother wished not to be found, and she had somehow convinced you to go into hiding, too."

"Called you? With what?" She showed him the cheap cell phone with the cracked screen she kept close by in case Rico was trying to get in touch. "I just got this burner last year."

Papa looked up at her through lowered lids. "Don't be ridiculous. You could have contacted me any number of ways. Every library has free public computers . . . the traditional way, with a stamp and a letter . . ."

"I could say the same thing to you!"

"Didn't you hear what I said? How can I contact you when your mother lives her life *comme un gitan*—like a—" he twirled an elegant hand while, impatiently, his eyes searched the ceiling for the right translation. "A *gypsy*, bartering herself for—" he bit his tongue and with visible effort, pressed his lips together.

The insult directed against Haha shot through Sake like a poisoned arrow, swelling the bitterness already lodged in her heart till it felt like her chest would explode.

Her father was every bit the bastard Haha had accused him of being. Sake'd be damned if she'd let Haha take the blame for their rift.

A bitter staring contest ensued. Papa thought he had a spine of steel? She was no slouch, herself—thanks to having to struggle for everything she'd ever got.

Finally he cleared his throat. "Very well. Moving on. On Friday you had begun to tell me what it is you have been doing with your life."

Ha. Round one: Sake. She brushed away the hint of confusion that brought with it. *If he hated her so much, why'd he cave so fast?*

"I already told you, I work at a bakery."

"How long have you been working at this bakery?"

"About nine months."

"And you claim that you do not know where Emma Grace is? Where she has been?"

She wished she did know. Thoughts of Haha's manic obsession with new places, new men, and new highs haunted Sake's thoughts and churned her stomach. And yet, she couldn't let go of her childish loyalty. Haha had brought her up pretty good until she'd been old enough to fend for herself. Anyway, show her the perfect mother. "I told you, I haven't seen her since my birthday, last September."

"You at least received my gift when you finished high school?"

Sake's cheeks burned.

Papa's eyes bored a hole through her. "Which is it? You did not receive it? Or"—with visible effort, he forced himself to voice the unthinkable—"you did not graduate?"

Papa's face flooded with red. He leaned in. "All three of your sisters excelled at fine schools, and now they have successful careers. *How do you expect to get anywhere in this life without an education?*" he roared.

Sake felt her shoulders slump. Nothing made her feel lower than being compared with her sisters.

Papa must've noticed her lower lip quivering. With obvious effort, he pulled back. "How long has it been since Haha stopped providing for you?"

Limply, her hands in her lap turned palms up. "Sixteen?"

"You have received none of the money I sent to her through my lawyer for the past six years for your care, your education?" Again, his hazel eyes grew dark with anger.

"I thought you said you didn't know where Haha was?" snapped Sake.

"I didn't say she didn't cash my checks, faithfully mailed to her post office box. If not for that indication that she was alive and well, I'd have had the help of the authorities long ago."

The sudden pang of a sharp childhood memory jolted Sake. Waiting alone in the locked car, eyes glued on the door of the check cashing place Haha had disappeared into, while just outside her window sullen young men with bad posture slinked by, and discarded candy bar wrappers skittered across the cracked pavement on a breeze.

Yet even though Haha would never be mother of the year, ratting on her felt like a massive betrayal of something deep and primal. Back where Sake was from, there was a code: you don't rat on your crew. Simple as that.

She said nothing.

Across from Sake, her father massaged his close-trimmed beard thoughtfully, barely containing his wrath. "Never mind your mother. Let me be certain I understand. You have been employed steadily for the past nine months. You are not abusing drugs—"

The little Chihuahua bitch inside Sake clawed to get out. "I don't even touch alcohol!"

"—and never before have been in trouble with the police?"

She wasn't some kid; she'd be twenty-three in September. Been taking care of herself since forever. "No," she bit out.

"Or simply have never been caught?"

"I've had enough of trouble heaped on me by other people! Why make more for myself?" She flounced back into the downy-soft cushions, folding her arms protectively across her breasts, though she knew acting childish only spoiled the impression she was trying to make.

She felt Papa's hard gaze studying her secondhand dress. For the first time, she noticed that the heel of her bootie jouncing nervously across one knee was worn down to the quick.

"What about that—*place* where you live? Are you bound by a lease?"

"No."

He sighed and his head sagged momentarily. "Something tells me that if I knew what kind of arrangement you have there it would only make me hate this Rico character more, so I won't ask." He gave her a slanted look. "So, here is what I propose. Number one. In preparation for your arraignment, along with the DA, my lawyers will be looking into your past to see if you speak the truth . . . that this is indeed your first scrape with the law."

Sake's mouth dropped open. "You don't believe me!"

"Second, you must prove to me that you are as mature and responsible as you say you are by maintaining a respectable lifestyle. Here, under my roof, where I can observe you."

Sake huffed her indignation. "You heard the lawyer—he already got the restraining order dropped. I can go back right now if I want."

But Papa wasn't hearing it. "And last, I refuse to accept that any daughter of mine would fail to achieve the minimum of obtaining a high school diploma."

"I don't need no diploma! I already have a job!"

"I will accept nothing less. You should be able to do all of your studying online, in this day and age. After that, if it is baking that you want to do, there is a fine culinary school—"

"I don't have time for college!"

"—just north of town. Its name is CIA . . . Culinary Institute of America, and it will make you an expert in the field."

She couldn't believe it. Rico was the one who'd started this whole debacle. Was it her fault the bar down the street had refused to serve him because he was intoxicated?

"Tell me this. Do you have friends in the city, other than this degenerate, this Rico?"

"Of course I have friends."

"Who?"

She threw up a hand. "People I know, who know me."

"What people?"

"My coworkers at Bunz. The people who live downstairs." *Who drank with Rico while she was at work. The very same people who'd called the cops that night.*

"It is as I thought, *chérie,* I have worked very hard so that I could provide you and your sisters with a roof over your head, an education. You would have these already, if your mother had fulfilled her promise to me. To attend to you as a mother should."

She lashed out in a knee-jerk reaction. "Maybe if you'd stuck around after you'd gotten her knocked up, Haha wouldn't have gone off with all those other—" She snapped her mouth closed.

Papa curled his lips inward. "Are you quite finished?"

She sighed with frustration. "Say I get my GED. What's in it for me?"

"That all depends."

"If I'm going to walk away from everything I've ever known, I need to know exactly what I'm getting in return."

"You have nerve, just like your papa." He shrugged. "Very well. A number comparable with what I gave your sisters would be in the realm of, say, a quarter of a million dollars."

"A quart—" Sake choked out, salivating like a starving animal getting a whiff of steak on the grill. She'd lived on next to nothing for so long.

"One lump sum to replace the monthly checks which I sent to Emma Grace, which she was to have used to provide for you all this time."

"That's a lot of cheddar."

"Consider. A private college costs in the neighborhood of fifty thousand a year. And an advanced degree, such as Sauvignon's? Make the math.

"But before I give you a centime, you must prove to me that you can fulfill the minimum requirements I have set forth. After that, I hope you will reconsider and further your education, either here or somewhere else. If not, you can use the money to start a business or live on until you find a real career."

"What's the catch?" There was always a catch.

"You have until your twenty-third birthday—coincidentally, the same date as your arraignment. By then the lawyers will be ready with their findings."

September first. Two and a half months.

Sake uncrossed her leg and planted it on the carpet. "I told you, I have a job I have to get back to—tonight," she said evenly. "A three a.m. shift. How's that for responsible?"

Teeny was meaner than a pit bull on crack. She'd already missed one shift. She couldn't miss another.

"The bakery."

His thoughts were transparent. A bakery job meant nothing to a man like Xavier St. Pierre.

"What is the name of this bakery?"

He was merciless. "Bunz." What seemed so hip down in The Mission sounded so lame when she said it *here*, in this fancy room, to *him,* her self-righteous father. She felt no more related to Xavier St. Pierre than she did to the president of the United States. Already her head was back home. Life in the Mission District might be not easy, but at least it was familiar, and she knew her place in it. Here, she could never measure up.

And what about Rico? Now that he'd sobered up, was he sorry he'd let her be taken away after the neighbors called the cops on their mouth battle? She'd been checking her phone nonstop all weekend for a text or missed call. Maybe Rico'd run out of minutes. That would be just like him.

"I can't do three months. I gotta get back now, today."

"And is this your life's goal? To bake bread?"

"It's not just baking bread," she huffed.

"Of course. Then tell me. What else is it?"

"We do croissants, éclairs, macarons . . ."

"The 's' is silent."

"Come back?"

"Even when you are talking about more than one, the words are pronounced like croissant, éclair, macaron."

He was going to make this hard. So hard. *And fine.* So she didn't get to create the fancier pastries at Bunz. All Teeny let Sake do was mix up the dough for baguettes, proof it, then scale it out, shape, and bake it. But she'd looked over Teeny's sweaty, white T-shirted shoulder countless times. She was sure she could make all those confections and more, given half the chance.

"This is exactly what I've been trying to tell you. Why you need an education. How much do they pay you at this bakery?"

Sake gave him a withering stare, knowing he'd only scoff if she told him.

"Allow me to hazard a guess: not much more than minimum wage. All that aside, *chérie,* do you really want to return to a man who would have you locked up for abuse?"

Papa stood then, towering over her. "I am finished discussing it for now. I was on my way out to meet with my vineyard manager when you arrived, to oversee the spraying before the sun gets too hot. I will have Jeanne show you your room.

"While you're in Napa, there are any number of charming venues to explore nearby, vehicles at your disposal in the garage. You will find all the keys hanging next to the kitchen door. And you still have the credit card I gave you when you bought the dress for the wedding, do you not?

"Your sisters come and go frequently. I hope you will become better acquainted with them while you work toward your diploma. Is there something else you have need of?"

Sake's tongue felt all cottony. She scrambled for any excuse she could find to get him to change his mind. "What about all my stuff?

All I had time to do Friday was grab enough for the weekend." It was none of Papa's business, but she still had pay waiting for her at Bunz. She wasn't about to let that slide.

"Have your things packed up. I will send a truck for them."

"*Have it packed up*," *he says*. Who did he think was going to "pack it up" for her? Her maid? And a truck? How much stuff did he think she had? Everything she owned fit in her old moving box. It might only be an hour's drive, but this world might as well be on the other side of the ocean from hers. Papa had no clue.

"I repeat: you have until your birthday, September first. In the meantime, if you have need of clothing or other personal items, you have the card."

"I'll stay on the streets before I'll live without Taylor." *Wouldn't be the first time.*

Papa thought for a second. "I will leave that problem to you and Madame Jeanne. I am confident you two can work something out." With that, he bellowed for his cook.

While the seconds ticked by, Sake and her father looked around the room at anything and everything but each other.

"Monsieur." A slight, clean-cut man in a navy suit appeared in a doorway, hands clasped behind his back. "Madame is in the herb garden. May I help?"

"Bruno," Papa said with some relief, "I would like you to meet my daughter Sake. Jeanne has prepared the west guest room for her. Would you be so kind . . . ?"

"Of course." Bruno turned to Sake with a polite smile. "Mademoiselle." He looked around the floor. "Your bags?"

Sake slapped her backpack over her shoulder, with a look defying him to comment on her extreme luggage deficit.

Bruno just nodded and spun on his heel. "Follow me."

Chapter 5

Bill Diamond and his parents watched Taylor delicately lick the sides of the bowl Bill's mother had set on the floor near the dining table.

"Poor little thing. She's starving," Mom said.

"Who, Taylor? She's a beast, aren'cha, girl?" Bill said, reaching down to give her sturdy body a pat.

Mom was always overfeeding everyone. One glance at her whale of a Persian would tell you that.

Bill himself had been a stocky teenager till he turned twenty-one, moved into his own place six blocks away, and joined the gym. That was eight years and twenty pounds ago. These days he only succumbed to Mom's ritual force-feedings occasionally.

"Give her another little piece of meat," said his dad, nodding to Taylor's bowl, and Mom wasted no time complying. "How long do you have her?"

"Don't know. I'll find out more when I call Sake later on."

"What kind of a name is Sake?" Mom kvetched.

"All the SPs have wine-related names. You know that. I'm guessing Sake's mom must be Japanese."

"How do you get yourself mixed up with these kinds of people, William?"

"How else? Everyone wants him. He's a mensch," said Dad without looking up from his plate.

"First it was that slutty Sylvia Goldsmith back in high school, then Brittany, then crazy Dynise, with the eating disorder."

Mom's borderline invasive ways had clashed big time with the last girl he'd brought to dinner. Dynise had asked about the ingredients in all the dishes Mom had set on the table.

"That girl was so skinny she could have hula hooped with a Cheerio. Now you've somehow got yourself all tangled up with the surprise love child of Xavier St. Pierre."

Unperturbed, Bill scooped up a second helping of roasted vegetables from the serving dish in the middle of the table.

"There's more in the pan on the stove," said Mom.

"Could you pass the salt, Dad? Dynise didn't have an eating disorder. She was just vegetarian," said Bill, sprinkling his carrots. But ultimately there had been something about Dynise he couldn't live with . . . something that would have freaked Mom out more than just someone shunning her brisket. And that was that Dynise spent every free minute working on her Wiccan blog.

Behold: you didn't have to be one of the Chosen People to date Bill Diamond. Call him prejudiced. It's not that he hated witches. He just didn't want one to be the mother of his children.

"How is Sake, after the accident? It was on the local news last night. David, pull it up for him."

"Don't get up, Dad," said Bill, scraping his own chair back to get his phone. He wouldn't mind reading for himself the secondhand version of Sake that the town folk were getting.

The Napa County Sherriff's office is investigating why a BO-105 helicopter crash-landed in fair weather just short of the landing pad at a Napa Valley winery last Saturday.

The chopper, piloted by prominent vintner Xavier St. Pierre, took off from San Francisco International Airport with one passenger, Sake, the youngest of his four daughters. They were headed for the Napa wedding of St. Pierre's eldest child, attorney Sauvignon. But something went wrong on approach, and the chopper landed hard, snapping off its right skid.

Ms. St. Pierre was taken to Queen of the Valley Medical Center by private transport and released the following day. Mr. St. Pierre refused treatment, claiming he was not injured.

Bill returned to the table. "Sake's fine. And I'm not 'tangled up' with her, not in any way, shape, or form. I'm just doing her a favor."

"That's how it all starts. Trust me, that's how I met your father. We were in Encino, in nineteen—"

"Rachel! Spare us—he's heard it a thousand times," groaned Dad, reaching to drop yet another scrap of fat into Taylor's dish.

"All I'm saying is it's beyond me how you ended up being closer than roaches on a Bacon Bit with all those wine heiresses. Chardonnay, Merlot, now Sake. If they weren't already famous, people would never believe me when I tell them about—"

"So then, don't tell them!" said Dad. "D'you ever think of that?"

Bill sighed. "Chardonnay and Merlot St. Pierre are clients, Mom, just clients. We have a professional relationship. I helped Char get her building for her children's charity, and I found Meri a jewelry workshop. That's it."

His watch said it was time to go. He left a small quantity of food on his plate, just as his trainer down at the gym had instructed him to do, folded his napkin, and scraped back his chair. "Thanks for dinner, Mom."

"But what about pie?" She put on her best guilt-inducing face. "Strawberry, your favorite. Got them fresh yesterday from Mrs. Morales down at the market."

"Told the guys I'd hit some balls with them before I take Sake's dog back."

"Wait, I'll wrap up a piece for you to take with. And some more meat for the puppy. Look at her, she's practically wasting away to nothing."

Chapter 6

The minute she was alone in her guest room, Sake let her backpack slump onto the nearest chair, pulled out her phone, and punched in Rico's number. She'd only half paid attention to her father's assistant when he'd showed her around her bedroom suite with the whirlpool tub, the heated towel bar. Something about the forever view out the floor-to-ceiling windows filled her with a familiar bitterness. The evenly spaced rows of well-nurtured grapevines represented deep roots, continuity, and promise for the future. Luxuries her sisters took for granted, but that had always been missing from Sake's world.

While she listened to Rico's phone ringing across the line, she paced the springy carpeting—twelve paces across! Bigger than most entire apartments she'd lived in, and she'd lived in a lot of them—then, when he didn't pick up, she spat out a message: "Call me. I need a lift." Wouldn't he be surprised to find out she needed a ride from Napa County, not the nearest city jail.

Then she called Bunz to tell Teeny that she might be late getting in in the morning, but lost her nerve and hung up when Francine, the counter girl, answered. Sake knew she was already on Teeny's shit list for calling off last Friday.

She had to get back to the city tonight, but how? No way could she do three-month penance up here in this green prison. By then, there wouldn't be anything left to go back to. Her job would be long gone. And what about Rico? Would he wait a quarter of a year for her, when he measured time by the bottle? Without him, where would she stay? Her mind flew to all sorts of awful scenarios—Rico skipping out, leaving her belongings behind to be raked through by the strangers who occasionally crashed there, or thrown out by the next tenant. She knew Rico. If he was shot to the curb, he might even sell what clothes of hers that he could for booze money.

She touched an earlobe, seeking the reassuring presence of a diamond stud. At least she had her most valuable possession with her. Of course, no one but she and Haha knew they weren't fake—otherwise everyone in The Mission would have been trying to get at them. She guarded those earrings with her life, knowing that if things ever got really bad, she could always pawn them as a last resort.

She lowered herself to the utmost edge of the embroidered duvet and racked her brain for ideas.

First thing she needed to do was get Taylor back. Unlike Rico, Bill Diamond picked up on the first ring, almost as if he'd been waiting for her call.

"Hi Sake. How's your afternoon going? How's your head?"

"Taylor okay?"

"Under the coffee table, sleeping off Mom's brisket."

In the background, she heard a metallic *whack*. "You can bring her back to me now?"

"Did you get things straightened out with your dad's housekeeper or whatever?"

"So, yeah, it's all good. She can come back anytime."

"Right this minute? I'm on the driving range with some guys. The 'rents went gaga over Taylor. We used to have a dog, back when I was a kid. Don't think any of us ever got over losing her. Little buff-colored pug named Mollie."

There was a knock on the bedroom door.

"Hold still," she hissed into the phone. Maybe whoever it was would go away if she stood quietly.

"Sake?" The bedroom door opened and a woman's head appeared through the crack.

"I'll call you back," she told Bill.

The woman stepped inside as Sake lowered the phone. "Forgive me for interrupting. I am Jeanne. Your papa said I would find you here."

Jeanne didn't look like any cook Sake had ever seen. Slender and tailored in her button-down blouse and gold hoops, she was one of those women who could pass for anything between late forties and early sixties. It was hard to tell. Because, unlike many attractive older women Sake passed in Union Square, Jeanne's face didn't appear to be shot full of Botox. Two faint vertical lines marked the space between her brows, but they did nothing to detract from her appearance. She looked refreshingly natural.

Jeanne placed her hands on Sake's shoulders and kissed both her cheeks, Papa-style. Must be a thing, here among the high rollers.

"Welcome. We're happy you're here. Have you recovered from the accident?"

She'd be better if people stopped asking her how she was every five seconds. "Hey. Look, what's the deal with you and dogs?"

"Pardon?" Jeanne blinked.

"I hear you have some kind of issue with dogs."

"Well. Er . . . it's true . . . dogs do make me—shall we say, uncomfortable."

"As in, chaps-your-hide uncomfortable, or you have a freak-out party every time you see one of those little teacup Pomeranians pop his head out of some rich bitch's bag?"

Jeanne gave her a frosty glare, then went to the window. When she spoke again, her voice came from far away. "When I was twelve and my brother was two, we were playing outside when we were attacked by our neighbor's German shepherd. I lifted Jacques up over my head to protect him and began to walk home. I was not able to run; Jacques was too heavy." She turned back to face Sake. "The dog bit the backs of my legs again and again, until I finally reached the safety of my house. He bit straight through the muscles, the nerves."

Da fuq. Sake winced.

"In my village in rural France, we did not have access to the best medical care. It was only years later, when I came to California, that I finally received the proper treatment. For that I owe a debt of gratitude to your papa. Unfortunately, it was much too late to make a full recovery."

"That is some serious shit."

"I'm told the only way I was able to hold Jacques over my head as long as I did was due to the rush of adrenaline."

Sake sat down. "Whew. I'ma be sending positive vibes your way for that."

"Is this how you always greet people? By asking about their tolerance for dogs?"

"No." Sake shrugged. "It's just that I have one. She's not a shepherd, nothing like that. Not even a purebred. Taylor's just a mutt with a sweet face and a mad underbite."

Jeanne's eyes widened and scanned the room.

"Bill Diamond is watching her for me right now. But he's bringing her back. We're, like, totally inseparable."

"I see."

"Okay? So I'm assuming it's okay if I keep her here with me."

The lines between Jeanne's brow intensified. "It is not okay. Not okay at all. Despite ongoing therapy, I have never conquered my fear of dogs. So no, Sake, I am sorry, but your dog and I cannot reside in the same house together. I would constantly be on my guard."

Well, la di. Sake's first impulse was to play the employer-versus-employee card to get her way, but on second thought, she kind of appreciated Jeanne keeping it real. She well knew what it was like to not get what you needed when you needed it. Besides, somehow she felt more from the same tribe as this cook than her bona fide blood relatives.

Jeanne brought her hands together, prayer-like. "Dinner is at seven. Of course, the newlyweds will not be here tonight; Sauvignon and Esteban are still on their honeymoon. When they return, they will live at their ranch.

"The design business of Merlot has taken off, with the help of her friend Mark. They spend much of their time in the city to be near Merlot's workshop and Mark's office.

"And Chardonnay all but lives at her foundation. She is affianced to Ryder McBride. Perhaps you have heard of him? He is known mainly for his role in the *First Responders* film, but he has humble roots, here in the valley."

Oh, Sake knew. It was creepy how much she knew, from years of stalking her sisters on the Net. The question was: What did her sisters know about her?

"Seven," repeated Sake. She had no intention of showing up for a cozy dinner with the fam. If Taylor couldn't stay here, neither could she.

"So. I have prepared a large family repast. Your papa, he cares about such things a great deal—more than he cares to admit. I do the best I can to keep his daughters together. But you know yourself how unpredictable the young are. One can never be certain who will show up until the very last minute." She shrugged, pursing her lips. *"C'est la vie."*

As soon as Jeanne left, Sake called Bill Diamond back. *C'mon, pick up!* She treaded the floor, picturing Bill busy with other things while Taylor stood at the door pining for Sake, wondering when— *if*—she'd come for her. She'd pegged Bill Diamond as way too anal to let his phone battery die—unlike Rico. So why didn't he answer? She hit redial, but again, no luck.

Now all she could do was wait. She slid down the side of the bed onto her haunches. No sense in messing it up too bad since she wouldn't be sleeping in it, anyway. Plus, there was the housekeeper to consider. She didn't want to give her needless work.

She tried calling Rico again without success, and then got up her nerve to leave word for Teeny, tensing when Francine told her to hang on, he was right there.

"Yeah?" came Teeny's gruff voice.

"Teen! Whoody. Hey, I got a situation. I might need to take another day. I'll be back Tuesday, latest."

"Again?"

"In nine months, when have I ever called off before? C'mon, man, cut me some slack. I'ma try to make it, but I'm just telling you, in case I don't. If not tonight, definitely tomorrow. Definitely."

Holding her breath, she heard a grunt, then Francine got back on the line. "Okay?"

"What'd he say?" Sake asked, phone bruising her cheekbone.

"Nothing. He just went back to the kitchen."

Teeny never cut anyone a break.

When Bill called back to say he was on his way, Sake went outside to wait for him.

Taylor bounded out of Bill's car, looking totally on point in a shiny new red collar.

Bill beamed attractively, watching Taylor jump into Sake's arms. Sake took note of a dimple in his right cheek.

"Whaddya think? I was only going to buy a leash, but then I caved and bought the matching collar. And then I thought I'd surprise you and give her a bath. The water running in the tub must've drowned out your phone calls."

Sake hid her guilt in Taylor's neck. Why hadn't she gotten her act together enough to bathe Taylor before today? True, Rico's place had no tub, and those folks down at the pet mart were robbers, charging what they did for a doggie shampoo.

"Did you get a bath?" she cooed. "Did you? Look at you, all bezeled out!"

Taylor wriggled away from her to race circles in the sunshine while she and Bill watched.

"Jeanne didn't give you too hard a time about keeping her here?"

Sake let out a big sigh. "Not so much. Turns out Jeanne got run up on by a dog when she was a kid, so now she can't handle them. No one said Taylor couldn't stay outside, though."

"She won't run away?"

"Never has yet." They'd be long gone by nightfall, anyway.

Concern darkened his expression. "Might want to put her under cover on the porch. Hard to believe from that sky right now, but there's a chance of rain later."

"Well, I guess I'll get going then," he said, unexpectedly. "Nice meeting you." He stuck out his hand. "If you ever need some commercial real estate, I'm your man."

She shook woodenly. The warm, sturdy quality of his handshake shouldn't have come as a surprise, given how he'd taken care of her and Taylor the past twenty-four hours, but Sake had learned the hard way not to fall into the trap of trusting people. She went so far as to scour his eyes for the usual hint of chicanery while she had him in her sights. But all she saw was a complete lack of guile. A wistful feeling washed over her, like when she spotted a dress in a shop window she knew she'd look bangin' in, but couldn't afford and wouldn't have any place to wear it to even if she could. She had to let him go.

Sake watched Bill drive away in his logo-plastered car. Hoping he'd look back . . . knowing he wouldn't.

Taylor was still giddy with her recent bath and their reunion, so Sake didn't have the heart to tie her to the porch just yet. Besides, this place was even better than the dog park, Taylor's special treat in the city. Here, on the private grounds of her father's estate, there was no one else around. No need to be on the lookout for creepers of the canine or human variety. Safe, but strange. It would take a lot of getting used to—assuming she was staying here, which she wasn't.

Now that she had Taylor back, she considered splitting before dinner, but it would be smarter to leave with a full stomach. Otherwise her next meal wouldn't be until tomorrow morning.

At seven, Sake sat down at a long mahogany dining table sporting more silverware than Bunz had in its entire inventory. Both Meri and Char had shown up. Sake watched her sisters to see which utensil to use first—damned if she'd give them more evidence of her lack of refinement—and listened with hidden fascination to her family—*her family*—make small talk.

She didn't know what she'd expected, but she ended up being shocked at how ordinary they were. Char asked Jeanne if she had a good recipe for her upcoming benefit, selling soup from handmade ceramic bowls donated by a local high school. Papa was all bent about something called downy mildew brought on by the wet winter and spring and his argument with his vineyard manager over whether the best thing to fix it with was lime sulfur or copper spray.

Sake took in every word that was said while quietly devouring her baked potato and broccolini and half her chicken, and slipping the other half into her napkin for Taylor to eat later. She was painfully aware that she had nothing to contribute to the dinner conversation except maybe how bad she was going to get bitched out by Teeny for sticking him with the bread ovens over the busy weekend. Or how much she hoped she'd find Rico in a good state when she got back. Rico wasn't a monster. When he was sober, he could be really sweet. The problem was he was only sober in the early mornings. By the time Sake got off her shift at eleven a.m., he'd already started drinking. But his apartment was right around the corner from the bakery and he let her and Taylor live there rent-free. Sure, she shared his bed and he had everyone believing she was his bae, but that was all a scam. It'd been a long time since they'd done anything, which was just fine with Sake. He was always too wasted.

Sipping from her water glass, Merlot caught Sake eyeing her arm party. She held out her wrist. "These are part of my Entwined collection, and these other three are from the Olive Branch line." She slowly rotated the bracelets to show off their wavy lines, their uneven surfaces designed to resemble natural vines and leaves. "Which one do you like most?"

Embarrassed at having been busted for staring, Sake replied, "This rose gold one is epic."

Merlot slid it off. "Here."

Against her better judgment, Sake accepted it. The metal was still warm from Meri's arm. The arm of *her sister,* who shared the same blood.

"Put it on. Let's see how it looks on you."

"That's okay." Even Sake could tell it was real gold. She handed it back. Merlot was a big-time jewelry mogulista, but Sake was only a minder of the bread ovens . . . lower than her sister's toenail clippings.

"Please? It helps with my designing to see how they look on other people."

Reluctantly, Sake slipped it on, unable to contain her grin when she saw how amazing it looked next to her tats. She started removing it after a few seconds, though. Better not to get attached to something you could never have. But Merlot laid a stilling hand on her wrist.

"Keep it," she said.

"No." Sake chuckled self-consciously.

"I want you to have it," Merlot insisted, her eyes aglow with sincerity.

Everyone's forks stilled midair to see how the thug sister would react. She didn't deserve a present as valuable as this. Was Merlot stupid, despite her impressive career achievements? Couldn't she add? Didn't she get that Sake was the result of an affair her father had had when he was still married to Merlot's movie-star mother?

"Well! Who wants dessert?" Merlot stood up, indicating that it was a done deal. The table breathed a collective sigh of relief. Chardonnay raised her napkin to her lips too late to hide her smile, and Jeanne and Papa exchanged satisfied glances. "Stay there, Jeanne. I'll get it."

Newsflash: it got *dark* out here in the sticks at night. The clouds Bill Diamond had predicted had rolled in at dusk, and now there was no moon, no stars, no city lights, only the rush of headlights zooming past, mere feet from where Sake and Taylor trudged along the stony berm.

It had taken forever just to trek out here to the main road, and though there was plenty of Sunday-night traffic—hungover wine country tourists heading south in time for work tomorrow morning, no doubt—Sake had been thumbing for twenty minutes and no one had stopped to give her a ride. Maybe it was because nobody wanted a dog in his car. Taylor was panting, looking up at Sake like she was out of her mind for dragging her out here when she should be curled up on her rug back in the room they shared with Rico.

"I know. I'm trying to get you there," Sake told her.

Okay, so thumbing wasn't the classiest way to go, but what other choice did she have? The city was only an hour away—she could almost see the lights on the hills, smell the unique blend of jasmine and sewage, hear the ding-ding-ding of the cable car bells—and yet so far away when you didn't have wheels.

She kept talking, pretending it was her pet she was reassuring. "Do you even remember your grandma, girl? Too bad you're not a bloodhound. You could track her down in a minute, couldn't you?"

Sake caught the glitter of phosphorescent yellow eyes. A wolf-like creature streaked across the highway, disappearing so fast she thought she might have imagined it. *Coyote.* She'd heard about them. Sometimes they even ventured down into the urban areas, looking for food. Her heart pounding like a jackhammer, she reached down and snatched Taylor up. "It's okay, calm down. He's gone." Coyotes were scared of people, everyone knew that. On the other hand, they might find terriers tempting. She strained her eyes toward the vineyards, but she couldn't see more than ten feet into the blackness of the night.

She set Taylor down on a patch of grass and, with a trembling hand, poured her some water from the bottle in her backpack. Waiting for her to lap it up, she felt the first raindrops. "Come on, now," she said when Taylor had drunk her fill and licked her muzzle. "I promise someone'll stop for us in the next few minutes."

Like magic, she heard gravel crunching just ahead.

"See, what'd I tell you?" With relief, she looked up to see who had finally given them a break.

"Evening!" called the man in blue, slamming his door as the colored lights atop his roof started to swirl. Cautiously, he approached Sake as if she were a dangerous criminal, taking the precaution of ducking his chin to report his location into the radio attached to his shoulder.

"What're you doing out here this time of night, young lady?"

"Just trying to get home."

"And where would that be?"

"Samfrancisco," she heard herself say nervously, in the local vernacular.

"How old are you?"

"Twenty-two."

She felt her pupils contract in his flashlight's powerful beam.

"Don't you know hitchhiking is illegal on this highway? Come on back to the car with me a minute. Here. Walk out in front of me."

She and Taylor followed the column of light he shone on the road. The cop held open the door to his back seat. "Why don't you and your dog hop in for a minute while I ask you a few questions? Safer that way."

Like she had a choice. She climbed in and slung her backpack off her shoulder onto the seat by the door. Maybe if she obeyed his every instruction to the letter he'd let her go. Papa couldn't find out about this! She couldn't go back to jail. She pictured Taylor hauled off to the pound, cold and afraid, while she sat helpless in yet another police station.

"Mind if I take a look in here?" he asked. Before she could answer, he hooked one finger around the strap of her pack and locked her in with a foreboding ka-chunk, reminiscent of last Thursday night.

Her heart sank.

The cop slid into the front seat and from behind the metal grid she watched him pick up his iPad.

He asked for her name and typed that in.

"You got any identification?"

"No," she said glumly.

"No driver's license, school ID, bank cards?"

"I don't drive." *Or go to school, or have a bank account.*

He picked up his receiver and clicked in the button. "Base, this is Charlie-hotel-one-nine. Got an Asian female, approximately twenty-two years of age, five-foot-three—"

"Four," Sake corrected him.

"Five-foot-three, hitchhiking at Twenty-nine and Hoffman, goes by name of Sake St. Pierre. No ID." He turned to her. "Izzat S-O-K-I?"

Taylor whined while Sake corrected the cop's spelling.

"I think my dog has to go to the bathroom," she said. But he held up a shushing finger to listen to the result of her background check crackling in over the speaker.

"Sake St. Pierre, Fog City, no known street address, criminal record one count simple assault June twenty-five, awaiting court date."

"Ten-four."

The cop pulled on some blue latex gloves and reached into her backpack. "Anything bad in here? Weapons, syringes, needles that could poke me?"

"No," she sighed, watching him unzip zippers and dig through her makeup and dirty underwear and the new dress she'd gotten for the wedding, all balled up.

"What's this?" he asked.

"My father's credit card."

"And this?" he added, holding Merlot's bracelet up to the dashboard lights.

"It's mine."

"Pretty fancy. Looks like real gold."

"My sister gave it to me."

"Uh-huh. And what's *her* name?

"Merlot St. Pierre."

It hit him then. He whipped his head around, eyeing her tattoos, her Sal Val dress. "You the one that was in the helicopter crash Saturday up at the winery?"

Taylor yipped her *I have to pee, NOW* yip.

"Cheese-oh-man. We were going to get in touch with you anyway, sooner or later. It's routine to interview the pilot and passengers after a plane crash. During preliminary questioning, seems your father couldn't locate his pilot's logbook—er, scratch that, that's confidential. You sustain any injuries?"

Her headache was coming back with a vengeance. She closed her eyes. *Modulate.* "No."

"I'm going to ask you again, what are you doing out here along the highway at night, in the rain? Are you running away from something? A domestic dispute?" His flashlight traveled across her body. "Your father hurt you? He's no stranger to the sheriff's department, you know."

"No! Look, I won't hitchhike. Just let me out, would you?" she asked, rattling the locked door. "My dog really has to go."

"Now, you just hold your horses a minute, young lady." He got back on the horn. "Yeah, Judy, gimme the sheriff. He's gonna want to know about this, ten-eighteen."

A half hour later, Sake stood dripping rain onto the marble floor of the foyer at Domaine St. Pierre under the disapproving gaze of

Jeanne, who was clutching her long velour robe closed at the throat, Papa, and her wide-eyed, perfect sisters. Sure as shit none of *them* had ever seen the inside of a police cruiser. Thanks to Deputy Dawg here, any good headway Sake had made at dinner was now shot to pieces.

"Thank you again for returning my daughter," said Papa, peering down his nose. Despite her predicament, she had to bite back a smile at that special gift Papa had of making it seem like it was the cop's fault Sake was in trouble instead of her own.

The deputy saluted and reached for the brass doorknob. "No problem, sir." He glanced at Jeanne. "Thanks for the paper towels, ma'am."

Sake had *told* him Taylor had to pee.

"Sheriff'll be out pretty soon with some more questions about the plane crash as a result of the inspection."

The yellow police tape was gone, the chopper towed away. But apparently it still wasn't over.

"I welcome him. As I have said repeatedly to your office and the press, I have nothing to hide. I did nothing wrong. No one was injured."

Meri studied her feet, Char rubbed the back of her neck, and Jeanne raised a brow and pursed her lips, anything to avoid drawing attention to Papa's obvious black eye.

The deputy grimaced, sucking air through his teeth. "Any time an aircraft sustains damage on impact, that's cause for an investigation, sir. Maybe you've heard, there's been lots of controversy about small plane crashes last couple of years. The authorities are starting to take a closer look. Especially when it's high profile."

After the deputy left and her sisters drifted back to their beds, there was still the issue of what to do with Taylor out on the front porch, barking her head off. She wasn't used to being tied up in a strange place at night, on top of all the other recent upheaval.

"She can spend the night in the vestibule off the kitchen," Papa said. Though he acted like the shot caller most of the time, Sake saw him eyeing Jeanne for her approval. "That is a compromise."

"You know how I feel about dogs," Jeanne told him gravely.

"For one night only." He turned and peered sternly at Sake through lowered brows.

She nodded. Better than outside. She'd think of something else by tomorrow.

But an hour later, confined in what Papa referred to as a vestibule but Sake would call a mudroom, Taylor still wouldn't stop barking. Even after Sake smuggled her up to her bedroom, she wouldn't settle. A sharp rap startled her.

"Sake!" called Papa from the other side of the door. "It is after twelve! That animal is keeping the whole house awake!"

Sake had tried and tried to hush her. But all this was too much. Taylor wanted her rug, her snug corner.

There was only one thing Sake could think of to do.

Chapter 7

When Bill's phone rang, he automatically raised his head from his pillow and scrabbled for the glowing rectangle lying on his bedside table. He was used to getting work calls at all hours, but seriously?

He looked at the screen, then answered with a confused, "Sake?"

"Yeah. You can come get me?"

"It's the middle of the night!" He was conferring with Russ Cross tomorrow. He needed sleep to be on his game.

Was that a sigh of impatience he heard?

"Either you can or you can't."

"What's wrong?"

"Taylor won't stop barking."

Bill scrubbed a hand through his thick crop of short hair, trying to shift from dreaming to waking mode. His big meeting was in—*let's see*—seven and a half hours. But whom else did Sake have to depend on?

Sighing, he swung his feet onto the floor. "Give me a chance to pull on a pair of jeans."

Bill hung up and shook his head at himself. Name one other person he'd get up in the middle of the night for.

Six hours later, Bill stood buttoning up his white shirt, fresh from the cleaners. He peered down at a sleep-rumpled Sake, stretched out on his sectional, and wondered what his mom would think if she could see the sight of the unorthodox wine heiress in nothing but his T-shirt, one slender leg wound around the afghan she'd knitted for him, while at the same time he tried to ignore the effect that leg was having on him. He couldn't afford any more distractions this morning.

He'd already fed Taylor, and lacking a backyard, taken her out for a short walk to do her business, all the while hoping that his morning routine—making coffee, showering—would wake Sake up. But she was out like a light. No wonder, after last night. He could have used a few more winks, himself.

On the coffee table, Sake's phone buzzed. Bill checked the screen where it lay, then nudged Sake's shoulder. "Wake up. Your father's on the phone."

"Nnnn."

"Sake. It's your dad."

"Sake!" He picked up her phone, wrapped her hand around it, and went back to the bathroom.

"Hullo?"

As Bill tugged his tie this way and that in front of the mirror, all he could see in his mind's eye was her outrageously sexy bed head. While he went about straightening the towels and yanking his comforter up over his pillows, he overheard Xavier St. Pierre ranting through the phone in his rapid Franglais.

When he returned to the living room, Sake had tossed off the afghan and was gathering her clothes from where they had been strewn helter-skelter during the wee hours of the morning.

His breath caught at the sight of her girlish curves bouncing beneath his T-shirt . . . her black panties peeking out from underneath.

"He wants me there, but I can't have my dog with me, and now he's all up in my grill about leaving in the middle of the night."

Bill checked his watch as he slid into his loafers. "I was just going to wake you anyway. I gotta be at a meeting. Can you be ready in ten so I can drop you off first?"

It was raining again when Bill Diamond pulled up to Domaine St. Pierre, but just like before, he still insisted on walking Sake up the slick steps to the door, even though he was all dressed up for work. After he said good-bye to her and Taylor for the last time beneath the porch roof and she watched him drive away, she looped Taylor's leash around the balustrade and sternly ordered her not to bark. She went in and stood very still, listening.

Incredibly, all remained quiet outside. Must have been the dark that had made Taylor act out before. Who could blame her? She didn't know where she was or what she was doing here.

Sake wandered through the maze of rooms, following the sounds of life into the most tricked-out kitchen she'd ever laid eyes on. There, on the wall hooks near the door, dangled the sets of car keys Papa had told her about. Her gaze traveled over the tall glass-front cupboards, the polished copper pots suspended over an island, to Jeanne, stirring a pot on the flame of a six-burner AGA with a quad oven.

Jeanne startled when she saw Sake standing there.

"Where is he?" asked Sake, hiding her awe of the workspace, the primo equipment.

Jeanne countered with, "Where is the dog?"

"Don't have a seizure. She's tied out on the porch."

"You will find your papa in his lab," Jeanne said coolly. "Go out the front door and follow the signs."

It was starting to sink in—this was really Sake's family's property, and she technically had the run of the place. Still, neither the gardeners nor the field workers in their rain gear and hats looked up when she and Taylor walked by. To them, she was still nobody.

She followed the signs to the lab. Behind a glass door sat Papa at a long white table, surrounded by the kind of odd-shaped cylinders and beakers she'd only ever seen back in science class at Bal High. The atmosphere was musty with the mysterious smells of grapes and earth.

"I thought we had an understanding, *mademoiselle,*" Papa said sternly, peeling off his reading glasses when she entered, tossing them on the table with a clatter. He sat back in his chair and pierced her with his eyes.

Taylor shook the raindrops off her coat onto the lab floor. The sound drew her father's attention to Sake's own stringy, wet locks.

"Where is your umbrella?"

Umbrella? Before she laid down cash money for an umbrella, there were about ninety-seven other things she needed first. But then, why would Papa get that? Under those preppy corduroys, he probably was sporting golden underpants.

"I'm here, aren't I?"

"Evidently I did not make myself clear when I told you that you needed to prove yourself for the next three months, here at home. *Your* home."

"*Swerve*, okay? I don't need to prove myself to you or anyone else. Just lemme and my dog go back and live our lives."

"Is that really what you want? To return to the *crétin* who would have you still sitting behind prison bars? I happen to know what it is like to sleep in a prison cell. What kind of man would allow a woman—any woman—to spend a single second there?"

Sake started to make the excuse that Rico had been mad turnt that night when the cops came—but before the thought reached her lips, she was struck by the weakness of that argument.

"Answer me! What kind?" Papa's eyes burned through her.

Sake couldn't admit that Papa might be right. It was too hard to wrap her head around the concept that she might deserve better than Rico. So she responded in her habitual way, by lashing out in self-defense. "It's my life. You can't make me stay here!"

Papa jumped up from his chair so fast its front legs left the floor. "Go then!" He snatched up his phone. "Bruno, drop what you're doing and bring the car around." He stabbed a button to end the call. "Leave the credit card on the table."

Sake swung her backpack around to land on the pristine table with a thud that rattled the delicate glassware and rifled through it until she found Papa's card. Catching a glimpse of the bracelet on her wrist, she made another impulsive decision: she'd do him one better. She'd ungift Meri's bling, too. Slipping off the bracelet and tossing it on the hard surface, where it gyrated with a high-pitched ring, gave her a warped sense of satisfaction. But mingling with the sense of martyrdom was a twinge of regret. That gold had looked so sweet next to her tats. Why couldn't she just accept it at face value?

Chapter 8

In the back seat of Papa's car, Sake stewed. She'd made it this far on her own. She didn't need no overbearing man telling her how to live, even if she did share his genes. Or her fancy sisters, giving her charity.

"Where are we going?" asked Papa's driver, Bruno, an hour later, when they were breaking out of the clot of traffic coming off the Golden Gate Bridge.

It was almost eleven. She had missed her shift at the bakery. But she needed her pay. And it wouldn't be a bad idea to score some face time with Teeny, just to prove to him that she really was back. She gave Bruno the address of Bunz.

There were no parking spaces to be found along the street. "Drive around the block while I pick up my pay real quick. Meet you on the corner," said Sake.

"I'll be back," she promised Taylor, touching her wet black nose with the tip of her finger.

As she walked through the shop on her way to the kitchen, Sake waved to Francine, just like always.

"Hold on," Francine said from behind the register, where she was stuffing a bag full of croissants for a waiting customer.

Something in the woman's rheumy old eyes—despite Teeny referring to her as his counter girl, Francine claimed she'd been at Bunz since the quake of eighty-nine, and she looked every day of it—sent a bolt of dread through Sake. What Francine had to say could only be bad. So she kept going, stopping short on the other side of the swinging kitchen door when she saw Teeny showing some stranger how to slide the proofed baguettes from the metal tray to the wooden peel, score the tops at an angle with a knife, and slide them onto the bare oven rack to brown.

Teeny slammed the oven door shut, set the timer, and looked up at the wall clock. "As soon as these are done, your shift's over. Be back tomorrow at three a.m., and don't be late."

The new man glanced at Sake with indifference before peeling his paper hairnet off his blond dreads, throwing it into the trash and untying his apron—*Sake's* apron—and hanging it on the wall hook.

Sake took a step toward her boss. "What are you doing? The baguettes are *my* job."

Teeny picked up a dishcloth and started wiping down the pastry counter with sweeping strokes. "Not anymore."

"You can't give my job away! I'm back." She held her breath.

"Not only can I—I just did."

"I told you, I had a situation!"

"You told me you'd be back yesterday. I'm only hiring men from now on. Bitches—so un-fucking-reliable. Think they can just show up whenever they're not on the rag."

She clamped her mouth shut to keep from blurting out what Teeny could do with his job and rose up on her toes to feel along the top shelf for her envelope of cash, but it was empty.

"Where's my money?"

With meaty hands, Teeny dunked his cloth into a bucket of gray water and wrung the life out of it. "What money."

"For the past two weeks."

"You don't show up, you forfeit. You didn't read the fine print in your contract?"

What contract? Sake breached Teeny's personal space, catching her breath at his overripe aroma. "I earned that pay fair and square! You can't take it back!"

"You got balls comin' in here tellin' me what I can and can't do after you leave me to do your job *and mine* all weekend."

"It's my money! I worked for it!"

"Get the hell out of my kitchen." Teeny jerked a thumb toward the door.

That money was all Sake had to get by on. She didn't know where she'd get more.

"I'm not leaving until you pay me." Sake stood her ground, but

Teeny just stepped around her as if she weren't there and got the dough bowl and the sack of flour for donuts.

Sake bit her lip, creating a substitute pain to distract herself from the dejection blooming in her heart. *Don't cry.*

How was he supposed to know treating her like she didn't exist was the worst possible thing he could do to her? First Papa and her sisters, then Rico. And a gnawing dread over the past few months that now even her own mother didn't think Sake was worth recognition.

A girl could only take so much rejection before she had to face facts—she wasn't *worth* accepting.

She was invisible.

She wasn't ready to accept it yet. Tasting blood from her lip, she thought of a new tack. She lowered her voice and forced a smile, though it felt as though she was grinning through false teeth.

"C'mon, Teen. That's not fair. You owe me my pay. You know you do."

In response, Teeny lumbered out to the front of the house. Tentatively, Sake followed, daring to hope he was caving, going to get her some cash. But instead of opening the register drawer, he picked up the sticky shop cell phone off the counter. Skimming his finger down the list of phone numbers kept under the glass, he began punching in numbers with a fat index finger.

"This's Teeny over at Bunz on Valencia. You wanna send a badge down here? Gotta little problem with employee theft. . . ." He twisted from his barrel waist to make sure Sake was hearing him.

She'd been arrested once already. Was he really piling on some bum rap, even before her court hearing?

Numb, Sake's feet somehow carried her past Teeny, feeling his swine-like eyes boring a hole in her back.

"False alarm, found it," she overheard him say as she pushed out the door.

Sake stumbled down the sidewalk toward the intersection where Bruno was to pick her up, hurrying to put as much distance between herself and the real crook, Teeny, as she could.

"Sake!" Behind her, she heard the hoarse yell from Francine's cigarette-ruined voice. "He don't mean it."

A passerby turned to look.

"He's just pissed off. He'll get over it. You've heard how many helpers he went through before you. Two, three a month. They all quit on account of he's so mean. You're the best worker he ever had. Come back in a week or so when he cools down. He'll beg you to stay."

Sake kept on moving.

"Here." Francine jogged up behind her, withdrew a wrinkled bill from her apron pocket and thrust it toward her. "Take this. It's all I got, but you can have it."

Sake half-turned. "You keep it," she said in a meek voice she didn't recognize. She pushed back Francine's hand holding the twenty. "I'm not taking what's yours."

"Come back when he cools off!" Francine called after her, concern deepening the wrinkles on her leathery face.

She was still standing there when Sake got back in the sedan.

"All is well?" asked Bruno.

"Peachy."

Now what? She had no job, no money. She told Bruno the way to Rico's as she sat stiffly in the back seat, watching the streets of her neighborhood go by. Once-bright murals decorating whole sides of buildings, the Spanish taquerias, the sleepy-eyed guy selling bags of pot on the corner. After Napa, she saw them all through different eyes.

Coasting up to Rico's concrete building, Papa's Cadillac stuck out like an emerald in a goat's ass. It drew the curious gaze of an approaching male figure.

Rico couldn't ID Sake from where she was, all the way in the back seat. By the time he reached his building, he'd lost interest in the car and stepped through his nondescript doorway.

Bruno turned around. "This is it?" he asked, clearly skeptical that Xavier St. Pierre would really want him to drop off his own flesh and blood outside this sketchy-looking place.

"This is it. Whelp, it's been real," she said, opening the door.

"I will wait here for a few minutes," Bruno said.

The ringing of her footsteps on the metal steps filled Sake's ears. She couldn't help but compare that to the muted slap of her soles on the marble staircase at Domaine St. Pierre. The usual smells of curry and onions stung her nostrils. Inside the apartment, nothing had changed since she'd been gone. Over on the couch, some vaguely familiar guy with bloodshot eyes was watching cartoons with the sound off, and a fixture Sake knew simply as The App Queen still sat cross-legged, only looking up from her phone to scrutinize Sake so hard she felt like *she* was the intruder. Rico had never been particular about who he let hang at his place.

"Sake! Baby!" Rico came out of his bedroom with open arms. "You're back!"

She accepted the requisite hug from his angular body.

"Where you been?"

"My dad's place. He got me out of jail. Where've *you* been? How come didn't you answer your phone?"

"Huh? Oh, I musta lost it somewhere. Who knows. Went over to look for you at booking and release the next day and you were gone. I been asking all over. Talked to Francine down at your work, and everything."

He couldn't have borrowed a phone to call her? Rico's screwed-up logic was an insult to her intelligence that was hard to swallow, but no matter how bitter the taste it left in her mouth, now wasn't the time to get into an argument. Not when she needed a place to crash.

"How's Taylor? How are ya, boy?" he asked, giving Taylor's back a brisk, back-and-forth scrub.

"She's a girl," said Sake wearily. How many times did she have to tell him that? Usually Rico ignored Taylor. Why was he showering attention on her now?

"Yeah, about that night. Get a little over-served, act the fool, you know?"

His words left her feeling hollow. Sake well knew what getting wasted looked like, but not how it felt.

"It ain't like *I* called the cops. It was those *mofos* next door. People need to mind their own business, *youknowhatI'msayin'*?"

Sake got a close-up of the swollen red stripe that marred his cheekbone, above the line where his beard would have started if he had one. "That looks *hurt*. You got any Neosporin?" she asked with more than a twinge of guilt that something she had done might scar anybody, not just Rico.

"Forget about it. All in the past," he said charitably. He circled her waist with his hands and backed her into the bedroom. "Hey," he said, softening his voice.

Rico kissed her neck, without regard for the jammed backpack still weighing down her shoulder. "I missed you." She felt a sudden draft on her behind, then cool palms sliding down her lower back into the waistband of her panties.

She shivered. Over his shoulder, she stared dully into the corner of the room. Rico's place was no mansion, but at least there were no surprises here, no unspoken rules she was supposed to conform to. Here, the only expectations imposed on her were her own.

Rico squeezed handfuls of Sake's rear end while he bit her neck in a long-neglected move he knew she used to like. That suddenly seemed like a long time ago.

She felt her traitorous body respond, molding to Rico's with the basic need for simple human contact, source be damned. Her backpack slid down her arm to the floor with a dull thump and her arms returned his embrace. The depth of her emptiness surprised her. So maybe Rico was no prince. Even if he was drunk sometimes—okay, most of the time—she could usually count on him to be there. Unlike Haha, Rico was as constant as the sea lions at Pier 39, as permanent as the Filbert Street Steps. So what if it was only because he didn't have the gumption to up and leave for something better or more interesting. *All good to the gracious.* As long as she could put up with Rico, she'd have a place to lay her head. And in her world, that was saying something.

She heard her dog noisily lapping up stale water from her dish in its regular spot on the kitchen floor. Taylor knew where home was, too.

But wait—the corner of the bedroom wasn't entirely empty. Up near the ceiling, a fly trapped in an invisible web strained and struggled for its very life.

"You get paid, babe?" Rico's mouth left her shoulder to murmur in her ear. "I just wanna run down and get a six-pack. I'll give it back to you first of the month. Promise."

Sake stepped out of his groping hands. "I was just at Bunz to get my pay and Teeny wouldn't give it to me." She didn't bother to fight the distress that came welling up in her throat. Here, in the real world, everyone had problems. It was nothing to be embarrassed about. "Then he fired me for calling off."

"That sucks."

"What am I going to do?"

"You can't let him do that. Go on back and ask him for it again."

He'd have her beg?

"Let's go, I'll walk you back over." From the doorway, he stopped, waited, and tossed his head toward the street. "C'mon."

She really needed her money. "Will you go in with me?"

He averted his eyes, rubbing at an imaginary smudge on the door-frame. "Teeny don't like me much."

"Teeny doesn't like anyone."

And then Sake pictured the convenience store where Rico bought his beer, strategically located right between the apartment and Bunz. If she got Teeny to give her her cash, Rico could stop and buy his six-pack on the way home.

Quick as an Embarcadero pickpocket, Sake made a decision. She breezed past Rico on her way to the kitchen, where a weekend's worth of dirty dishes piled up in the sink only strengthened her resolve. From underneath it, she snatched a fresh trash bag, then turned and strode back to the bedroom, white plastic flapping after her like a seagull over the Bay. While Rico stared, she started stuffing clothes into it from out of her box.

"What are you doing?"

"Going back to my dad's place for a while. What else can I do? I got no money! Just till I come up with a plan."

"That who was in that Caddy dropped you off? Damn. Nice whip."

Like a fool, Sake had mentioned once in passing that her dad was well off. But no real harm done. To Rico, "well off" meant a little rental in the Cole Valley with a couple of nice cars in the driveway. Other than the Social Services websites, Rico never got online, didn't care squat about the world outside The Mission. He'd probably never even heard of wine country.

"Hold up. We'll get The App Queen to show you how to play the system. You don't have to ever work again."

That's what The App Queen did. She used to work for the govern-ment, until she "wised up"—Rico's words.

"I'm not taking your check, and I'm not going on the dole my-self." Save welfare for the people who really needed it. Besides, work was totally her jam. The one thing that made her feel good about her-self.

"What about Haha? You giving up looking for her?"

Sake froze. Looking for her mother was a never-ending quest, and no one knew that better than Rico. She'd charged Rico with keeping an eye out for Haha every place he went, too. That's how she'd met him, looking for Haha in one of the dives those two had in common. Rico was under strict instructions to get in touch with Sake immediately if Haha showed up at any of their regular joints. Unlike other jobs, he actually seemed into it, if only because it gave him an excuse to drink.

Now he was using it to make her feel guilty.

"I do want to find her. I will. I just can't do it right now. I told you, I'm just taking a little break. I'll be back."

She left some things behind to get later, but not Taylor's rug. That, she rolled up and wedged under her arm. "Time to go," she told her.

From where her head rested on her paws, Taylor peered up at Sake with a sheepish expression.

Sake tsked and gave the leash a tug.

Still, Taylor wouldn't budge. *We just got home, and now we have to leave again?*

Impatiently, Sake reached down and scooped her up. "We'll be back," she repeated.

Rico stood there with his arms hanging limply at his sides when she brushed by him, laden with her bags and the rug and her dog. She could almost hear his brain calculating as she steadfastly picked her way back down the steps before she could change her mind.

"Get back here," he called halfheartedly, in a feeble attempt to restore normalcy, his voice ricocheting off the walls of the stairwell.

Sake's heart raced with conflicting emotions. What if, later on, something happened and Rico didn't let her come back? Where would she go? At the same time, she was hoping against hope that Caddy would still be waiting out at the curb.

"If things don't work out, I'll run you to your dad's myself."

I don't think so. Rico might not be evil, but that didn't mean he was reliable. He had a DWI, for one thing. It'd be a while before he was legit again. And that car of his? Papa would freak if he saw her pull up to the mansion in that murdered-out hooptie.

"I love you."

That stopped her. It had taken a lot for Rico to say that.

In the doorway to the street, Sake halted to turn and look at him. She saw again the wound she'd inflicted on his cheek. She even saw a flicker of what might pass for genuine emotion.

Then, in an instant, she remembered all the times Rico had sent her into stores to return items so he could use the money for beer, instructing her to claim the items were defective. He'd done it so many times himself that he was on some kind of list where they wouldn't let him return things anymore.

She picked up her feet again.

Bruno hopped out to take her gear and get her door the moment he spotted her. He saw to her and Taylor's comfort in the back, then sprinted back around to his seat. But as he was checking his side mirror for an opening to pull away from the curb, Rico came tearing out of the apartment, calling Sake's name.

Bruno hit the automatic door locks.

"Sake!" Rico pounded on the window. That set Taylor off.

"Don't go! Don't leave me, baby!"

While Taylor barked and barked, there was a break in the stream of traffic. Bruno caught Sake's eye in the rearview mirror, reading her unspoken *yes*, and he pulled out.

Sake heard Rico's professions of love coming from the middle of the street behind them. But the Caddy was soon forced to slow behind other cars. Rico could easily have caught up with them on foot, but he apparently drew the line at that.

Bruno gave her a block or two to collect her thoughts before he again sought her eyes at a red light.

"Are you quite all right, Mademoiselle Sake?"

All right? She was turning her back on the city of her birth, a man who professed to love her, and everything she owned except for the clothes she'd managed to stuff into the trash bag.

As the car turned northward toward wine country, all Sake could do was watch passively as the only place she'd ever belonged slipped by outside her window.

Somewhere out there, amid all the gingerbread Victorians, the gay bars, the food trucks, and the tourists, was her mother. She told herself that Haha was just on an extra-long binge this time. Maybe some high roller like Papa had parked her in his crib. There'd been a few of those in Haha's life, wedged in among every other class of man imaginable. The more different one was from the last, the more Haha liked him. Fanciest mansion or divey-est dive, though, Haha was born with itchy feet. She never stayed with one man, in one place, for long.

For the second time in mere hours, Sake was crossing the Bay.

But this time it felt different. The rain had tapered off; the fog was lifting. Far below, brave little sailboats bobbed and dipped among the swells, giving themselves up to whichever way the winds might blow them. All they had to do was stay upright and let the wind do the rest. Her head fell back on the seat while her finger stroked absentmindedly under Taylor's chin. Maybe, right this very minute, Haha was in one of those sailboats. Or just out of sight, livin' chilly with a drink in her hand on the patio of one of those cliff-side Marin County showplaces. She pushed away the thought that any picture of a happy Haha wasn't complete without her being totally demolished—on something more potent than mai tais.

In a few months, though, Sake would turn twenty-three. One thing she could count on no matter what was Haha not missing her birthday.

There was an old Japanese superstition: a child's third, fifth, and seventh birthdays were auspicious. Starting with those birthdays, Haha had bought Sake all new clothes and took her to the Shichi-Go-San ceremony at the Sokoji temple, even though she complained each time that it cost sixty bucks. There, the priest gave her and the other boys and girls long, skinny sticks of thousand-year candy wrapped in red and white, along with good-luck pictures of cranes and turtles.

After that, birthdays at the temple had turned into a ritual. Every year, even after they'd gone their separate ways for all intents and purposes, Haha met Sake at the temple at noon, to celebrate with tea and candy.

She pulled out her phone and Googled *GED: sample test questions.*

Find a pair of numbers with:
a) a sum of 11 and a product of 24.
b) a sum of 40 and a product of 400.
c) a sum of 15 and a product of 54.

That didn't seem too hard. She scrolled down to the next problem.

What is the primary function of chloroplasts?
a) captures energy from sunlight
b) carries proteins to parts of the cell
c) stores water and food for a cell

The answer was A. She knew that without even studying.

Maybe this GED thing wasn't so tricky.

Fine. Who couldn't use a long vacation? She'd go back to ye olde homestead long enough to get the loot Papa had promised her. But she'd be back on September first. Haha would be looking for her at the temple. Imagine how proud she'd be if Sake had a shiny new diploma to show her.

Since she'd been working regular at Bunz and living at Rico's, Sake had been able stop fretting about how she was going to buy Taylor's next bag of dog chow. But was that really enough?

Imagine the apartment she could rent with a quarter of a million dollars! Maybe even a pretty townhouse in Cole Valley. She could get Haha to quit her vagabond ways, move in with her, settle down once and for all. And wouldn't Rico love her then, for real? Maybe even enough to stop drinking.

She'd buy Haha a new cell phone so they never had to be out of touch again. After all, Haha was no spring chicken anymore. She couldn't keep drifting from man to man, apartment to apartment, forever. Could she?

Didn't Haha want—didn't she *need*—her only child, as Sake wanted and needed her?

Chapter 9

"You ever been in love?" inquired Russ Cross from where he and Bill stood in the parking lot of Cross's strip center.

Cross's recent divorce settlement had left him bitter and disillusioned. Now the silver-haired investor was anxious to liquidate his assets so he could live on the sailboat he kept docked in St. Maarten.

Bill jammed his hands into his pockets and kicked at the macadam. With Sylvia, he'd only been a kid. He and Brittany had had fun together, but in the end, what she'd done had been a little bizarre, to say the least. And Dynise, the witch? She'd been . . . *interesting*— in the short run. "Might've come close a time or two."

"Let me guess. As soon as you thought you knew a woman, *bam!*" Cross smacked his fist into his palm. "She ended up a loose cannon, leaving you high and dry on your beam ends."

Bill grinned wryly.

Cross threw a deeply tanned arm around Bill. "Take it from me, mate. Don't ever get married. Marriage sucks the life out of you." Then he took him by the shoulders and gave him a shake. "Just get my building sold so I can cut my losses . . . spend the rest of my days fishing, drinking rum, and screwing island girls."

"There's nothing I'd like better than to sell your property, man." The same transaction that would allow Cross to spend his golden years with a perpetual piña colada in hand would earn Bill his biggest commission ever. That, plus the savings Bill had been squirreling away since he was a kid, would be more than enough for a substantial down payment on the house on Elm Street. That is, if some other lucky buyer hadn't already snapped it up by then.

Remnants of last weekend had infiltrated all of today's meetings and phone calls and showings. The helicopter crash at Domaine St.

Pierre was the talk of the valley. Since word got out that Bill was an actual eyewitness, everyone he ran into hounded him for details. But when asked about Xavier's biracial love child, he found her impossible to explain. How did you describe a woman who looked as sweet as cotton candy, but when she opened her mouth, Eminem came out?

Even now, locking his car in the parking lot of his apartment building, precious signed contract safely tucked into his briefcase, Bill couldn't stop thinking about Sake. Good thing he'd got rid of her before he got too wrapped up in her drama. The last thing he needed was someone who had no compunction about phoning him at all hours of the day and night to be at her beck and call. Hadn't he already had more than his share of crazy chicks? Mom was right. He needed to find someone nice and normal to settle down with. Especially now that his goal of home ownership dangled tantalizingly within reach.

He stepped over the threshold of his dark, quiet apartment, dropped his keys into the plate by the door—and immediately experienced a letdown. No friendly dog jumped up to greet him. No one asked about his day. Bill was a people person. What was he doing here all alone when there were dozens of wine bars and taverns within a twenty-mile radius? He grabbed his keys, turned right around, and walked out again.

But none of the guys were down at Toasted, the pub nearest the golf course. He eased onto one of three empty seats at the bar and ordered a beer anyway. No sooner did his draft arrive than two women in scrubs and practical, rubber-heeled shoes sat down next to him.

Bill loved golf, but he wasn't especially good at it. Something he *was* good at, though, was small talk. Within minutes, he knew the women's names and that they worked at Queen of the Valley hospital. Marissa liked Moscato and Deborah, a physical therapist with a confident demeanor, was drinking pinot. When Marissa got up to use the ladies' room, Deborah scooted over to keep Bill company.

Deb was in the middle of repeating a patient's funny story when Bill's phone rang, the name on the screen hitting him with a cocktail of elation and dread. "Excuse me." He faked an apologetic face. "Client." And then immediately felt guilty for lying.

"Sake?" Bill answered, walking away to talk in privacy.

"'Wassup?"

"Er, what's up with you?" He frowned. "Where *are* you?"

"Back at Papa's house. I'ma be hanging out with you, after all."

"What—how—?"

"You can come get me?"

She had a way of turning a question around into a demand. Who did she think he was? Her personal assistant?

He glanced over his shoulder at Deborah, picturing her in the doorway of the house on Elm Street, a baby on her hip, dinner on the stove, welcoming him home from a hard day of selling real estate. Was it a premonition, or just his age talking? He'd be thirty this year. He'd sown his mild oats, and everyone knew what came after that.

"Now?"

"You got somethin' better to do?"

The *chutzpah!* With sudden certainty, it hit him that Deborah, even after knowing Bill an entire year, wouldn't have had the gall to ask him to do the favors Sake had asked of him within mere days of meeting each other. "Actually, yes. I mean no. I can't come get you. I'm busy."

"Whatevs."

"Why? What is it this time?" He couldn't just leave it at that, could he?

"Doesn't matter now."

"Can't you just—?" Bill huffed through his nose, resolute. "No. I can't come get you right now, at the drop of a hat."

"I said, *it's cool.*"

"Wait—" But she had hung up.

Bill walked back to the bar and Deborah's indulgent smile. "You were saying?" he asked. But his laugh at the end of her story was forced. All he could think about was Sake and wonder what kind of trouble she'd gotten herself into this time.

He bought the women a second round, thinking it would keep him there longer, but when there were still a couple of inches of wine left in their glasses he made an excuse to leave.

One beer, and your common sense is shot.

From the parking lot, he returned Sake's phone call.

"So what's your crisis this time?" He hated that he was grinning.

"I got something to ask you."

"Did you eat yet?"

"No."

"Want to grab something?"

"A girl can always eat."

On his way to the winery to pick up Sake, Bill considered a dozen places to take her before deciding on Bottega, equally beloved by tourists and locals alike.

"They've got an unbelievable cellar here," Bill said after they'd been seated.

"I don't drink."

Bill looked up from his menu. She was a Californian who didn't drive, and now the daughter of the most notorious vintner in Napa Valley didn't drink?

"I'll just order me a pot of herb tea."

"You can get anything you want. My treat."

When Bill was nervous, he tended to talk even more than usual. And something about Sake made him anxious to please. He found himself opening up about his work, then his colorful parents. While he moved on from his family tree to the NorCal real estate market and then the current state of the local, state, and world economy, he couldn't take his eyes off Sake, who was carefully peeling apart the layers of her dinner roll.

"Do you actually find that roll more interesting than the Fed's plan to normalize interest rates?"

"That is a croissant, not a roll. Look at these layers! Whoever made this got some mad lamination skills."

How did she do that? Always knock him off track? "Tell me. Exactly what happened after I dropped you off at the winery this morning?"

Sake popped a morsel of perfectly baked dough into her mouth and chewed, swooning. "Mm. So flaky . . . so buttery." She swallowed. "So, here's how it went down. Papa gets all *assholian* 'bout how I cut hair in the middle of the night—like he's layin' down some kinda curfew on me, twenty-two years old!—and then I was all like, I'm not about to ride your leg like everyone else around here—"

"Wait. You *said* that to him?"

Sake looked at him like he had an IQ of about ten. "You think I'd actually say that to my father? That was, you know, just a metaphor.

"Then he was like, da da da school, woompty woomp work, somethin' somethin'. Finally, he let up. Sent me back downtown, like I wanted in the first place." She sipped daintily from her teacup. "Copped a ride from my man Bruno."

"But then"—Bill spread his hands—"what're you doing here, now?"

"Gimme time. So I went in to my work to tell my boss I was back, and do you know, that heartless thug was already training my replacement?"

"You got fired?"

"For taking off to go to my sister's wedding. Can you believe that?"

"You'd given advance notice, right? How far ahead did you tell him that you needed time off?"

"See, that's just it," she said, analyzing her second roll—er, croissant—as she separated it. "I didn't have any notice to give 'cause I didn't even know about no wedding till the day before."

Bill frowned. "I don't understand."

She made an impatient face. "I only found out about it when Papa bailed me—"

Bill's eyes flew open wide.

Sake licked her fingers. "Nothing. All you need to know is, I lost my job. And then, my damn boss wouldn't give me my back pay."

"He can't do that." The more Sake talked, the more Bill's head spun with questions.

"Oh. Yes. He. Did," she said, cocking her head from side to side with each word.

Bill's shyster radar rang like a fire alarm. Was she about to hit him up for cash?

"Papa told me if I stay up here till my birthday, get my life on lock, I can go back and press restart."

"Then what do you need me for?"

"Back me up. Taylor's gonna need a place to stay for a while."

Bill released his held breath. "I think I can handle that. I don't mind having a dog around." Truth was, he liked the company. But then he remembered—this was Sake. With her, nothing was straightforward. He envisioned her coming around at times that might be . . . let's say, inconvenient.

"We can set up some sort of visitation schedule."

Sake scowled. "What do you mean, visitation schedule? I got to see Taylor every day."

Bill used his objective voice, the one he used when he was negotiating with clients. "Well," he said reasonably, "you might have to compromise there . . ."

"Compromise? You telling me when I can and when I can't see my own dog?"

Was she going to make him spell it out for her? "It's just that, well, you know. I have a life."

"Everyone's got a life. I got a life, too: *Taylor*. Taylor is my life. Especially now that I had to give everything else up.

"You gotta work. I get that." Her face was open, her eyes candid. So how could she not see his point?

"Riiiight . . . there's work, and then there's life *after* work. There are times when I might want to, you know, go out on a date or something."

"Date? People still *date?*"

Bill shrugged. "I do." *Note to self: Look up alternative word for "date" in Urban Dictionary.*

She slanted him a suspicious look. "You got a girlfriend?"

"Well, no, not exactly."

"What do you mean, 'not exactly'? Do you or do you not have a girlfriend, Bill Diamond?"

Earlier, at Toasted, Bill had made a prudent investment in his future by asking Deborah to go out on Friday night.

"If you got a girlfriend, what're you doing buying me dinner at this fancy restaurant?" She looked around for her bag and slung it over her shoulder, ready to bolt.

"I don't have a girlfriend." He planted a staying hand atop hers. "But I may *get* a girlfriend at some point. . . ."

"And if I'm hanging around, you're afraid I'll be in the way, izzat what you're saying? Throw salt on your game?"

"Well, no, I—"

"Yes, you are."

Bill's hand slipped off of Sake's and went palm up as he leaned back. He had nothing.

Sake took a moment, then lifted her chin and bored her eyes into his. "Okay. I tell you what. I'll compromise. On nights you got a booty call—"

Booty call? Furtively, he looked around to make sure no one had overheard. He had his reputation to protect. *"I don't have booty calls—"* he said in an undertone.

"On nights when you do what it is that you do, you just let me know, and we can skip visitation."

"You're forgetting," he added, pumped that another good excuse had come to him, "every time you come to my apartment to see your dog, first I have to pick you up, then, when visiting hours are over, drop you off again. Why? Because *you don't drive*."

He sat back again with a satisfied smirk.

Sake's face fell. She looked up through lowered lids. "You're real proud of yourself for that shiv in the kidney, aren't you?"

Immediately Bill regretted cutting her. There she went again, buffeting his emotions like a whipsaw.

But a man had to stand his ground. "Look, I'm sorry, Sake, but you can't expect to just drop into my life and start running the show. Three days ago I didn't even know Sake St. Pierre existed. Now all of a sudden you're planning to be omnipresent."

She lifted a brow. "Somebody's being negative. You didn't hear me? I said, let's compromise. Whenever you got something better to do, just lemme know."

The server arrived, balancing their plates on his arm. "Who's got the Patatine Fritte?"

"Right here." Sake lit up, eagerly taking her plate from the waiter's hands before he had the chance to properly set it down, and from that moment on, all the bad stuff melted away like a snowball in an oven. Starting with the way she closed her cat eyes to savor her first crunch of the parmesan-coated fries, to the careless way she sat with her elbows on the table, one crossed leg jutting out from beneath the tablecloth, where it almost tripped two waiters, every move Sake made fascinated him, leading him to drag out his meal with more rambling talk long after Sake's plate was clean and she had started stealing forkfuls of his neglected duck confit.

Later that night, Bill realized he couldn't even recall the taste of his meal. Usually when he couldn't sleep, it was because he was wrestling down a fine point on some deal—making a case for a zoning variance, crafting some creative financing. But ever since dinner, he was preoccupied with visions of Sake—the way her pride hung on, even when he'd hurt her feelings . . . her easy grace offsetting her cheap dress . . . right down to the way her slender fingers tapered to hold a greasy French fry. . . . What was it about her that had him losing his usually well-ordered mind? He couldn't let his guard down for a second when she was around.

Irritably, Bill flipped his pillow over to the cool side. *Sake St. Pierre is a royal pain in the ass.*

Time to distance himself from cheats and wack jobs, stick to his plan to settle down in that house on Elm. Thanks to Russ Cross, he was halfway there. He couldn't get sidetracked by a quirky, captivating little sprite. That was just asking for trouble.

So why couldn't he wipe that stupid grin off his face, alone in his room in the dark?

Chapter 10

The following Friday, Sake heard determined footsteps padding into her darkened room. On a scrape of metal, the heavy drapes swept across the carpet. Even with her eyes still closed, the strong summer light made her squint.

"Up, up, up!"

Sake gave Jeanne a glazed look. "You trippin'."

"It is one o'clock in the afternoon. All week you have done nothing but lie in bed or laze by the pool all day and stay up all night."

"Like that's a bad thing. I'm ill-suited for day shift."

For the past five days she'd stuck to pretty much the same waking and sleeping schedule she'd had when she worked at Bunz—except for the working part. Slept till two. Got up. Put on her swimsuit, and trod barefoot down the palatial staircase. Then she held the door of the well-stocked fridge open until Jeanne scolded her for letting out all the cold air. Was it Sake's fault she found it almost impossible to decide from among all the juices and nut butters and flavored yogurts and fruits in there? She'd never had so many choices.

Eventually she would compose a plate and carry it out to the pool. After she ate, she'd lower her leopard sunners, close her eyes, and lie back in the chaise longue with a satisfied sigh.

Ahhh. This is the life.

Except that it wasn't.

After only a few minutes of lying there, Sake's eyes would pop open again of their own accord. Because after fourteen hours in bed, the last thing she needed was rest.

Not only that, wasn't sponging off of Papa the same as relying on the state to take care of you? Without a job, she was no better than Rico.

"That was the past," said Jeanne. "Here, you must adapt to your new life."

"Looks like I'm well on my way, thanks to you," she said, holding back a smirk.

"Your papa tells me you worked in a bakery."

That brought Sake to a sitting position. "So?" She yawned without covering her mouth.

"I need your help in the kitchen. Your papa is having a business dinner tonight, and I was hoping you could bake some bread."

"What, you don't got no froufrou bakeries in this neck of the woods?"

"Napa has many fine bakeries. But I thought you might appreciate the opportunity to do something concrete."

Studying for her GED at night in bed was a workout for her mind, but Sake was a hands-on learner. Jeanne was right. She needed something to do before she went off the rails.

From hanging around the past few days, watching her family and the people who helped run the house, she had started to get a handle on life at Domaine St. Pierre. Early each morning she heard someone—presumably, one of her sisters—in the upstairs hallways getting ready for work, then the click of the front door closing when she left for the day.

Papa seemed to have no set schedule at all. You never knew when you might pass him late at night in the foyer, or spot him in the afternoon rifling through the stack of mail Jeanne pre-sorted for him. He was never still for long . . . always on his way either in or out. Jeanne said he traveled a lot.

And then there was Jeanne herself. She had a lot on her plate, running a house the size of this one, where the mood was one of subdued bustle. Its serenity was deceiving, though. Keeping it that way required a lot of behind-the-scenes planning and delegation and supervision. Jeanne rarely sat down before the dinner dishes were rinsed and put in the dishwasher.

"You know, Sake, your sisters may have grown up with all of this"—Jeanne swept an arm across the guest room, looking for the word she wanted—"*lavishness,* but they are not lazy. Each of them has worked exceedingly hard to—"

Sake sprang from her bed. In two steps she was standing nose to nose with Jeanne. "Who you callin' lazy? These past five days is the longest stretch I haven't worked since I was thirteen years old. I was waitin' tables before I was even legal, then up at two a.m. to get to work by three. So don't you be calling *me* lazy. 'Least lemme get cleaned up and throw some clothes on."

Jeanne raised a brow. "Fortunately, even *you* know that going downstairs in the nude would not be appropriate," she muttered on her way out.

After she showered and dressed, Sake sidled into the spacious kitchen with all its gleaming appliances.

Like, whoa. Love. "This AGA is off the hook," she murmured, stroking a fingertip across its black enamel surface.

"Make yourself at home," said Jeanne, adding, "After all, this *is* your home, is it not? I've set out the bowls and some flour. Feel free to look around if I have forgotten something. I must supervise the staff with their preparations for tonight's dinner, but I will be wandering in and out if you need me. Do you need a recipe?"

Sake shook her head. "No, ma'am." She was used to mixing large quantities, but she knew how to reduce the proportions. Maybe she hadn't graduated high school, but math had never given her any trouble.

Whew. School seemed like eons ago.

"Well, if you do, the cookbooks are on that shelf. Here"—she reached into a drawer—"an apron."

It felt good to slip the loop over her head and tie the strings behind her back. Jeanne hung around for a minute or so, watching Sake, probably to make sure she wouldn't slip a butter knife into her pocket or something. Finally, when Jeanne left, Sake relaxed a little. She peeked into the nearest cupboard. Alongside the expected canned goods and boxes of pasta, she found bags of jasmine rice and yellow lentils and quinoa, almonds and walnuts. She closed that door and opened another cupboard crammed with just as many exotic things.

Sake was a baker, not a cook. There was a difference. But all those riches were enough to make her want to set a pot to boiling on every one of the AGA's burners.

Instinct told her that the use of this kitchen was a fleeting high point. She wished she could just enjoy it without automatically comparing it to some of the lower ones.

Coming up, her life had always been dictated by whichever man

Haha was on a thing with. Sake had liked some of them . . . the ones who had let her tag along on trips to the Pier, or on long drives down the coast, or to restaurants overlooking the Pacific.

But not all of them.

In between the good guys that wove in and out of their lives, Haha lived for the long white official-looking envelope to arrive in her post office box. She'd stuff it in her purse, load Sake into the car, and drive to the check-cashing place. From inside the locked car—Haha said she'd be safer waiting there than going in with her—Sake would sit petrified with fear, holding her breath until Haha made it back to the car without getting jumped.

After that, Haha would drop Sake off at the house of one of her constantly changing cast of "friends." They would feed her rice or noodles or toast and, if she was lucky, let her be to chill for a couple of days, until either Haha came back or they got tired of the added burden of an odd, introverted girl, and then bitter at Haha for having taken advantage, the weight of their resentment as uncomfortable as a cold, wet blanket on Sake's shoulders.

The worst of them treated Sake like a free babysitter, going out for hours, sometimes days, leaving her behind in their sour-smelling apartments where the beds were never made, to mind their kids, with not enough milk or diapers on hand and no way for her to get more. . . .

But that was a long time ago. Now, Sake concentrated on getting to know the AGA, adjusting the flame on the burners, peeking into the ovens . . . pulling gently on a drawer to feel it glide smooth and silent on its track.

She began measuring out flour and honey and yeast. As always, kneading the stiff bread dough until it reached the ideal degree of smoothness and elasticity kept her grounded in the moment. The next step was shaping it into a ball, placing it in its greased bowl to rest, and covering it with a linen towel to eventually double in size. That was another thing Sake loved about baking—if you used proper technique and followed the recipe, the dough could be counted on to turn out the same way every time. Bread and pastry didn't give you painful surprises, like you got with people. Just warm, fragrant, soul-soothing results that filled the emptiness, if only for a while.

Later that evening, Sake sat alone in one of the mansion's living rooms, studying.

Jeanne was having dinner with Papa and his guests. Clearly, Jeanne was way more than just another employee. At the very least, she played hostess to Papa's parties.

Evidently, Rico still hadn't found his phone. Sake would worry about that later. Being incommunicado might not be bad, anyway, at least for a while. It might even help him get past her taking a break from them.

Tired of studying, Sake laid the iPad on the coffee table, rose from the couch, and walked to the window.

Bill Diamond had begged off seeing her tonight. She tried not to think about what he was doing.

The high points of the past week had been the daily hour or two she'd spent with Bill and her dog. That said something about life in the valley in general, when all she and Bill ever did was walk Taylor around the block, toss a ball to her a few times on the tiny patch of lawn in front of his apartment building, and then go inside and have tea or pizza and watch the evening news before he drove her home again.

At least it wasn't as quiet at Bill's place as it was here. Bill never ran out of things to say. He was interested in everything. Local gossip and global climate change. Store openings and what to do about the unending problems in the Middle East. Concepts and ideas that Sake had never paid any attention to. When it took all your energy just to keep your head above water, it tended to narrow your focus. But hearing Bill talk made Sake think.

She wondered if another woman was there, at his place right now, listening to Bill ramble, petting Sake's dog. How would Bill explain Taylor away?

The colors of the half-dozen, high-class cars lining the driveway had become indistinguishable in the descending darkness. She turned from the window, wondering absently how her baguettes had gone down at the party. Might as well go upstairs and try out that super-sized Jacuzzi while she could.

Sake reached the staircase as Jeanne came out of the dining room. "Do you have a moment? Come, meet your papa's guests."

Sake halted, immediately uncomfortable. "I've already met their type, at Savvy's wedding."

"Sake." Jeanne came to her and placed her hand on her arm. Lowering her voice, she said, "The way to happiness is to open yourself up to new people, new experiences."

"How do you know what will make me happy?"

"You have won them over with your baguettes," said Jeanne.

Still, she hesitated. Could she take Jeanne at her word?

"You have a true talent for baking. They can't stop talking about it."

The sounds of laughter and conversation drifted into the foyer.

"You hear that?" Jeanne clucked. "Come, come."

When Jeanne and Sake walked into the dining room, Papa and all the other gentlemen immediately rose from their chairs.

Papa put his hand lightly on Sake's back. "My friends, I present to you my youngest daughter."

Those standing nearest to Sake reached out to shake her hand, while those farther away nodded their respects.

"Ernst Volant," said the jolly-looking, round guy whose voice she'd heard earlier. "Only one time have I had French bread as good as this: in Lyon. It is absolute perfection. A crusty exterior, yet soft inside. That bread would have my customers standing in line."

What did I tell you? said Jeanne's sly, encouraging wink.

"Nice to meet you," Sake replied politely.

Everyone but Mr. Volant went back to their seats and the coffee that a server was pouring.

"Will you share with us your secret to making this fantastic baguette?"

"Er, it's simple, really. First: treat it rough."

By their guffaws, the men clearly thought that was a riot, their wives not so much. She caught them exchanging dubious glances. But Sake knew what she was talking about when it came to baking bread. She wasn't cowed.

"When you're punching it down, you gotta let some air out and give the yeast more sugars to feed on without wrecking all of the work they've already done—that is, without letting *all* the air out."

Mr. Volant nodded in rapt attention. "Go on."

"Second, knead it by hand instead of machine, and walk away from it for twenty minutes before you mix in the salt and the yeast, to let the flour absorb the water and the gluten strands develop. Letting it rest like that makes your crumb come out whiter too."

"Where did you learn to bake?"

"Sake apprenticed to a baker in the city," Papa interjected.

"No, I mean, where'd you get your schooling?"

"Balboa High," replied Sake.

Far down the table, a woman ducked her chin in a mock attempt to hide her smirk, peering up at the other women through her eyelashes. *Isn't she precious?* her expression said. And not in a good way.

"Sake is looking for a position with a reputable local establishment," Jeanne announced, breaking the resulting, awkward silence.

She was?

"I am trying to convince Sake to attend the CIA, to obtain a degree," added Papa. "But I'm afraid my daughter has a stubborn streak when it comes to my advice. Perhaps she'll listen to someone else."

"Just like her papa," said Mr. Volant good-naturedly. "I gather you'll be staying here with your family for the foreseeable future?"

"Maybe."

"Absolutely," Papa stepped on her reply, negating it.

Sake gave Papa dagger eyes.

"We should talk. Give me a call tomorrow morning. Here's my card."

Mr. Volant's card was sky blue with white clouds. *Mon Rêve— Patisserie Francaise.*

"My dream," he translated.

Like, whoa. Working in a real French bakery was way *beyond* anything Sake had ever dared to dream of. But wearing her heart on her sleeve was just asking for it. "Cool whip. Thanks," was all she said, before turning and leaving.

As she walked away, the room fell silent. She paused at the newel post at the foot of the stairs, to eavesdrop.

"Ahem. Well," came the initial deep-voiced comment, followed by more masculine throat-clearing and restrained coughs.

"I don't know how you did it, St. Pierre," said an authoritative tone. "Raised four brilliant, beautiful daughters, each one more fascinating than the last."

"So artless, so ingenuous," said the bitch who'd snickered at Sake's expense.

Crazy how the same comment that smacked women between the eyes could pass right over men's heads. "Artless" and "ingenuous" were just fancy code for unsophisticated.

Speaking of bitches, who'd given Jeanne the green light to tell folks Sake was looking for work, up here in the hinterlands? Sake had to hand it to her. It was genius. Just what she needed—something to keep her from going stir-crazy till she could go back to civilization.

Sake sprang up the stairs two at a time, all but skipping down the long hallway to her suite. Thanks to Jeanne, Papa's friend had practically promised her a job—in public, no less!

Her steps slowed again when she realized she now faced another problem. Wherever this Mon Rêve was, it sure wasn't within walking distance of the mansion. Nothing was. And there were no cable cars out here in Timbuktu. Assuming she did get hired, how was she supposed to get to work?

Like anyone else, Sake had assumed she might get her license one day, had already gone through the preliminary steps—before discovering that she was terrified every time she got behind the wheel. But in the city, it wasn't really essential. Maybe if she weren't surrounded by freeways, it wouldn't be so scary. Up here on Napa's country roads, where she could go slow and there weren't any other cars zooming around on all sides, maybe she could learn to relax.

Papa said a car was hers for the asking, as long as she lived at the winery. Jeanne had already wondered out loud why Sake never went anywhere except with Bill Diamond. Not even *he* knew she was terrified to drive herself.

Sake sat down on the bed, pulled out her phone, and punched in Bill's number. She took a preparatory breath while it rang, cursing Papa yet again for blackmailing her. She could have lived the rest of her life in San Francisco, walking or taking BART everywhere. But here? She couldn't stay stuck inside this house with nothing to do but lounge by the pool for the next two months. What was she? A damn hostage?

"Sake?"

"You can teach me to drive?"

"Me? Teach you? To drive?"

"I can do most anything I want when I set to it. But I'ma need some help with this one, seein's how they want you to practice with a licensed driver and all. So picky."

Chapter 11

The next afternoon, Bill and Sake sat at his dinette table, polishing off the last of a take-out pizza.

Bill pulled up the website of the California Department of Motor Vehicles while Sake dunked her tea bag in and out of her second cup of tea.

"Props to you for getting hired at another bakery, after only being in the valley a week," he said, while searching for the requirements for getting a driver's license.

"So," she said leaning over his screen, sipping her tea, "what do I got to do?"

At first, Bill had almost blown a fuse when Sake had had the gall to ask him to give her driving lessons, on top everything else he'd done for her—heck, was still doing. Boarding Taylor, taxiing Sake back and forth almost every day so she and her dog could spend time together . . . when was enough, enough? Where did a guy draw the line between being a mensch and a patsy? With a word, Xavier St. Pierre would gladly pay for professional driving lessons. Or why couldn't her sisters help out?

But if Bill had learned one thing about Sake this past week, it was that beneath that who-gives-a-darn attitude and the indecipherable tattoos was a deep well of pride. If Bill were a betting man—which he wasn't—he'd wager her family wasn't even savvy to the fact that she couldn't drive. She already had an inferiority complex from comparing herself with them. It seemed cruel to ask her to add to her long list of perceived shortcomings.

Anyway, Bill supposed he could sacrifice a couple golf matches this summer. He believed in lending a helping hand. And getting her license would be a positive step up for Sake. Wouldn't take long.

Once she could drive on her own, he could retire his chauffer's cap, maybe sign up for something more staid, like the Rotary. Something that better suited his style.

"A lot's changed since I learned to drive. Brings back memories. Dad always made sure we ended up at the ice cream place as a reward for a job well done.

"This says you need thirty hours of classroom instruction and six hours of behind the wheel."

"Already did that back in school," said Sake, from over by the sink where she dumped their soggy paper plates in the trash.

He looked up, frowning. "Wait a minute. If you had six hours professional driving instruction, how come you froze when I asked you to take the wheel that time when Russ Cross called me and I had to get my briefcase?"

"Okay, no, that's a lie. I never got around to the actual driving. But I did sit through the boring book part."

"Jeez! Do you go around lying like that all the time?"

Sake squared off in front of him, hands on her hips. "Why do you make such a big deal about every little thing? Didn't you ever tell a lie, Bill Diamond?"

"Other than the little white ones designed to keep from hurting peoples' feelings? No."

"Not even once? Yes, you did. Everybody lies sometimes. Come on. Tell me something you lied about."

He snorted. "This is ridiculous."

"Tell me!"

His hands flew up. "I don't know!"

She cocked a hip, lifting a condescending brow. "What's it like, Bill Diamond? Being so perfect?"

"Okay! Here's something. When I was in third grade, I lied to my mom. I said I wrote that tree poem. You know, the one that goes, *I think that I shall never see, a poem as lovely as a tree.* There. Happy?"

"Like, whoa, jump back. You are some bad-ass, Bill Diamond. Lying about a damn poem. I bet all the other Realtors run and hide when they see you comin'."

Bill bit down on his smile and went back to his screen. "But then, once you get your permit, you need fifty more hours of practice driving with a licensed driver."

She slid into the seat next to his, bringing the amber scent of her Oriental perfume with her. "That's only for minors. If you're over eighteen, you can take the test anytime you're ready, long as it's within a year of getting your permit. After that, though, the permit expires and you gotta start the process all over again."

That scent.

"Are you sure?"

"I can't drive, but I know how to read."

"I didn't say you didn't. So you have taken the classroom part about what the signs mean and everything, right?"

"You don't believe me?"

Bill gestured like, *duh.*

She pulled a face in response. "Anyway. I only got two months left till my permit expires, on my birthday, and I haven't had no on-road practice. At. All." Sake smiled brightly, and Bill forgot about his intent to ask her why that was.

Mentally, he shook his head. Dad was right. He was too damn nice.

"So, you mad now?" she asked.

"No, I'm not mad."

"You want some more tea?"

Bill never drank tea. "Sure."

She took his half-empty mug back out to the kitchen.

He heard water running in the sink, the clink of china. A homey warmth that came from sharing a meal, conversation, and a dog snoring under the table enveloped him.

"Lemme do the driving when you pick me up to come see Taylor till I get used to the feel of it, then it's just take my test for my Ls, right? And I'm in there like swimwear."

"Ls?" he repeated, like "ells."

"Ls. License." He heard her giggle over the kitchen sounds. "Don't you know nothin'?"

Bill bowed his head over his laptop to hide his amusement until he noticed a shape gliding slowly toward him in his peripheral vision. When it loomed too close to ignore, he looked up to see Sake pulling her T-shirt over her head, followed by a mass of dark hair tumbling down across her bare shoulders. Above her skirt, all she had on was a sheer black bra, held up by the thinnest of straps.

On his keyboard, Bill's hands went still.

Sake reached behind her back, and in the next second her bra was gone, too. Then, in a move a professional stripper would envy, she swept her mane up over her head, letting her hair drift back down across her pert breasts in a shower of jet. She cocked her head and, eyed him with a come-on that both repelled and aroused him, all at the same time.

Slowly, Bill stood up. "What are you *doing?*"

A laugh gurgled in the back of her throat. "Paying you back, what else? You think I'm some freshman at life? I know how it works. No such thing as a free ride."

She backed Bill up until he was practically bowed over the table backward, his hands braced on its edge. Then she slinked her arms around his neck.

Robot-like, his hands went to her waist. Her skin felt soft and warm, obliques yielding to his fingertips, and here, up close, the exotic blend of amber and spices hit him full force. His thumbs pressed into the twin curves of her lowermost ribs.

Sake lifted her eyes and parted her lips in an invitation.

His hands sprang back like they'd been singed. "What is *that?* What's going on?"

Sake stumbled backward, her brow furrowed. "Serious?"

"I'm seriously not joking. What the hell, Sake? What are you doing?"

Crimson crept up her neck. She sniffed, "If you don't know—"

"It's not that—it's . . . *why?*" Why was she suddenly hurling herself at him? The only day they'd been apart all week was yesterday, for his date with Deborah. Still, he was practically a stranger to her. Didn't she have any higher opinion of herself than that?

"What's with you, Bill Diamond? You gay?" she snapped, cheeks flooding with embarrassment.

"Gay?!? Hell no, I'm not gay! I just . . ." One hand scraped his fingers through his hair while the other dipped to retrieve her bra off the floor. He held it out to her by a string, looking away for the sake of modesty. "Christ! Put this thing back on!"

He looked away until she retrieved her shirt from where it had landed on the floor and tugged herself back together.

"Now, would you mind telling me what that was all about?" he huffed.

"Shut up!" She straightened her skirt with a jerk, camouflaging her rejection with scorn. "I never met no man as stupid as you. I'm tryin' to be nice, and you make me feel like a fool."

Half of him wanted to shake some sense into her, the other half to pick her up, toss her on his bed, and have his way with her. But he was older and wiser. He couldn't send the message that it was cool to throw herself at men as payback for favors, freely given.

Besides, being anything more than a friend to Sake was out of the question. Bill had plans. Long-term plans. Solid-as-a-rock plans.

"I think I'd better take you home now."

"Holla." The pink had reached her cheeks now.

She grabbed her bag.

"You can sit in the driver's seat."

She stopped. "Now?"

"Might as well start."

"Today?"

He shrugged his shoulders. "Why not? No reason to put it off." Things were getting out of hand. The sooner he weaned her off him and his enabling, the better.

She finished packing up her things, snapped on Taylor's leash, and followed Bill out the door.

Bill paused on the stoop to unwrap his American flag where it had furled around itself in the breeze.

"Rule number one, always wear your seat belt," he said when he eased in next to her, fastening his own. "Never go anywhere without it."

Bill watched Sake fumble inserting the male part of the buckle into the female slot. Surely she knew how to fasten a seat belt. Then, seeing how her hands trembled, it hit him. "Are you scared?"

"I'm not scared of nothing." She scowled. Bracing herself, she sucked in a breath, applied a death grip to the steering wheel, and waited for further instruction.

"Okay, rule two: you can't learn to drive with a dog on your lap. Here. Do you want me to hold her?"

She hesitated. "Maybe she'd be safer the back seat."

Yup. That's definitely fear.

"You're more worried about your dog than you are me?" he chuckled, keeping things light to ease her nerves.

She sighed and let Taylor go to him. "Just tell me what to do."

"Your hands are good there, at ten and two. But first you need to turn it on."

Her eyes swept over the dashboard.

"The ignition button's right there."

She jumped when the motor came to life.

"Now, check your mirrors and when no cars are coming, ease your foot onto the gas and steer away from the curb."

Bill checked, too, to be sure. "Easy does it. *Niiiiice* and easy."

When it was clear, Sake pulled out, and they were on their way.

"That's it. Now relax your grip. You're about to pull the wheel out of the gearbox. Lower your shoulders."

She bit her lip, tucked her chin, and furrowed her brow in concentration.

"Don't forget to breathe. Let's take a couple of passes around the side streets where it's quiet and there aren't many cars. I'll tell you where to turn.

"So, tell me more about your phone interview. When does your job start?"

"The person I'm replacing just gave her two weeks' notice, so not until then."

"Full time?"

"Six-thirty a.m. to one p.m."

"Not quite full time, but it's a start. Benefits?"

"God, are you always this practical?"

"These are things you have to think about, Sake. It's all part of being an adult. For instance, I'm what's called an independent contractor." Bill didn't let Sake's eye roll deter him. "If I got sick or hurt, I'd have no income. That's why I purchased disability insurance."

"Papa put me on his health plan."

"Good." He nodded.

"Glad you approve."

At the edge of his vision, he saw her hint of a teasing smile. His attempt at distracting her from her driving phobia was working.

"It's not your approval I'm after. I'm telling you these things because I care, Sake." With a start, Bill realized he was speaking the truth. "What kind of work will you be doing?"

"I'm straight up into baking, but Mr. Volant said I'ma be working the counter, ringing up custys. All his bakers have their associate degrees or some such thing, no idea."

"There's a degree in baking? Who knew. Well, that's something to aspire to. Assuming that's your main—*stop!*" Bill's right foot shot forward on a reflex. "Stop sign! Brake!"

The car lurched, his seat belt locked down on him, and Taylor yipped at his reflexive squeeze to keep her from falling off his lap.

"You said you knew the signs!"

Who doesn't know what a stop sign is?!

"How long ago was it that you took driver's ed?"

"Who the hell knows? Years . . ."

"How *many* years?"

"I *told* you, I don't *know*."

"Well, think. It was probably your junior or senior year. When did you graduate?"

Sake paused at the next corner. Beneath her flimsy top, her breasts rose and fell visibly. "Now what?" she demanded.

"Right. Wait—put your turn signal on. What year did you get your diploma?" he repeated.

Her lips tightened into a line.

"You didn't graduate." The words left Bill's mouth before he could censor them.

"I can pull over around here? I've had it with this for today," she said, wiping her brow with the back of her hand. "It's freaking roasting in here."

"How can it be roasting when you've got the A/C on full blast? Okay. We just made a loop. There's my apartment complex, straight ahead. Think you can parallel park if you have empty spaces around you?"

"What's parallel park?"

"Never mind. Just turn into one of these alleys and we'll trade seats."

Chapter 12

Once they stopped moving, Sake tried to catch the breath she'd been holding since they'd started out. By the way her heart hammered inside her chest, she might be having a heart attack; her face and torso were awash in a dewy film.

"Hey." Bill's voice held concern.

Warmth atop her icy right hand jarred her back into the present.

"You okay?"

She looked down at Bill's hand covering hers, still clenching the wheel.

And then something crashed that was even worse than the car: her composure. Her hands, sticky with anxiety, flew up to hide her face.

"What is it? Hey. Don't cry." Bill's hand slid up to rub her forearm.

His pity only proved how pathetic she was.

"Sake."

An ugly-sounding sob escaped from her core.

She heard Taylor being deposited onto the floor mat with a thump, felt Bill's arms slide around her as best they could within the confines of the vehicle.

"What are you crying about?"

Thinking about that only made it worse.

"Don't be so hard on yourself. This was your first time. You'll get a handle on it."

"Maybe it's not the driving. Maybe it's every other shitty thing." The unholy mess that was her life. "I'm so tired," she cried. "I've been trying so hard, for so long."

"Trying to do what?"

"I came this close to losing it when Teeny fired me," she cried. "And now, here I am in a new place, leaning on people again, just like before. Papa. Another boss. And you, who had the serious bad luck to be in the blast zone when my world blew up. You don't need the likes of me. What if I can't do it?"

What if she was doomed to repeat Haha's mistakes?

Above her sobs, she heard the click of his seat belt coming apart. Then the tension on her own belt relaxed as she realized he'd undone hers, too.

"Shhh." Bill eased the belt over her shoulder and took her into his arms, stroking her hair, gently rocking her as she let loose her emotion into his neck. When was the last time she'd been held like that, with no strings, no expectations? She barely noticed when another vehicle squeezed through the narrow alleyway to get around them.

"You're going to do it, sweetie. I'm going to help you." When she quieted, he drew back to examine her face. But she still couldn't meet his eyes. She felt his finger under her chin.

"Look at me."

No. To let someone see how bad you hurt was to be vulnerable.

Bill angled in until his mouth was so close to hers she could feel his breath on her skin. Softly, he kissed the track of a tear on the right side of her nose. Beneath her left eye, he kissed away another tear. Then a third, where it was about to fall from her chin.

He smelled like warm cedar and ginger.

"There," he said, wiping both cheeks with the pads of his thumbs.

For the first time since she'd stopped the car, she looked at him. His heavy-lidded eyes shone. He smiled crookedly, right cheek dimpling.

The sight of him had a miraculous calming effect. She sniffed and wiped her nose with the back of her hand.

"That's better." He cupped her face and touched his forehead to hers, while his fingertips massaged slow circles on the base of her skull . . . rubbing her problems away. Sake melted into the sensation.

And then Bill brushed her lips with his.

Her mouth responded by opening a little, and the tip of his tongue slid in, tasting . . . prodding . . . deeper. Deeper still.

Sake's insides went limp and gooey. She put her hands on Bill's shoulders, barely touching him, wary of spooking him away.

But as the kisses went on . . . their mouths experimenting together, trying this, then that, she forgot to be careful. She took his head in her hands.

Sure, she'd bumped fuzzies with Rico. At first, out of curiosity, and after that, from of some unspoken sense of obligation. During most of those so-called sexy times, Sake thought of nothing spicier than cinnamon. And though she didn't have much experience to draw on, she didn't imagine Rico had felt any more of a burning desire for her than she did for him. Still, when all the other aspects of life were such a grind, it was a relief to have at least one thing sorted out.

But Sake had never felt like *this* before—like she couldn't get close enough to Bill even if she crawled inside his skin. Need fired white-hot between them. She wanted him surrounding her, on top of her, around her, every inch of him. But he'd already rejected her once today. She'd die if he pushed her away agai—

Ping!

Bill slowly withdrew from their kiss. "Should you get that?" he breathed, face flushed, eyes dreamy-soft.

"No." She pulled him back in for more.

"What if it's your papa?"

She sighed impatiently. Was anyone really *that* responsible?

Before she could stop him, Bill reached between the seats. With a glimpse at the name RICO filling the screen, he frowned and handed her her phone.

Reality smacked Sake in the face like a wet towel.

"Hey. This my bae?"

She could hardly hear Rico above the heavy metal blasting in the background. Picturing one of his many hangouts in her mind, she flicked a glance Bill's way. Typically, by this time of day, Rico had been drinking for hours.

Sake switched the phone to her far hand. "It's me," she mumbled into her shoulder.

"Baby, where you at? Izza Fourth of July. I'm out here celebratin'. You been gone a week. Thought you were comin' back by now." He had to talk so loud to be heard above the music, no way Bill couldn't hear him.

"I know. I am. Just . . . not yet."

"*Whatthehell?* Wha's taking so long?"

"I got . . . stuff to take care of. It's gonna take some time." Haha had taught her from a young age never to argue with a drunk.

"How much time?"

"Not too much longer. Any sign of Haha?" If there were, Sake would drop everything and *run* to San Francisco.

"Not yet. But hey, you know that new guy Teeny hired? He quit already."

Sake tucked that factoid away. "Thanks for letting me know. I gotta go. I'll call you, 'kay?"

"But—"

"I gotta go."

She pushed end.

"Who's Rico?" asked Bill.

Ha. She paused. Easy question, complicated answer. "The guy I stay with."

"*Used* to stay with."

Was Bill right? Where was her real home? Whose life was so out-of-control that she wasn't even sure where she lived?

"What did he want?"

"The guy that Teeny hired to replace me at Bunz quit already."

He snorted, confused. "Why should you care?"

"Means I can probably get my job back."

"Is that what you want?"

Was it?

Bill's eyes burned a hole through her, demanding an answer.

Her pulse pounded. What did she think she was doing up here . . . rumbling around in an empty mansion with only the hired help for company, imposing on this innocent guy she barely knew, thinking she could overcome years of ingrained fear and learn to drive?

She hid her face in her hands. "I don't know."

"What's this Rico guy really want?"

"Nothing." She looked up. "He's been drinking. Celebrating the Fourth." That explained the flags flying everywhere. Not that the holiday was especially meaningful to her, but it was as good a way as she could think of to get Bill off the subject of her life.

"You don't have plans, an all-American guy like you? Barbecue, parade, fireworks or something?"

"No."

"No? That's it? What, you once get burned by a sparkler or something?"

"You could say that."

She'd been trying to make a joke. Sake smoothed down her dress, now curious about what had happened to Bill Diamond on some past July fourth. "So what happened?"

"Brittany Wilson happened." He looked out the window, as if looking into the past. "We were together for over a year. She worked down at the bank. Pretty blonde. She liked cooking, talked about having kids someday, dissed tattoos. Britt was about as regular as they come. Heck, we double dated with Britt's best friend Jessica and her boyfriend—until last July."

"Then what happened?"

Bill huffed and let Taylor hop back up onto his lap, fluffing her fur. "Britt and Jess showed up arm-in-arm in front of the whole town at the July Fourth celebration sporting matching blue rings, inked around the fourth fingers of their left hands."

"Ouch."

He exhaled. "Guess we ought to get going." He opened his door to trade seats.

Once the car was back in Bill's capable hands and Taylor was in hers, he said, "Sometimes I wish I had a brother or a sister, like you do. You've got a ready-made support system. Why won't you confide in them?"

"I'm not in their business and they're not in mine. Besides, those wine princesses would never get my problems," she sniffed.

Bill reached back between the seats for his trusty box of tissues. "How do you know?"

"Figure it out. Their mother's dead—*now*. But she was alive until Meri was eight years old and I was seven. Which means that Papa cheated on their mother with *my* mother when Meri was only a year old," she said, honking into the tissue.

From lips swollen with kissing, Bill let out a low whistle. "That's rough," he said, surprising Sake by reaching over to tuck a wisp of hair behind her ear.

The only time Rico ever touched her was when he wanted something from her.

"It's a shame you all can't get along, though. You're all so close in age. Think about it. If they resent you so much, then why'd they bother to visit you at the hospital?"

"How should I know? Maybe Papa ordered them to. Maybe they

wanted to look good in front of Savvy's wedding guests. Or could be they just wanted to throw it in my face, how much better they are than I am."

Doubt filled Bill's eyes. "I've done work for Char and Merlot. They don't strike me as the vindictive type. Can't imagine Savvy is, either."

"To them I'm nothing but a skid mark."

"Don't be so hard on yourself. You're a smart, capable woman. Your sisters have got nothing on you."

She huffed. "Nothing? What you don't know . . ."

"What I do know is, you can be a little . . . snarky, yourself. Maybe *they're* walking on eggshells around *you*. Ever think of that?"

Her head whipped back around. "Me? *Swerve*. You'd be snarky too if—" She snapped her mouth shut at the last second. There were some secrets she would never tell.

"I'm never going to fit into Napa, where everyone's nice and polite and rich."

"Sorry," said Bill. "You didn't ask for my opinion." They sat in silence as he continued driving. "You like ice cream?"

She granted him the merest of nods.

"That's as good a Fourth of July tradition as any."

Chapter 13

Bill Diamond had gotten himself into a bit of a pickle.

He owed it to himself to see where this thing with Deborah might lead, but at the same time, he didn't have it in him to further injure Sake's already-ragged feelings by keeping her apart from Taylor in the evenings.

Bottom line: Sake needed him. Despite a bloodline to one of the most famous wine families in the valley, all he saw when he looked at her was a lost soul who needed saving.

And no. It had nothing to do with the sport of matching wits, the contrast of black hair on pearly skin, or the way his heart threatened to thud out of his chest at the sight of her pink tongue doing a number on that swirl of butter pecan.

But a successful real estate man didn't let doubts get in his way. He cobbled crumbling deals back together. Solving problems was Bill's forte. So, as usual, he came up with a plan: he'd take Deb out for lunch. What made it a particularly brilliant plan was that a lunchtime date wouldn't interfere with Sake time. Plus, there was an excellent deli, Aaron's, conveniently located right next to the medical center where Deb worked. Bill's family had been going there for years.

He arranged a date for the middle of the following week.

Bill met Deb inside the restaurant.

"What did you do this morning?" asked Bill, holding out her plastic chair for her.

"Nothing much. I've been working on developing an appropriate intervention strategy for a patient with a medical diagnosis of Athetoid cerebral palsy. I've determined that his PT diagnosis is motor incoordination resulting in gait abnormalities and inability to negotiate uneven surfaces. He also shows signs of lower extremity weakness, leaning to inability to transition from floor to standing independently," she said distractedly, eyes darting over the menu.

"Oh," said Bill.

Deb snapped her menu shut. "I'll have the Reuben."

Bill's eyebrows shot up in surprise. "Can't go wrong with that."

Apparently, ordering lunch was child's play compared with executing a PT plan. As for him, it usually took longer to decide what to get than it did to actually eat his meal.

"And you? What have you been up to?" Her sharp gaze dissected him.

"I just came from putting a sign on my newest listing." He'd had to wrestle the metal legs into the hard-packed ground, hoping the entire time that nobody was watching. It hadn't been pretty.

"I see." Deborah nodded, but her tone was a reminder that schlepping real estate, while a perfectly respectable profession, wasn't exactly on a par with helping people walk.

After they ordered, Bill, rarely at a loss for words, could suddenly find nothing to say.

While he watched, hands folded, Deb pulled out her phone and scrolled until their plates arrived. Just as he was salivating over his first, luscious-looking bite, he heard a familiar voice.

"William! Billy!"

He lowered his intact sandwich. "Hi, Mom, Dad."

"Son," said Dad. "What are you doing here?"

"Having lunch. What are you doing?"

"Same thing. What a coincidence."

Bill turned to his date. "My parents, Rachel and David Diamond."

"And who is your lovely friend?" asked Mom, taking in every detail, from the top of Deb's short brown curls down to her Crocs, giving special scrutiny to the naked third finger of her left hand.

"Deborah. Pleased to meet you."

"*Doctor* Deborah?" asked Mom, zooming in on the name stitched into the breast pocket of her lab coat.

Deb threw back her shoulders. "Technically I'm a DPT—doctor of physical therapy."

"Very nice!" At Deb's shelf-like chest, Dad's eyes grew round as saucers.

Bill gave Dad a pass. A man would have to be dead not to notice that.

Mom whacked Dad's arm. "Feinstein, is it?"

"That's right."

"Feinstein! Wonderful!" Mom crowed, calculating eyes flitting from Deborah to Bill and back again.

Inside that head of hers, Bill was pretty sure Mom was already debating whether to go short or long for her mother-of-the-groom dress.

Dad left to go to the counter and Deborah lunged into her sandwich.

"How's the Reuben?" Mom asked.

"*Noh bah,*" Deborah murmured.

"Bill, you should have told her to get the pastrami." Then she addressed Deborah. "I'm telling you, Aaron here, the owner, is like the pastrami whisperer. He makes the best pastrami sandwiches I've ever tasted."

"*Gooh bahance oh fah an leah?*"

Bill touched his own mouth with his finger in a discreet signal to Deb to wipe the little glob of Russian dressing from the corner of her lips.

"A terrific balance of fat and lean! And they pile it high, but not too bulgy, you know what I mean?"

Finally, Deb swallowed. "Layered, so the meat bites away cleanly? Because that's how my mother taught me."

"And you cook, too!" Her eyes met Bill's. "She cooks!" She returned to Deborah. "Yes. That's it. That's exactly how Aaron makes it. The way it *should* be done."

"Rachel," called Dad from over at the counter. "Can we stop talking about pastrami and start ordering it? I'm starving over here."

"Very nice meeting you, Doctor. I hope to see you again soon," said Mom, leaving Bill with a look that meant, *What are you waiting for? You should have proposed yesterday!*

"I'll have to try the pastrami, next time," called Deborah.

"I'll be waiting to hear how you like it."

"Rachel! I'm ordering. Do you want the chips or the fries alongside?"

* * *

Though Sake couldn't forget about her lame attempt at coming on to Bill that day in his apartment, he had never again brought it up. That was the thing about Bill Diamond. *He* never made you feel "less than." Judged.

But there was another thing he hadn't repeated after that day, either. He hadn't touched her. Had those kisses in the alleyway just been sympathy kisses, after all?

She'd weighed that question over and over. There were only two explanations: either he wasn't attracted to her at all, or he was *more* interested in his other so-called "dates."

Now that their times together always included driving around, it only made sense for them to stop and get a bite somewhere. People-watching next to Bill as they dined al fresco, Taylor lying contentedly at her feet, was her favorite new thing. From one of Napa's many outdoor restaurants, she could observe her new environment without feeling obliged to interact with any of the fancy people up here, and risk saying the wrong thing in the wrong way.

On Friday evening, as they sat eating clams, Sake noticed Bill eyeing something—or someone—over her shoulder. The café tables jutted into the sidewalk, making it impossible for passersby to go unnoticed. He put down his fork, wiped his mouth with his napkin, and looked up.

"Sylvia," Bill said. Sake looked over her shoulder to see a woman with heavy dark brows, long wavy hair parted in the middle, and a straight, if melancholy, smile.

"Hi, Bill, how are you?" Her voice was soft and breathy.

Bill stood up, ever the gentleman, and gave her a hug. "Fine. You?"

"Great!" she said with forced enthusiasm. "Pete Junior's playing JV next fall."

"Chip off the old block."

"Yeah . . ." With curiosity, the woman looked down at where Sake sat.

"Oh, pardon me. This is Sake."

A glint of recognition—and was that jealousy?—swept over her features. "Sake St. Pierre?"

Sake smiled. "Nice to meet you," she heard herself mumble.

It was hard for two women to hide hate at first sight.

"Well, better scoot. . . . Call me sometime." She kissed Bill's cheek before flouncing off, giving Sake the view of her hips swishing from side to side that Bill had been treated to moments earlier.

"Who was that?"

Bill resumed eating. "Sylvia Goldsmith. Er, Johnson, now. Or was, until she got divorced," he said, not looking up from his plate. "Not sure which name she's going by these days."

He wasn't going to get away with acting like nothing momentous had happened. Sake circled her fork in the air. "And?"

Nonchalant, he chewed his mouthful of salad. "And what?"

"Seriously? *'Better scoot. . . . Call me sometime,'*" Sake aped, with a flip of her hair. "What happened between you two?"

He sipped his beer. "It was over between us years ago."

"What? What was over?"

Resigned, he set the bottle down. "I grew up with Sylvia. We dated all through high school. Our families just assumed we would go the whole happily-ever-after route. That is, until the morning of prom, when I came down with a bad case of the flu. Sylvia already had the dress and all, and after hours of handwringing and a tearful apology, she made the brave decision to go to the dance by herself, with my blessing. Fine with me. Done and done, right?"

"Then what happened?"

"Then August rolls around, and I'm as shocked as the rest of the school when Sylvia announces she's no longer going to college in the fall. Turns out she got knocked up at the after-prom party by Petey Johnson. From the football team."

"Nuh-uh."

"You think she cried about the prom?" Bill buttered a chunk of bread and let his knife clatter to his plate. "That was nothing."

"She regretted it."

"She couldn't say she was sorry enough. But that didn't stop her from marrying the guy."

"But now she's divorced, you said."

"Just this summer."

Sake was dying to ask him how he knew that, but that wouldn't be cool.

She couldn't stop thinking about Sylvia Goldsmith Johnson though, even after Bill took her home. Why should she care if Bill called Sylvia? What had gotten into her? It was ridiculous, when she'd probably never see him again after September first . . . after her world was set to rights.

Only she wasn't sure exactly what "right" looked like anymore.

Chapter 14

A few days later, Sake handed Bill Papa's credit card when they pulled into the gas station. Bill had been running late and hadn't taken time out to stop for fuel before he picked her up.

"What's this?"

"Snaps for the petro."

Bill waved it away. "I got it. Save that for something else."

"You always get it. You never let me pay for gas once in the past week. Only thing I've charged since I've been in Napa is Taylor's food. I hate sponging off Papa, even for that."

Bill directed the attendant to fill it up, then told Sake, "I can afford the gas. And I hardly think a couple bags of dog chow are going to break Xavier St. Pierre's bank."

"Just because Papa has money doesn't mean I'm going to throw it away on every little thing." Sake had a lot of respect for money. At least while she was confined here in the Valley of the Wine, she didn't have to worry about what she was going to eat and where she'd sleep. She still couldn't wrap her head around the fact that her father had simply handed over his card. Was it some kind of a test? Would his disapproval come storming down on her once she reached a certain arbitrary spending limit known only to him?

Welp, he wouldn't catch her abusing his hospitality.

"All set to switch seats? High time we got you out on the highway."

Sake's breath froze in her lungs. Driving in town was one thing. What with all those stop signs and red lights, she never got going fast enough to fear losing control.

"I haven't driven on the freeway before, remember?"

"Twenty-nine hardly qualifies. The speed limit's only forty-five along this stretch and it's only two lanes. Nothing to get bent of shape about.

"Besides," he added, settling back on the passenger side, "it's a beautiful summer evening. We'll find someplace good to eat at in St. Helena."

He leaned forward to help her gauge the traffic. "Now's as good a time as any."

Sake took a deep breath and stepped on the gas.

"How do you ever get used to looking at everything at once? The road, the instrument panel, the mirrors, back to the road . . ."

"Practice. You just keep doing it, and one day, you realize you're not even thinking about it."

"Promise?" She laughed nervously.

"Sure. You'll see."

"But how do you know everyone else on the road's gonna do what he's supposed to do, at the same time?"

"Ah, there's the rub. Driving is kind of like living. It takes a certain amount of faith to make it work."

"Just one problem with that. How're you supposed to have faith when everyone you ever knew let you down?"

"How come you ask such tough questions?" He chuckled softly. "I don't have all the answers. All I know is what's right for me, and that is if you stay on the straight and narrow and watch out for the other guy, you're putting yourself in the best possible position for good things to happen. That make sense?"

"You mean, be defensive? Now you're talking. I can do defensive."

"Believe me. I know." He gave her a look, but she couldn't spare the attention to argue.

"You can pick it up a little. You're only going forty."

"Give me a break. I'm a little nervous here." Nevertheless, she squeezed down harder with the ball of her foot. "Speed isn't exactly my jam. Hard enough to do all that needs done while going slow. Don't know how I'm expected to do it while I'm on the fly. What am I? Wonder Woman?"

"Hm. And here all this time, I thought it was your love of restaurants that kept us close to town."

A smile sneaked out of Sake. "You know I like to eat."

"Ditto. St. Helena's only about fifteen miles north of here. There are restaurants up there we haven't tried yet."

"Fifteen miles?" All her fear came rushing back. "I got to drive fifteen miles?"

Bill felt a rush of empathy. "I know you're uncomfortable with highway driving. But don't you think we've been putting this off way too long?"

"Is that why you didn't want Taylor to come tonight?"

"Sake. You're going to be driving to work every day, starting Monday."

"I know," she admitted. "I set up my appointment for Saturday at ten."

"Saturday," he replied "Perfect timing to start your new job. The officer might even take you out here on the highway for your test. Get used to that idea so you don't freak when it happens."

"Too late."

"You just need to build your self-confidence. Do you want me to pick you up a little early tomorrow morning? Let you drive to the test site to warm you up?"

"That'd be cool."

"You'll be fine. I promise. While we're headed in this direction, I want to stop and check on my new listing while it's still light outside. Meant to run over this afternoon, but work was crazy. Seems like all I got done today was putting out fires."

She turned on the radio and a tune she liked filled the car.

"Watch for the sign that says El Camino."

Why hadn't she thought of playing music while she drove before? Gradually, she accelerated until the speedometer read fifty.

"You think they'll let me listen to my tunes when I take my test?"

"Don't see why not, as long as you keep it down to a reasonable volume."

Before she knew it, they were turning off the highway onto El Camino. Then he guided her into to a shopping plaza.

"You see this? This mall is my future," Bill said from where they idled in a far corner of the lot with a wide-angle view of the adjoining storefronts.

Sake peered out at a dry cleaner, an acute care place, an insurance agency, a wine store, and a couple of cafés.

"Looks like any other bunch of stores to me."

"It's fully leased, well-maintained, and has a great mix of services for the people who live in the surrounding developments. That's what makes it so valuable."

With his usual enthusiasm, Bill buzzed on about cost per square foot, something something, return on investment, and so on. He had no idea his face glowed in the summer sun slanting through the windshield.

To be real, there was nothing outstanding about Bill's appearance. Medium build, dark hair, clean-shaven . . . he was more gravitas than glitz. The best words to describe Bill Diamond were *solid* and *trustworthy*.

But this evening, as he rambled on in his undecipherable real estate-ese, those late-day rays highlighted his best features: his square-cut jaw, his great skin . . . the clarity of purpose in his green eyes. Abruptly, his monologue ended and that laid-back, boyish grin of his split his cheeks, punctuated by the dimple on the right.

When had she started looking for that dimple?

"Looks like all the lessees are doing well this time of day. Parking lot's full, customers are patronizing the cafés. That's what I came to see."

"Okay. But what makes it 'your future'?"

"You remember that house we drove by the first time we met?"

"The one with the big trees and the little backyard?"

Bill nodded. "If I can sell this center, I can afford to buy that house." There it was again, that look of wistful determination.

He turned to her. "What about you?"

"Me?"

"What are your long-term goals?"

Sake sniffed. "Been too busy figuring out what I'm doing today to worry about tomorrow."

"Dude! There must be *something* you want more than anything else."

"I've never even lived in the same place for more than six months. You really think I'd have long-term goals?"

"Everyone needs goals. And to reach them, you have to be proactive, not reactive. Look at your sist—"

Sake felt her face fall.

"Sorry. Not comparing." They sat in uncomfortable silence for a moment until Bill spoke up again.

"Ready to go? I'm starved. I just remembered there's this place up in St. Helena that looks like a castle, serves great food."

Bill was right—the restaurant did look like a castle. A sprawling, Gothic stone castle, complete with towers.

Peering up at it, Sake followed Bill along the walkway toward a courtyard shaded with olive trees and orange umbrellas.

A perky woman about Sake's age wearing a pristine white shirt and black vest handed them menus. "Welcome to the Culinary Institute. I'm Chris, and I'm also a student."

Sake had only glanced in passing at the sign out front.

"I've heard of this place," blurted Sake. Papa's words came back to her: *It's a fine school . . . and it will make you an expert in the field.*

"You like to cook?" Chris fairly bubbled over with enthusiasm.

"Actually, I'm more of a baker."

"The Institute offers an associate's in pastry arts." Chris leaned close and cupped the side of her mouth, letting Sake in on a secret. "We culinary majors call the bakers 'pastry princesses.' " She straightened again. "All kidding aside, though, you ought to check it out. Its graduates are placed all over the world."

"For me it's just a place to get awesome grub," said Bill, showing more interest in his menu than hearing about the cooking school.

Sake looked around, cautiously curious. "Where are the classrooms?"

"We share the same cooking facilities with the restaurants here. Before you leave, go inside and watch the chefs at work in the open kitchen, and you'll want to check out the shop, too. It's chock-full of everything having to do with cooking.

"Tonight we have some lovely appetizers, starting with a lovely burrata with creamy fresh mozzarella, local heirloom tomatoes, and an olive relish. If that sounds good, I'll be right back with them."

Watching Chris bop away, Sake told Bill, "The staff sure doesn't dress like that back at Bunz. And if Francine acted that chipper, Teeny would accuse her of being on something."

"Did you say you'd heard about this place?"

Sake had never been one to put her business out on Front Street.

She'd never told Bill the details of her deal with Papa. All Bill knew was the date she was going back home, and that until then, she was expected to stick close by the mansion so Papa could keep an eye on her.

"Papa mentioned it. It really chaps his hide that I left school without finishing. He made me promise to get my high school equivalency before I leave here. I been working toward it online."

"That's an excellent idea, Sake. I'm glad to hear it."

"But you know my father—he couldn't just leave it at that. He wants me to go on and get my associate's degree. Just because my sisters went to college doesn't mean *I* have to. I wish he'd get that through his head."

"Maybe he has a point. . . ." He shrugged, fingering the edge of his place mat.

Sake soaked in her surroundings. The gray stone architecture, the swaying palm trees . . . the sweet scent of magnolias and the mellow strains of guitar music. The idea of actually studying baking here, in this place—assuming she could get in, which wasn't likely . . . she couldn't *even*.

But then the server was back with the breadbasket and the starters and all thoughts of college were forgotten, as she sat outside in the sultry summer evening next to Bill Diamond.

Bill wasn't the kind of guy whose face stopped traffic, like Rico, but he took care always to be neatly pulled together. Bill Diamond was a decent, respected man. A man of integrity. Plus, he smelled like dark woods and warm spices, a deeply sensuous smell that made Sake want to curl herself around him.

Did Bill notice details about her, too? Or to him, were all of their dinners out over the past weeks nothing more than an extension of driving lessons? She thought back, looking for signs that he thought of her as anything more than a poor little rich girl who needed his help. He never would've kissed her that day in the alley if she hadn't totally wigged out. All he'd meant to do was calm her down.

Still, when Bill's shoulder lightly bumped into hers when they finally left the cooking shop for the car, she wanted more than anything to believe he'd done it on purpose.

"It got dark," Sake said with a start.

"You didn't notice while we were eating?"

She'd been too busy noticing how round the shoulder muscles inside his shirt were from working out at the gym. The way he always held her chair for her and spoke with kindness and confidence to everyone, lowliest server to wine mogul.

But now that she had to drive back—*in the dark*—all the usual fears sprang to life. Then a brand-new, irrational one joined the others. *What if a coyote runs out in front of the car?*

No sooner had Sake pulled out onto the main road, than Bill's Bluetooth rang, cutting off her music.

"When will he be back?" asked Bill, suddenly all business. He reached around to snag his briefcase out of the back and began rummaging blindly through it.

Without the music, Sake's heartbeat ratcheted up again. This was the first time Bill had taken a call while she was driving. He knew she was even less sure of herself driving in the dark. Shouldn't he be keeping an eye on her?

"After Labor Day?" He switched on the interior light to study an important-looking paper. *Shit,* he mouthed emphatically, brows knit together in a frown.

Whoa. Salty language, for Bill. That scowl on his face was worrisome. He was usually so in command.

He stuffed the paper back into his case and shut off the light.

"Who's handling his business while he's gone?"

Sake couldn't resist another glance his way, to see if that look was still there, in the dashboard light.

"Yeah, I've tried, but he's hard to get hold of too. Hold on—"

Bill jerked his head toward her, muffling the phone in his shoulder. *"Watch where you're going."*

Startled, Sake stiff-armed the car back into her lane. But she must have overcompensated because—*oh, no*—from out of nowhere, a car rushing by on her left blared out an angry warning.

Her heart started pounding. She tried not to look Bill's way again. But the glare of headlights that seemed to be coming straight toward her was blinding.

In her side vision she saw Bill pinch the bridge of his nose and try to refocus on his call. "Is he taking messages while he's away?"

She could hear the measured restraint in his voice.

"Next time you talk to him, I'd appreciate you filling him in. It's a primo location. I know he'd be interested."

When the call was over, he turned to Sake. "Dude! How many times do I have to tell you? This car is my life! Nothing can happen to it! When you're driving, the only thing you should be looking at is the road. Not me. Nothing else but the road!"

Everything—keeping a fast car on an unfamiliar road in the dark while remembering all the things he'd taught her, the possibility of wandering coyotes, the sheer terror of damaging the car of the man whose opinion she valued, and now, getting yelled at by said man—rushed together to incite a panic attack.

Blood roared in her ears. *How much farther?* Cars started passing her.

"Why are you slowing down? You have to go with the flow of traffic! Otherwise you become a hazard."

He was obviously still irritated, and though it might not be all because of her, he sure made her feel that way.

But she'd deal with Bill later. Sometimes you just had to stop the bleeding, and this was one of those times. Right now it was going to take everything she had to get them back to Napa alive—and intact.

God, she hated to drive. She would never pass the test for her Ls. That meant she couldn't take the job at Mon Rêve. Couldn't take *any* job up here in the outback, where everything was spread out all over creation and they didn't have the most basic modern conveniences to help you to get from A to B.

Tense silence blanketed the car's interior. The twenty minutes it took to get back to Dry Creek Road seemed like twenty years.

"Sorry I got so bent out of shape," sighed Bill when Sake finally turned into Domain St. Pierre.

He was bent out of shape? The moment she braked, she pounced. "Hear this, Bill Diamond. You best save Mr. Bossy for the office. The last man who talked down to me got himself mollywhopped and I ended up in the gray bar motel. So get off my bumper, like *now*."

"I said I was sorry," he said, miserably. "I've been trying to get ahold of this guy I want to sell the strip mall to for weeks, but he's been tied up back east. Now they're telling me he just left for vacation—"

"You think that's all you have to do is say 'I'm sorry' and it's all gravy? That's like trying to drink from a fire hose."

She swung open her door and stamped one booted foot on the ground.

"Sake—wait. There's something I have to tell you."

Oh, God. Sake braced herself. *Here it comes.*

"I'm sorry to be telling you this now when you're already so upset, but I was planning on telling you tonight anyway because it's the right thing to do. I have no problem keeping Taylor for you and teaching you to drive. But that's it. I'm not interested in anything more serious."

"You think I'm interested in you? Don't be giving yourself props where they're not deserved."

"Good. I hope you won't take it personally."

Then how was she supposed to take it? He was done with her. She was too much of a hassle. His life had been so much simpler—so much *better*—before she'd crashed into it.

"It's just that I'm a lot older than you. We're in different places in our lives, you know? You're just starting out, and I'm, well, thinking about settling down. And now, for the first time, with this listing . . . it's within the realm of possibility."

"You're not *that* old. Not with that baby face." Okay, no, that was a lie. He didn't have a baby face. He had a sweet, lovable face. But she wasn't exactly in the mood to dole out compliments.

"I'm no macho man. You think I don't know that? It doesn't matter. It's more of a stage than an actual age I'm talking about."

And to think she'd begun to feel something for him! She was such a loser.

"I just wanted to make it perfectly clear that you're not the only woman I've been, er, going out with, before things went any further."

"Understand *this*, Bill Diamond," Sake lashed back without missing a beat. "You're putting way too much on this. I don't care who you go out with—tonight, tomorrow night, or any night, you get me?" She braced her left hand on the seat to hoist herself out.

Bill reached for her forearm. "Sake, stop. Wait. You're a beautiful young woman, but you're just starting out. You're going to go through a lot of guys before you're ready to settle down."

Sake huffed. "I've done fine till now without your advice. I'll figure out how to get my dog back tomorrow." She got out and slammed the door.

"Sake, wait! Du—"

She whirled around, pointing a threatening finger. "Say 'dude'

again. One more time!" she dared him. And then, at his silence, she
spun away and marched off toward the house.

Bill called to her from over the roof of the car.

"What about your driver's test?"

"Game over," she yelled without bothering to turn around. "I'm
not taking no test. I'm going back to civilization, where they got decent public transportation."

Where she didn't need Bill Diamond.

Chapter 15

Bill watched Sake jog up the stairs, slam the door, and disappear into her father's house. Then, on a sigh, he climbed back into his car and leaned against the headrest to puzzle out what had just happened.

They'd had a great time tonight—an awesome time—right up until he got that call from the assistant at Cornerstone Properties about the strip mall.

He hadn't meant to snap at Sake while she was driving. But there was going to be an open house at the property on Elm Street this coming Sunday. That meant lots of potential buyers trooping through it. All it took was the right offer from a well-qualified buyer, and his dream house would be gone—poof.

But the truth was, putting Sake on notice had been the right thing to do. It wasn't fair to string her along. Deb could handle it. Hell, Deb could handle anything. Besides, Deb was so preoccupied with fixing people she didn't even realize she'd been short-listed. But Sake was more sensitive. More . . . *damaged.*

She needs you. And you want her.

A fact which definitely got in the way of his mantra: *Success comes from putting off what you want now for what you want most.*

Okay—he'd admit it—Sake stirred something deep inside him. No sooner had he advised her to go out with other guys than he felt pierced by a self-inflicted stab of jealousy.

Which didn't compute with his failure to encourage Sake to go to the CIA when the waitress raved about how she should check it out. That was selfish of him, now that he thought about it. But sometimes you had to choose between the lesser of two evils. Bill couldn't let a troubled gypsy barely past the age of consent get in the way of his long-range goals. He'd worked too hard, for too long. The way things stood now, with Sake gone by September, Bill didn't have to be overly concerned about getting too attached to her. But if she hung around for another couple of years to get a degree? All bets were off. Bill circled the fountain and made his way back toward the road. He shoved a hand through his hair. Maybe losing it on her had been for the best. He'd probably let this Good Samaritan gig drag on way too long, anyway. He'd deliver Taylor to her tomorrow and be done with the whole affair.

Even if the Elm Street property didn't sell this weekend, there would be more open houses after that. Wouldn't be too long before some savvy buyer would recognize it for the little gem that it was.

All Bill needed was to get past the guy who ran Cornerstone's real estate to its elusive owner. This mall was exactly the type of property Cornerstone collected in its portfolio. But the owner was a semi-retired recluse with a reputation for being harder to reach than the Pope. His portfolio was already worth millions. He didn't need to re-turn calls from a small-town broker he'd never dealt with before . . . had never even heard of. He paid someone to take those calls for him. But that someone had just left for vacation and wasn't even accepting messages.

Still racking his brain, Bill turned onto the highway. He'd been putting all his efforts into Cornerstone. Suppose his message never reached the top? What other investors might be in the market for a profitable strip mall? Where was that list of prospects he'd drawn up earlier?

That's right. He remembered *exactly* where he'd placed that docu-ment: tucked neatly into an inside compartment of his briefcase. Congratulating himself on his awesome organizational skills, Bill leaned over to grasp its handle from the floor on the passenger side, never seeing the eighteen-wheeler stacked full of wine for distribu-tion to every point of the globe that bore down on him.

Pacing the floor of her guestroom, Sake pulled out her phone, fin-gers flying.

"Hello?" Rico raised his voice over the raucous background noise.

"Where are you?"

"The Black Orchid."

"Any sign of my mom?" She couldn't not ask. The Orchid used to be Haha's favorite. Even though you couldn't even carry on a conversation over the awful music they played, Sake and Rico had been going there for the past year in hopes of spotting her.

"Hold on. *Hey, Mike!*" Rico yelled.

Sake flinched and jerked her phone hand away from her ear.

"See Sake's mom around lately?" And then: "He says no."

"I'm coming back."

"When?"

"Tomorrow."

"What?"

"I said, tomorrow!"

"Cool! See you then!"

"Rico—can I still stay at your place?"

"Why not?"

Tomorrow, she would stuff her things back into her trash bag and figure out some way to get back to San Francisco, once and for all. Get a cab to take her to the bus station, beg Papa to have Bruno run her down, something. If worse came to worst, she'd even lower herself enough to hit up one of her sisters for a ride.

Chapter 16

Sake opened her eyes to a knock on her bedroom door. Weak light bathed the room.

Thanks to her fight with Bill Diamond, she'd barely slept. Why was Jeanne bugging her this early? And why didn't she just barge in like she usually did when she wanted something? She pulled her covers up over her head.

"Sake? It's me, Meri."

Sake eased down her blankets to see her sister's glossy head peeking through the doorway. Meri had never been in Sake's room. Not that Sake had ever invited her.

"Can I come in?"

Warily, Sake propped herself up on an elbow.

"Sorry to wake you." In her high-waisted pants, fringed leather top, and trademark bling, Merlot looked like one of the models you'd occasionally glimpse shooting in Union Square. To top it all off, she smelled like a rose garden.

Next to her, Sake must look like canned hell.

Halfway across the room, Meri stopped, ominously quiet.

"Wassup?" mumbled Sake, arranging her hair in a futile attempt to look presentable.

Her sister approached the bed gingerly. "May I sit?"

Something Bill had said came to mind: *Maybe your sisters are only walking on eggshells.* Sake moved her legs to give her room, though her gut told her she wasn't going to like what she was about to hear.

"Jeanne said Bill Diamond's been watching your little dog while you're here."

All at once Sake felt wide awake. Had something happened to Taylor since her fight with Bill? Could it be that she couldn't trust Bill, after all?

"I was reading the news like I do every morning, and I saw that Bill was in a car accident."

Sake sat up straight as a pole. Not Bill. Not *her* Bill, with the earnest green eyes and the square jaw and the dimple.

On top of the comforter, Meri reached out to touch Sake's calf. "He's hurt pretty bad. I thought you'd want to know."

"Where did it happen? When? Where is he now?"

"Here." Meri handed her the iPad. "You can read it yourself."

Tragedy on a Napa Valley highway last night after a trailer truck collided with a car, spilling wine out on to the roadway. The crash occurred around 10 p.m. Thursday night, and blocked all lanes on Southbound 29 until California Highway Patrol cleanup crews could bring out a sweeper truck to pick up the glass. The highway didn't completely reopen until around 7 a.m. today.

The truck driver was unhurt. He told police he was unable to stop when the car, driven by William Diamond of Napa, pulled out in front of him. Diamond was transported to Queen of the Valley Medical Center, where he was reported to be suffering from multiple injuries. The car was a total loss.

Bill's car . . . his rolling office.

"Bill helped me find my first jewelry atelier, and now he's on Chardonnay's board of directors. Ask anyone in the valley. He's a hardworking guy with a heart of gold."

"I have to go," said Sake, swinging her feet onto the floor.

Meri stood with her. "Jeanne said you two have spent practically every day together these past few weeks. I'm sure you're upset. Maybe you should let me drive you."

"Bill?" Sake whispered.

Was that really his body lying motionless in that hospital bed? One of his legs was encased in an electric-blue cast from his thigh to his toes, propped on a stack of pillows. His torso was swathed in thick bandages, and an oxygen mask obscured his nose and mouth.

The place where his dimple should be was flush with the rest of his cheek.

When Bill's eyelids fluttered open, Sake took what felt like her first breath since she'd heard the horrible news.

She bent closer. "It's me. Sake."

She was vaguely aware of more people bustling into the room. Behind her, an older female voice held subdued surprise. "You're two of the St. Pierre girls." That was followed by the sound of Meri's voice introducing the both of them.

A man dressed in muted green scrubs squeezed by to read the spiky graph on one of the machines Bill was hooked up to. "How you feeling this morning, Mr. Diamond?" he asked, his thumb pressing inside Bill's wrist. "Got the prettiest visitors on the floor, I see. Some guys have all the luck."

But Bill's eyes had fallen closed again.

"How are his signs, nurse?" the woman behind Sake inquired tremulously.

"Surprisingly strong, given the extent of his injuries."

"What . . . exactly . . . are his injuries?" Sake made herself ask.

From where he checked Bill's heart with his stethoscope, the nurse glanced back at the others.

"It's all right, you can talk in front of them," said the man who must have been Bill's dad.

"Shattered fibula, two broken ribs, and a collapsed lung," he replied matter-of-factly, inserting the nub of a thermometer into Bill's ear. "Antibiotics are doing their job. No fever. How we doing there, Bill?"

Bill grunted so faintly Sake almost thought she'd imagined it.

"Are you in any pain?"

His finger moved an inch.

"You have company. Want to say hello?" Carefully, the nurse eased back on the elastic strap holding up the oxygen mask.

Sake's eyes pored over Bill's face. He used to be so animated, always asking questions, telling her all sorts of things, half of which she didn't even pay attention to. She promised God that if He healed Bill enough to talk her ear off again, she'd cherish every word.

"He might take a sip of water for you if you hold the straw for him."

Sake took the Styrofoam cup the nurse handed her while he pressed a button to elevate the head of the bed.

She'd always found satisfaction in caring for Taylor, but even a dog could drink without help.

Tentatively, she guided the straw to Bill's lips. "Here. Want some water?" Somehow, this most basic of tasks felt intimate in front of all these witnesses. But looking down on him, she realized that it wasn't the act of helping Bill drink that moved her so powerfully. It was the sight of him lying there, helpless. She felt her love shining around her like an aura, for everyone to see.

Obediently, Bill tried to purse his lips around the opening, but he couldn't make a tight seal. Half the water ran down his chin.

Someone handed her a tissue.

"Tay," said Bill in a voice that sounded dust-choked.

"What's that? He's talking!" said his mother, edging in toward the head of the bed.

All eyes in the room went to Bill's face.

"What did you say, Billy?" His mom laid her hand on his shoulder.

"Tay. Lor."

"Taylor!" repeated Sake. Who was watching Taylor?

Taylor had scarcely crossed Sake's mind since she'd heard about the wreck, yet here was Bill, lucky to be alive, and all he could think of was making sure her dog was all right.

"That's right, he's boarding your puppy, isn't he? Leave him to us, dear. David and I will see to her. She loves us, doesn't she, Dave?"

But now Bill was mouthing something else.

"What's that?" asked his father. "Sounded like 'tess.'"

"Tess," Bill repeated, eyes meeting Sake's. "Goo. Luck."

Test. Was there no end to this man's thoughtfulness?

"If you're talking this much the morning after you punctured your lung, that tells me you're going to be one of those pesky patients who's yakking our ears off in another day or two," the nurse said briskly. "But for now we don't want to overdo it. Let's get that oxygen back on."

"What do you think Bill was talking about?" Meri asked Sake during the drive back to Domaine St. Pierre.

Next to her in Meri's Mercedes, Sake frantically debated her next move. Last night she'd been set on abandoning this valley. What now, after seeing Bill, unable to get out of bed, dependent on oxygen? How could she desert him after all he'd done for her and Taylor?

But this time, if she stayed, there would be no one to call on when she needed something. She gave her sister props for running her to the hospital this morning. But as Meri had already explained on their way to the hospital, if not for this emergency, she'd be at her jewelry bench right now, as usual. Folks didn't have time to be dropping everything for somebody else. Only one person was selfless enough to do that: Bill Diamond.

If Sake didn't keep her 10 a.m. appointment at the DMV tomorrow, first thing she'd have to do would be renege on the job at Mon Rêve. Make some lame excuse. Say she didn't want it, because no way would she admit she was turning it down because she couldn't drive and give everyone up here further confirmation of what a deadbeat she was.

And then she'd be stuck like Cinderella in the palace. At least Cindy had had shit to do. Sake would be bored out of her mind. Papa's fireplaces hadn't been used since she'd been there, and this mansion had a dishwasher. Come to think, *two* of them.

Still, that driving test terrified her. What if she didn't pass?

What if she did?

Meri glanced her way, waiting patiently for her to answer.

The vision of Bill staring earnestly up at Sake, wishing *her* luck after he'd just been mowed down by a semi, was what clinched it.

"I got an appointment tomorrow to get my driver's license."

Meri flashed Sake the precise look of disbelief she'd been expecting.

"No big deal. I had one before, it just expired." Sake hoped her lie sounded legit. She had no idea if expired licenses were even a thing.

"Oh, sure," Meri nodded, adding, "How were you planning on getting to the DMV? Was Bill going to take you?"

"Was." Sake held her breath. A ragged edge on a fingernail gave her an excuse to pull an emery board out of her bag. Anything to occupy her hands while she waited to see if Meri would take the bait . . . offer to go out of her way once again.

"Tomorrow's Saturday. I can take you."

Yes! "Cool whip." She didn't look up, just finished her filing on a controlled exhale and slipped her emery board back into her bag.

Chapter 17

The examiner pointed through the windshield toward the brick wall of the DMV building. "Pull into that space between those two vehicles and park."

No way had he not noticed how frothed up into a lather Sake was, sitting there right next to him for the past fifteen minutes. She could feel her thighs stuck together under her skirt. Then again, after what she'd been through this summer, the boys in blue were enough to send her to the ding wing on a *good* day.

On top of everything else, at the last minute Sake had been forced to take her test in an unfamiliar car—Meri's Mercedes, no less. Flunking would be bad enough. What if she ran into something with her sister's whip-hot Benz?

But at least the guy didn't make her turn off the radio, and after all her misgivings, the test had zoomed by fast, thanks in part to the music. Now it was almost over, and incredibly, Sake hadn't made one mistake—that is, none that she knew of.

While she oh-so-carefully completed her final task, the examiner busied himself ticking off items on his clipboard.

She came to a halt, let out her breath, and searched his face for his approval.

He looked up, checking her park job. "You can pull in a little farther," he motioned with his pen. "Your back end is sticking out about three feet," he added, returning his attention to his paperwork.

Sake barely touched the gas, but the Mercedes had a hella more power than Bill's hooptie. It jumped ahead, tapping the brick wall of the building a split second before she could slam on the brake.

"Snap!" Her eyes flew to the examiner's.

"Not *that* far." He scribbled something and peeled the top sheet of paper off, handing it to her.

That was that.

"Promise me you'll practice parking between the lines in a big public lot like a school or something."

While he climbed out of the car, Sake skimmed over the report. In her agitated state, all she saw was random black marks on a white ground.

"Wait. Then what?"

He ducked down into the door opening, bracing his hands on the edges of the car. "Whaddaya mean?"

"How soon can I come back and take it again?"

"Take what again? You passed," he replied with a slam of the door.

Sake slowly got out of the car and walked over to where Meri was waiting for her. A grin split her face. "Woohoo!"

"Success?"

"Yeah, baby! I passed!" She danced a circle, smacking her sister a stinging high five.

"But you knew you would, right?" Meri smiled bemusedly at the abrupt change in her sister.

"Never any doubt."

On their way home, Meri asked, "I guess you don't have a car, at least not up here in Napa. Have you been out to the garage yet? I swear, there are more cars out there than I can count."

"Papa showed me the board next to the kitchen door where all the keys are kept, but I couldn't take him up on it until now."

"There's a green SUV no one ever uses. That's the one I'd take."

For a time, there was no sound but the soft hum of Meri's tires on asphalt.

"I have a job," Sake volunteered with a modest shoulder shrug. Tooting her own horn didn't come easy, but only now that she had a means to get there was she starting to get pumped about something she'd known for two weeks.

"You do?"

"At Mon Rêve, starting Monday."

"I love that place! They make the most *amazing* croissants. I'd turn into a beach ball if I worked there."

Sake grinned at the absurdity of her slender sister putting on a single ounce.

"But, FYI, I'd be okay with it if you brought home the occasional bag of goodies," she chuckled. "That is, once you're a little more established. Did I hear something about you wanting to go to the CIA?"

Since when had she and Meri started talking like best friends—like the bad blood between them had simply drained away? Suddenly it was like the sky had cracked open and now all these opportunities were raining down on her.

"Let me guess. Papa."

"Be careful. Papa has a way of channeling his agenda onto others."

But some things even Papa couldn't manifest. "It's all pie in the sky."

"Why is that?"

"I never was one for books."

Meri sniffed with the authority of an older sibling, though they were practically the same age. "College is totally different from high school."

Sake waited for Meri to explain, too proud to admit that she was so clueless about college she didn't even know what the questions were, let alone the answers.

"You get to study what interests you, not some slate of required subjects. Before I quit Gates College of Art—"

"Hold still—"

"Pardon?"

"Reboot. You did what?"

"Quit. Gates College of Art and Design." She glanced over at Sake. "Is that so shocking? Don't you hold it against me too. I was ready. I'd had enough."

"No smoke? I thought none of you—you, Blondie, or Ms. Hot-Shot Attorney—ever made a mistake in your lives."

Meri laughed. "At the time, Papa and Char and Savvy were sure I was making a mistake, but looking back, I think they'd agree that dropping out of school was one of the best decisions I ever made."

Sake struggled to digest this stunning new development.

"At the end of my junior year, something happened that made me feel pretty down on myself. Then, out of the blue, something—some-one—good happened." She smiled, remembering. "That gave me the confidence I needed. I took a gamble and won."

Chapter 18

When Sake arrived at the hospital that afternoon, all the medicos hanging out at the nurses' station abruptly quit joking among themselves to stare at her—until Bill's friendly RN hopped up to escort her down the hallway toward Bill's room.

"Is there something wrong with me?" asked Sake, looking down at herself while they walked. "Do I have food on my face? Am I bleeding from some orifice?"

The nurse huffed a dry laugh. "You don't know? Honey"—his hand fluttered to his breastbone—"when the daughter of the man who gave the money for the St. Pierre Heart Center shows up, it does tend to give people pause. Especially when she's as hot as you are."

Bill *had* mentioned something about a St. Pierre wing when he'd brought her here after the helicopter crash. In all that had happened since, she'd forgotten about it.

"How's Bill doing today?"

"Your Bill Diamond is precious. The model patient. Takes his meds without a fuss, never interrupts the perpetual comedy routine out at the nurses' station. Then again, his morphine drip might have something to do with that."

Sake guessed a sense of humor helped when you were dealing with sick and injured people every day. "How much longer will he be on that?"

"If he continues to improve, the docs might start weaning him off as soon as tomorrow. Actually . . ." He checked his watch. "His dinner tray is coming in less than an hour. We dine unfashionably early, here at Queen of the Valley. If you stick around, maybe you could help him eat."

Dinner turned out to be a cup of chicken broth and Jell-O.

Sake aimed for Bill's mouth with the spoon. "Here comes the wine train. . . ."

Bill smiled weakly, shaking his head in protest. "No more," he rasped.

She'd only persuaded him to down half the cup. "You'll be sorry. The nurse is going to make you put the oxygen back on as soon as he gets here and I'm taking off to see my puppy, who I haven't seen for days. Here it comes, last chance. Choo choo . . ."

Sake followed Bill's line of sight to where his parents stood in the doorway.

She lowered the spoon. "Oh. Hi."

They didn't look happy to see her. In fact, Sake clearly sensed an air of uneasiness surrounding them. After a beat of hesitation, they ventured forward as one.

Rachel's smile was patently fake. "You're back, I see. How's he doing?"

"The nurse said it was okay if I tried to get him to eat some broth."

"That's very helpful. Isn't that helpful of her, David?"

"Yeah. Real helpful." David rammed his hands into his pockets, a gesture Sake had seen Bill make a dozen times. Now she knew where Bill got it.

"Is something wrong?"

His parents eyed each other again. "No! Nothing wrong, is there, David?"

David smudged the tile with the toe of his tennis shoe—another idiosyncrasy he shared with Bill. Surprising how well Sake had come to know his son in such a short time.

Rachel dropped her façade then. "Can we step outside the room for a minute?"

Bill's eyes were closed again. "I'll be right back," Sake said, with a pat to his shoulder.

Out in the hall, Sake asked, "What's going on?"

Rachel's mouth started to move, but she couldn't get the words out.

"Is it Bill? Is he worse off than we thought?"

David said, "It's Taylor."

Rachel pressed her lips together, resigned. "She ran out when I opened Bill's door yesterday. We can't find her anywhere."

* * *

It wasn't that Queen of the Valley was all that far from Bill's apartment. It was the fact that Sake had never driven between those two points that made it so hard. But she was determined to sweep Bill's entire neighborhood for signs of Taylor while it was still daylight. Following several wrong turns, she pulled into the lot of his complex, parked askew, and headed out at a trot.

"Taylor! Taylor, where are you?!"

Was Taylor running *away* from this place, or *back to* something? As cushy as life was up here, it was true what they said: there's no place like home. Yet going home wasn't always easy.

So many things could happen to a little dog in twenty-four hours. Luckily it was summer and the weather was dry, but . . . Sake imagined Taylor lying beside the road, injured . . . dog-napped by some bully, or picked up by a well-meaning traveler passing through, leaving Sake wondering for the rest of her life what had happened to her.

"Here, Taylor! C'mon, girl!"

She scoured the area surrounding Bill's apartment complex on foot, threading through backyards and alleys . . . trespassing in carports . . . asking everyone she met if they'd seen Taylor. But all she got were sympathetic looks and promises to call her if they did.

At dusk, Sake went back to Bill's and scavenged through his drawers for paper and markers to scribble some flyers.

Then, to save time, instead of walking she drove between the traffic signs where she hung her posters, spiraling outward until she'd used them up. If Taylor was still gone come tomorrow—a sickening dread accompanied the thought—she'd hang more.

Tomorrow. Thirty-six hours was a long time for her little girl to go without her favorite dog chow.

Sake whistled and called until well after dark. Finally, exhausted and hoarse, she dragged herself back to Bill's place for the last time that night.

On Sunday morning, she woke up fully dressed on Bill's couch. After splashing her face and brewing a to-go cup of coffee, she took up where she'd left off the day before, stiff this time from all the miles she'd already walked.

By eleven she was famished. Downcast, she plodded back to Bill's lonesome apartment once more and made herself a peanut butter sandwich. But all she could taste was the salt of her tears.

* * *

Bill felt strangely out of it, like he'd been hit by a truck.

Which, according to all reports, he had.

He'd have to take the doctors' word for it. From the time he'd woken up in the hospital, he couldn't quite separate dreams from reality.

He recalled the concern in Sake's eyes peering down at him. Where was she now? He strained to puzzle together his life before the crash. Lots of the pieces featured her. They must have spent a good deal of time together recently.

He heard a noise and squinted up at an approaching figure. Lo and behold: it was Sake.

"Hi." She looked tired, but she brightened a little the moment she saw him. "You're awake."

The sight of her close up was like manna from heaven. With the hand not tethered to the IV, he reached for her, and she returned his squeeze, not letting go.

"How are you?" she asked.

Sake hated it when people asked *her* how she was. He didn't know how he knew that, but he did. Then he recalled another piece of the puzzle: *They were here, in this hospital, but Sake was the one in bed and Bill was standing over her.*

"No more oxygen mask, I see." Shyly, she reached out and brushed a stray lock of hair off his forehead.

"I missed my appointment for my haircut yesterday."

"Only Bill Diamond would be thinking about that after he nearly got himself killed."

But relief at her presence transcended everything else. Somehow she made him feel whole again. His let his eyes drift closed, just for a minute.

When he opened them with a head that was clearer than it had been in a long time, the room was in shadow. Sake was gone, along with the IV, and his right leg was throbbing like all get out.

Chapter 19

Sake set her alarm for 5 a.m. She donned her new white coat embroidered with the Mon Rêve logo, checking herself out in the full-length mirror. Back at Bunz, she would have settled for slinging her hair into a messy bun, but that didn't seem good enough for a real French patisserie. This morning, she twisted her hair into a neat braid.

The whole time she was getting ready for work, she couldn't stop thinking about poor Taylor. *Where are you?*

Squeezing toothpaste onto the brush, Sake sighed. She'd lost track of so many things throughout her life: homes, people, her hometown, and now even her dog. But until the end of her shift today, there was nothing more she could do.

At least, working—having somewhere she had to be—gave her a sense of purpose. A feeling that she belonged, somewhere.

She grabbed some clothes to change into after work and tiptoed down the stairs of the mansion. At this hour, no one but a few staff was around. A housekeeper did a double take at seeing a St. Pierre daughter wearing a service uniform.

The commute to the bakery turned out to be a piece of cake, the traffic sparse in the still-sleepy town. That was another thing Sake loved about being a baker. Greeting the day . . . trying to catch the precise moment the dusky lavender sky morphed into pale yellow, while most of the world was still asleep. On the streets of San Francisco, she had occasionally bonded with another rare early bird passing by, gripping a coffee, in the space of a nod. This morning, from behind the wheel of the borrowed Subaru, a similar interaction took place at a red light when she caught the eye of another, random driver.

It felt good to be going to work again.

"Smells like heaven," exclaimed Sake the moment she set foot in the door.

"I just put a special-order cake into the oven," said her new boss, wiping his hands as he trundled out from the back. He was dressed in the piped jacked and toque signifying his exalted chef status.

Like the proverbial kid in the candy shop, Sake spread her fingers along the top of a slanted glass showcase, peering down into it with awe.

"We're known for our canéle, chocolate and raspberry cheese croissants, and brioche," the chef said, detailing the case's contents. "We always have macarons, beignets, and cheesecake. Our trademark savories are quiche, potato salad, and specialty sandwiches on artisan breads, baked fresh daily."

He showed her where she could put her things, and their system of making coffee and processing payments. The entire time, Sake kept half an eye on the opening to the kitchen.

"That's where the tour ends," he said, inadvertently blocking her view with his body. "We leave the baking to the professionals. They've earned the right."

Mon Rêve was superior to Bunz in every way except one: here, Sake wasn't allowed to do the one job that made her heart sing.

Chapter 20

B ill hobbled up the sidewalk, one arm around his dad's shoulders for support. Mom brought up the rear, carrying his crutches and a vase of flowers that wilted more by the minute. When they got close to Bill's front door, it became apparent that their double-wide configuration wasn't going to fit through the opening.

Eyeing their dilemma, Mom said, "Let William go in first, David."

Dad halted. "Maybe *I* should go first."

"Turn sideways," said Mom, revising her instructions.

Bill turned left and Dad right.

"Ow!" Dad's hand flew to his nose.

"Sorry, Dad. You okay?"

"Not that sideways!" Mom shook her head. "You two are the biggest klutzes I ever saw."

"Hey," said Sake from where she stood, just inside.

Bill's eyes grew wide at the outfit she sported for his homecoming: another one of her miniskirts paired with over-the-knee socks exposing a sweet twelve inches of thigh. When she bent over to whisk away the doormat so he wouldn't trip on it, the view almost gave him a coronary, on top of everything else.

"Welcome to life with the Diamonds," Bill said with a grin. "I hope you're ready for this."

Behind him and his entourage, she released the door from its spring and it drifted shut.

Bill looked around at his place. This would be his new office until his driving leg healed. Technically, his desk was at the real estate office, along with some file cabinets full of closed transactions and zoning maps lining the walls. But he spent most of his working hours driving between sites and to meetings, with everything he needed to work his important deals right there at his fingertips. Now, his beloved car sat crumpled up in some junkyard. "Pleated like an accordion," the cops had told Dad when he'd gone to the station to pick up what they'd been able to salvage, adding that the driver was lucky to be alive. Mom had scolded Dad for repeating that part to Bill.

That must the box, there on the coffee table. The corner of his briefcase stuck out of it, along with some other familiar-looking odds and ends.

His spirits sank a little lower. You couldn't sell real estate from an easy chair. It was all about being in the field. He was going to miss ferrying prospective buyers around the valley, scouting out new locations, and lunching with colleagues to keep abreast of the latest industry goings-on. But with a cast covering both his ankle and knee joints, fixing his right leg at a sixty-degree angle, Bill could barely get into a car, let alone drive one. He wouldn't even have a new phone until Dad had a chance to run to the electronics store for him.

While Mom and Dad got him situated in his recliner, Sake stood off to the side holding a throw pillow at the ready in case he needed extra elevation for his leg.

"What smells so good?"

"I made you some banana muffins for lunch," said Sake.

"Banana muffins. I don't know when's the last time I had banana muffins," said Dad.

"Billy likes piroshky best," said Mom. "They've always been his favorite, ever since he was a little boy."

"Pir-osh-ky?" Sake stuttered.

"Piroshky. Not the savory ones, the sweet kind. The ones with apples."

"I like banana muffins just fine, Mom."

"I'll make you some piroshky tomorrow."

"I don't need all those sweets while I'm recuperating. I'll blow up again like a balloon."

"Billy used to be fat," Mom explained to Sake.

"Mom!"

"For Chrissake, Rachel. Not in front of—" *A girl? His girl?* Dad wasn't sure what Sake was to Bill. But then, neither was Bill.

Mom shot back, "Don't blame me. I'm not the one who made you banana muffins."

"What's on TV?" Dad sat down on the sectional and picked up the remote. Some dark dystopian drama with futuristic characters came on.

"Look at those tattoos, wouldja," said Dad.

Bill caught Sake tugging her sleeves down over her kanji tats. He wondered again what they stood for. Then the oven timer went off and she went to finish her baking.

Dad changed the channel again.

An update now on the investigation of a helicopter crash that occurred last month at the Domaine St. Pierre winery. The FAA and the NTSB are deciding whether to fine Xavier St. Pierre, or even suspend his pilot's license, because his flight log cannot be located. Regulations require pilots to log the departure and arrival times and other pertinent information for every flight.

It is becoming more and more apparent that the majority of owner/pilot crashes are the result of pilot error or, in some cases, blatant disregard of basic safety procedures....

All heads turned toward Sake, frozen in front of the open oven door holding a muffin tin with one mitted hand, eyes glued to the TV screen.

"Hey, Dad, is the game on?"

"What game?"

"Any game."

After a final fussing over by Mom, his parents finally left, promising to be back later to check on him. Bill called Sake out of the kitchen, where she was rinsing plates.

"Sorry about my mom. She means well."

Sake came and perched on the edge of the couch. "She liked my muffins, surprise."

Bill chuckled. "How many'd she scarf down?"

"Two or three." She shrugged. "Who's counting?"

"At least, with Mom, you'll always know where you stand."

She smiled thinly.

"Hey. There's something I want to say to you."

He opened his mouth to explain, but something didn't feel right.

She was too far away, over there on the couch. "Come here." He reached for her.

She rose and slinked toward him, though there was nothing contrived about Sake's feline walk. She couldn't help it, she was sexy.

Bill kissed the back of her hand. "Thanks for everything you've done for me," he said, peering up at where she stood next to his recliner. "Keeping me company in the hospital. The muffins. Everything."

"It's nothing."

"No. It's something."

"You would have done the same for me."

"Maybe." His guilt made him shrink inside. *Maybe not, if I happened to be busy with Deb.* "All the same . . . thanks."

"You taught me to drive."

"Kudos again on passing your test. How much did you have to bribe him—the officer?"

She took back her hand to give his upper arm a slap. "I did you proud, Bill Diamond! Until I tapped the brick wall with Meri's Benz at the end." She smiled broadly. "Guess he liked me or something."

She was kidding, but that was probably close to the truth. No wonder the guy had passed her. He was probably as in love with her as—

She took a step back toward the couch. Bill lunged to recapture her hand, suddenly possessive. He tangled his fingers with hers.

"It's like some crazy role-reversal. Now you're the one who's stuck at home, and I'm the one driving and working. I have a whole new routine since you've been in the hospital."

He made an ironic face. "Best-laid plans, and all that."

Regretfully, he let her slip out of reach. "So tell me what you've been up to. I got nothing but time."

She sat facing him, leaning forward, hands clasped loosely between her knees. "I've been getting up before dawn to go to work at Mon Rêve from six-thirty to one, then as soon as I get off I hurry back here to look for Taylor." The light in her eyes dimmed at the mention of her dog.

"I'm really sorry about her getting out."

"Your mom said Taylor slipped right between her feet. But then, this was never her home to begin with." She touched the inner corner of her eye with a fingertip. "I moved her bowls of food and water outside by the door in case she comes back sometime when I'm not here."

"We'll keep her dishes out there. And now that I'm here, I'll keep a sharp eye out for her, too."

"You need a ride somewhere, I'll take you. Anything. Just name it."

Bill's lips slid into an honest grin. "I appreciate that."

But without a real estate license, she couldn't show prospective buyers his listings. She couldn't go on walk-throughs for him.

Commercial clients were notoriously impatient. Typically they were already successful in their own fields. They pushed themselves relentlessly and they expected the same amount of effort from the people they paid commissions to. It wasn't personal, it was just business.

"Finish what you were saying about your daily routine."

"I've been circling from work, to your apartment, to the hospital until you fall asleep, then back to the winery."

"How are things going at Domaine St. Pierre?"

"Papa was pretty chill the night Taylor went missing. I looked for her till it got too dark, then I crashed here. Not that there wasn't *any* push-back. He made it clear that that night was an exception. It's ridiculous for a woman my age to be told what she can and can't do, especially when half the time Papa's not around anyway. But all those hidden cameras and staff at the mansion? Like San Quentin."

Bill laughed. "Most people would think they'd died and gone to heaven if they were sentenced to life in Domaine St. Pierre." He looked at her closely. "You don't have to talk about this if you don't want to, but what about that news report? Might your dad really face a fine or lose his pilot's license?"

She sighed. "Who knows? That's his problem. I have enough of my own."

"What about your sisters? Any progress there?"

She struck a pose. "Why didn't you tell me Meri quit school?"

"Didn't know I was supposed to. Does it matter?"

"Hells to the yes, it matters! Here I was thinking they were bullet-proof all this time, then to find out one of them isn't."

"I've been trying to tell you—nobody's perfect."

"Nobody except them. Well, the rest of them."

"I'll bet if you look hard enough, you'll come across flaws in the others, too."

"I'll take that bet."

She made him smile, in spite of himself. She always had.

"How's the job going?"

At that, her face lit up. "That place is *on point.* They have six full-time chefs working there, and all their equipment is state of the art, and their raspberry croissants sell out before ten o'clock—" Bill chuckled and she caught herself, pinkening at her childish enthusiasm.

But Bill loved seeing her glow. "I'm proud of you, Sake. You're on your way."

He shifted his leg a centimeter to relieve the stiffness and winced.

"You hurting?"

"Naw."

But Sake was right. The balance of power had definitely shifted.

"Don't lie. I'll get you your pills. Your mama left them on the counter."

She returned with his meds and a fresh glass of water.

"You need another pillow?" Without waiting for a reply, she brought one over from the couch.

Bill leaned forward so she could tuck it behind his head.

"There," she said, plumping it up for him.

The scent of her, standing there close enough to touch, triggered a sudden, primitive urge to spring from his seat and prove he was still a man in the way that really counted.

Peering up into her face, he dropped his left arm over the recliner's armrest, the backs of his fingers dragging a lazy trail up the outside of her thigh.

She stood still and wary as a cat.

His inhalations deepened, stabbing at his damaged lung like the point of a knife. He ignored the pain.

Not only had he lost his common sense, he'd turned into a masochist.

His palm opened to cup the back of her leg, stroking slowly up and down between where her knee sock ended and her hem began. Risking that his brazenness might make her spring away from him at any moment.

Sake's irises melted into black disks.

The deep rumble of his own voice sounded unfamiliar to his own ears when he said, "You're lucky I can't get out of this chair." No wonder masochism was so popular, if it felt this good.

Now her chest was rising and falling visibly, too.

Bill let his hand travel higher, up under her skirt. Now he could feel the warm, smooth skin of her inner thigh with his fingertips. Any higher, and his thumb should be grazing the edge of her panties where her rear end curved outward.

His leg might be broken in two places, but his man parts were ready for launch.

"Am I?" she interrupted his flight of imagination. "Lucky?"

She chose that moment to step out of range. But just before she was out of arm's length he lunged out playfully with his finger to flick up her hem.

Agh! He let his head loll back on his pillow. One small step for her, one giant let-down for him.

What had Sake done to him? The old Bill Diamond would never have acted so brash.

Sake retrieved her bag and keys from the kitchen and returned to say good-bye, this time keeping a safe distance. She peered down at him with a cool smile.

Before, Sake had come onto him. He'd shunned her advances twice, once when she'd done a striptease right here in this very room, and again when he'd told her he wasn't interested, in the car, minutes before his wreck. Now, who was putting the moves on whom? Payback was proving to be hell.

To expel his built-up frustration, Bill took a lung-busting breath, which brought on a coughing spasm.

Sake's aloofness disappeared immediately. She flew to his side. "You okay?"

His cough sputtered out. "You better stay. I'm not long for this world." He grinned salaciously.

She pulled a face. "Seriously. You'll be okay here by yourself?"

"No worries," he said, feigning a casual air while shifting his hips within the confines of the recliner. He grabbed the pillow from behind his neck and plopped it onto his lap.

"The 'rents'll be around to check on me. Can't help themselves. Had to put up a fight to convince them to let me stay here instead of their house while I'm recuperating. The only thing that won them over was that my room at their place is upstairs. Here, everything's on the first floor."

"You'll call me if you need anything." With gratifying reluctance, she headed toward the door.

She was leaving. And he was helpless to go after her. He scrambled for the right words that would bring her back.

"Will you come back after work tomorrow?"

She stopped with her hand poised on the knob. "Are you asking me to?"

"I'm asking."

That brought back her Cheshire cat smile. "Then I will."

Chapter 21

At Mon Rêve, the disheveled guy in the denim shirt seated near the window caught Sake's eye. He held up his coffee mug in that universal signal that every waitress knew.

Seriously? He really expected her to lug the pot over to him, pour him a refill? Cater to him?

She wished she were back in the kitchen. With baking, all you had to contend with were non-human factors such as ingredients, equipment, temperature, and so on. But the morning rush was over and the lunch bunch hadn't yet arrived. She was getting off early today. Mon Rêve was closing at noon for a private party, planned before she'd been hired. She supposed it wouldn't kill her to powder one customer's behind.

"You look like you just got off the last bus from the old school," said Sake, filling his cup to the brim.

"Beg your pardon?"

"Somewhere, somebody spoiled you rotten."

"Heh heh heh." His grin was refreshingly normal, not professionally straightened and whitened like those of most of the other people she'd met lately. "You're right. Somebody did. You new?"

"Been here about a week. Wait a minute." Sake pointed at him. "You're that guy."

"What guy?"

"The one who nodded at me from his car on my first day of work."

He took a better look at her. "I'll be. I remember you. Where do you hail from?"

"The city. Don't tell the boss," she said, looking over her shoulder, "but I'm only here a couple of months, then I'm headed back."

"What's the matter? Fresh air and sunshine getting you down?"

She set the pot down on his table for a minute. "I'm ill-suited for country life. First thing I'm gonna do when I get back is go down to the Wharf and get me a smashed tsukune sandwich. Then I'm going to sit on a bench at Pier 33 with the tourists and eat it."

"The Pan Grill makes the best sandwiches, don't they?"

"You know the Pan Grill?" It thrilled her to have found a connection.

"I been around the block a time or two. Funny isn't it? How the city is so close in terms of miles, yet so far away in atmosphere?"

"Hysterical. Do you live here now?"

He chuckled again in his gravelly voice. "Sometimes. What brings a dyed-in-the-wool city girl to wine country? Let me guess: a boy."

The bell on the door clanged as a noisy knot of women entered the shop.

"It's complicated," said Sake, lifting her pot, turning away from him.

"It always is," he muttered, blowing a ripple across the top of his hot coffee.

Sake led the newcomers to a four-top. "Here are your menus. Can I bring you some water while you're deciding?"

Their inane chatter shut off like a faucet. Furtive, sidelong glances bounced around the table.

Sake lifted a brow. "Water?" she repeated.

"Excuse me—"

"Are you—?"

Two of the women spoke at once, collapsing into giggles.

"What's your name?" demanded a third.

"Sake."

Smugly, the woman said to her companions, "I *told* you that was her."

Sake turned her back on their rude stares to fetch their drinks.

A careless whisper reached her ears: "What's the daughter of Xavier St. Pierre doing waitressing?"

When she returned, the man was gone. But he'd left a twenty lying on the table, along with a note scribbled on the back of his check. *For your tsukune sandwich. But don't discount the country. It's not all bad.*

* * *

Sake was still trying to get over those fancy customers acting like she was a Kardashian or something—and thinking of how she could put a funny twist on the story to bring out Bill's dimple—when she walked into Bill's apartment to find him and his parents gathered around his kitchen table, along with a well-endowed brunette stuffed into a lab coat.

It was hard to tell who was more surprised: Sake or the others.

"I should have knocked."

Their awkward silence confirmed it.

"I got off work an hour early, so I thought it'd be all right. . . . I'll come back later," she said, turning to go.

"Don't go on my account," said Party Boobs. She came around the table with a hand thrust toward Sake. "I'm Deborah Feinstein."

"*Doctor* Feinstein," corrected Bill's mom.

Bill's doctor made house calls? One thing for sure—Doc had a grip like iron.

"Mom and Dad just brought me a sandwich, and they brought Deb along," Bill explained.

Deb? He called his doctor by her first name?

"I'd get up, but . . ." Bill smiled apologetically from his place at the table. His bad leg lay propped on an odd chair wedged between the others.

"It's all good." *No, it wasn't.* Something was off, and it wasn't just that there was no room at the table for Sake.

"Here, take my seat," David rose.

"Go ahead." She waved away his offer. "Finish your food." Then she asked Deb, "Did you see Bill in the hospital?"

"I did," said Deborah from back in her seat, munching French fries.

"Stopped by every morning, from the minute she heard he was a patient," added Bill's mom.

"I work mornings." *That's it, Sake. Dazzle them with your wit.*

David, still standing in deference to Sake, pushed his plate to the side, carving out an extra place.

"Dad, there's an ottoman in the bedroom, if you wouldn't mind."

David returned with a padded, elongated cube.

Bill braced himself to lift his heavy cast. "I'll use that. Give Sake this chair."

"Stop!" Dr. Feinstein threw up a hand and rose halfway. "Any abrupt movement may compromise your deep fibular nerve," she said, licking the salt from her lips. "You could end up with paralysis of the foot dorsiflexors and toe extensors. We don't want you ending up with a steppage gait, do we?

Hells to the no! Anything but a steppage gait.

Sake ended up sitting on the ottoman. The cube was so low that her chest only came up to the table edge, so that everyone looked down on her.

"So, what do *you* do . . . 'Sake,' did you say your name was? I once drank some sake at a Chinese restaurant. I found it rather insipid. Flavorless."

"It's Japanese, and I'd be more than happy to introduce you to a sake that would kick your ass. Oh, and I work at a bakery."

"I know all about food service. My cousin owns the Gold's Bakery franchise in the Midwest," said Deborah, sucking on her soda straw. "What's your store called?"

"Mon Rêve."

Deb smacked her lips, frowning. "Doesn't Ernst Volant own that coffee shop?"

"It's a patisserie. And I didn't say I owned it. I said I worked there."

"Back in med school, a bunch of us used to study at this one hangout. Sometimes, when I was exhausted from coming off a double and still had studying to do for a crucial exam, I used to think about chucking it all, doing something mindless—like waitressing."

Everyone stared at Deb.

"I'm kidding," she said, holding out her hands.

Nobody laughed.

Sake stood up. "Look—I'm going to, um, take off, okay?" she said, directing her comment at Bill. "Don't have much of an appetite. I only stopped to see if there was any sign of Taylor."

"I called for her earlier today, but . . ." Bill's face filled with regret.

Sake swallowed her disappointment. "Should have known it was too much to hope for."

That evening, Sake's phone rang.

"Sorry about today," said Bill.

"I got used to not knocking, those days when you were in the hospital and I came over to look for Taylor. Never thought I'd walk in on a 'doctor's appointment.'"

"Yeah . . . about that."

"Dr. Deb's not your *doctor* doctor, is she?"

"Not exactly."

"S'okay," she said, forcing herself to act more mature than she felt. "It's not like you didn't warn me."

Sitting cross-legged in the center of her California king bed centered in the spacious guest room, Sake felt very small. Grateful that at least Bill couldn't see her face, she concentrated hard on the décor: the curved lines of the matching chests of drawers, the spot on the carpet where the silk drapes puddled, the vase stuffed with pink peonies that dominated her nightstand.

"Besides, it's not like I'ma be around much longer anyway. Only four more weeks."

"Forget what I said before. It's a whole new ball game since the wreck. I'm no good to anyone in my condition. I've got to put all my energy into getting better."

What had she expected? For Bill to tell her that he'd been wrong before—he wasn't interested in anyone else? There she went again, raising her hopes too high.

"You got a way with words, Bill Diamond." She sniffed away a laugh. "You always know just what to say to smooth things over." *To leave his options open.* He was a salesman, after all.

Sake hit end, lowering her phone.

When would she ever learn? The only person she could count on was herself.

Over on the bureau, the borrowed iPad caught her eye. She walked over and retrieved it. And started looking up the requirements to get into the CIA.

A high school diploma or its equivalent; proof of six months of employment at a non-fast food restaurant with a professional kitchen; letter of recommendation.

She could ask Teeny to write her a letter vouching for the time she'd put in a Bunz. It probably wouldn't do any good, but she could ask.

And then this caught her eye:

So Think You Can Bake? The CIA Wants You! Show us how you spread the love with your own cake recipe and decorating skills. CIA will waive admission requirements for one lucky baker. The winner will be admitted to the fall semester of the CIA with a one-semester scholarship. Rules: Bring four-dozen cupcakes to the CIA on the day of the event between 1:00 and 4:00 p.m. Entries will be judged based on taste, presentation, and originality. Cupcakes will be sold to benefit the local food bank.

Chapter 22

Without Bill Diamond or Taylor in it, Sake's world narrowed down to only two things: working and studying.

Yet despite her best efforts, Bill was rarely out of her thoughts. It was all she could do not to pick up his calls. But judging by the casual tone of his texts saying lame things like, *how are you?* and *keep in touch,* nothing had changed.

She worried about Bill and wondered how he was recuperating, but between his parents and Dr. Deb, he had all the help he needed. She could only hope that if Taylor miraculously returned to his apartment, he'd have enough decency to spell that out in no uncertain terms.

"I've been thinking," commented Jeanne during one of their light suppers in the kitchen. Papa was gone somewhere, Char and Meri were working late, and Savvy was still on her honeymoon. "Sauvignon will soon be back. Wouldn't it be a good idea if her sisters planned a shower for her baby?"

"A baby shower? Savvy just got married. What makes you think she's pregnant?"

"But everyone knows that she was already two or three months along on the day of her wedding."

Sake couldn't believe it. First Meri wasn't perfect, and now Savvy wasn't either?

"I'm somebody, and I didn't know."

"Pardon me." Beneath an arched brow, Jeanne's eyes danced playfully. "You most definitely are somebody."

Since they'd been thrust together with only each other for company most of this summer, Jeanne had thawed toward her a bit. They'd even found a certain respect for each other.

"Now that you know you have a little niece or nephew on the way, don't you agree that a baby shower would be a lovely gesture for you three to make toward your oldest sister?"

"Um, sure." Around here, Jeanne's word was gospel. Even Papa deferred to her, weirdly enough. The longer she was here, the more Sake realized she had to learn about her family. "But do you really think Savvy would want me involved? And what about Meri and Char? Maybe they'd rather plan this fête without me."

Jeanne laid her hand atop Sake's. *"Au contraire, ma chérie."*

Sake looked up from her salad. Jeanne had never called her "dear" before.

"What better way to get to know one another than planning a party?"

With Jeanne vouching for her, maybe her sisters would be more receptive to including the outcast.

The next day was Saturday, Meri and Char's day off. Following Sake's shift at Mon Rêve, Jeanne met her inside the front door.

"We're out by the pool. Join us after you change out of your uniform."

When she got to her room, Sake found a garment bag draped across her bed with a handwritten note.

I saw this dress while shopping and thought it would complement your figure. I hope you will give me the pleasure of accepting this small gift. Jeanne.

The dress was black-and-white polka dotted with a short, swingy skirt, just the style she liked. She gulped when she saw the price tag.

Before she could change her mind, she slipped the soft fabric over her head and went down to join the others, hoping her nervousness didn't show.

"Wine?" Char asked, holding the bottle of St. Pierre poised over the glass at Sake's place setting.

Should she? That wasn't just a bottle of wine. It was a powerful symbol. Sharing the product of their own father's blood, sweat, and tears might help them to bond. She was already an outsider, and to turn it down might send the wrong message. But in her experience, the stuff inside that bottle tended to tear people apart, not tie them together.

"I'll stick with iced tea."

Char didn't even blink before passing the bottle over Sake's glass to Jeanne's. "Love those kitten-eared sunglasses. Where'd you get them?"

"A little vintage place in The Haight."

"I'll bet you know lots of good places to shop in the city." Char glanced at the others. "Sake should take us on a tour sometime. Wouldn't that be fun?"

"Awesome," said Meri. "I'm in the city all the time, but I didn't grow up there like you did, Sake. It would be great to see the city through the eyes of a home girl."

"Any time." Sake imagined the stares her sisters would get if they showed up in some of the holes-in-the-wall Sake frequented.

"Salut," said Jeanne when everyone had a drink.

"To sisters," added Char.

Sake had been living at Papa's for several weeks, but she still hadn't spent much time in the presence of both Meri and Char. Now, it felt to her as if she'd only just arrived. She sat quietly in her elegant surroundings—the outdoor living room, complete with rug, the fresh fruit heaped on the table between them—and drank in her sisters' every detail . . . the way they held their wineglasses, the soft, low registers of their eastern accents, their choices of words.

Meanwhile, Jeanne, in turn, watched Sake, noting her every reaction. That's when the real reason for the new dress hit her: it was a booster for her self-image. Jeanne wanted Sake to feel good, sitting next to these two glamazons. Sake sent Jeanne a smile of pure gratitude.

The shower business came first. Chardonnay volunteered to be in charge of the guest list, Merlot the décor, and Jeanne the catering.

Thanks to Jeanne's gift, Sake found the courage to raise her hand. "I can make cupcakes."

Once all that had been decided, Char asked Meri how her new line of jewelry was selling. Then Char talked about Juan and Amelia, her favorite kids down at her foundation.

"Sake is making progress toward her goals, too," said Jeanne.

Meri and Char turned to Sake with what appeared to be genuine interest.

"Tell them what you've been doing, Sake."

What was she supposed to say? She gulped. She couldn't make them understand what a monumental leap up her job at Mon Rêve was without going into some background. But how could she tell them that while they'd been at the best prep academies money could buy, she'd been washing dishes after school at Balboa High?

She began on a deep inhale. "Growing up, it was just Haha and me. My mother is kind of—eccentric? But back then, I didn't know any different. Where I come from, everybody's a little eccentric."

While Char smiled politely, Meri, who was younger and a skosh less proper, asked, "Haha?"

Sake had forgotten. "Like 'Mama.' It's what I've always called my mom."

"Oh." Her sisters nodded in unison.

They thought they understood, but they didn't. Not really. San Francisco *celebrated* eccentricity, but Haha was edgy, even by her city's standards.

"Sometimes Haha would go off on her own for a while, to do whatever it was that she did. When I was real little, she always dropped me off at someone's house to make sure I was taken care of, but when I got older and balked at staying with strangers, she would let me stay on my own. Well, not totally alone. She gave me a dagger that had belonged to her father and told me to keep it under my pillow, to use for protection."

Meri inhaled sharply.

Char's fingertips flew to cover her mouth.

"Mon Dieu," breathed Jeanne, hastily making the sign of the cross.

"I never meant to leave school. Just sort of drifted away after I turned sixteen, the winter that Haha went AWOL for so long. After a couple of months, the landlord ran out of patience. I found another place to stay, but it was outside my school district, and I didn't have enough money for even the student rates for MUNI or BART. I probably should've started at yet another new school, but just showing up at some principal's office by myself would've got Haha in trouble. That's when I started working more hours in restaurants."

Jeanne downed half a glass of wine in one gulp.

Like an automaton, never taking her eyes off Sake, Char refilled it.

"One day, the place where I was serving was short-handed, and they asked me to help out in the back of the house. The head pastry maker was no prince, but I totally 'got' baking. I loved the warmth of the ovens, that yeasty smell. The way pastry always comes out right if you follow the recipe . . ."

"Is that where Papa found you?" Meri whispered.

"Not exactly." Her sisters' faces looked like they'd just seen a horror movie. "It gets *worse*?" asked Char.

She wasn't about to describe the night before Savvy's wedding, when Papa had stormed into the jail with his lawyer and demanded that Sake be released or he'd sue the city.

She laughed wryly. "Let's just say, the place I was staying when he found me didn't look nothing like this." She gestured toward the water of the pool, twinkling aquamarine and white in the blinding August sun.

Char took a deep breath and said, "Savvy should probably be here for this conversation, but I can't not bring it up. It's been brushed under the rug for far too long."

In anticipation of what Char was about to say, Jeanne sat perfectly still, while Meri bit her upper lip.

"How long have you known about . . . us?"

Sake took off her sunglasses and laid them on the table. "I was probably, oh thirteen or fourteen. We were taking computer classes at school. Haha was staying away longer and longer. I missed her." She looked at the others. "I was in middle school, and I was practically raising myself. Maybe if she'd told me where she was going . . ." She shook her head. Too late to think about that now. "Finally, I had this great idea. If I couldn't find Haha, maybe I could find Papa, somewhere on the Internet."

Sake stared at the glittering pool, mesmerized, recalling the image on the screen burned into in her mind's eye. "That day, I saw a photo of him with his arms around three girls about my age, standing in front of this very pool. The caption said they were the St. Pierre family."

Char closed her eyes. Meri's hand went to her forehead.

"But Xavier visited you after that," said Jeanne. "You didn't bring up the picture?"

"And say what? 'Hey, Dad, how come you keep me separate from your other kids?' I had eyes. I could see that I didn't belong. If I did, he'd have brought it up long before then."

Char put her hand on Sake's arm. "We never knew," she said, shaking her head slowly, gazing earnestly into her eyes.

Sake's lips twitched with an attempt at a smile, but just ended up trembling instead.

"No," agreed Meri. "He only told us when Savvy got pregnant and decided to get married. He said he'd always planned for us girls to meet when the first of us got married, but he'd lost track of you. He had a team of lawyers looking for you. We assumed that's why you were here now—because they'd found you."

"Hmph. Something like that." Sake did smile then, a smile filled with irony. Before asking the next thing she needed to know, she looked down, to gather hope and strength. "So you aren't mad at me?" she ventured, gazing from one sister to the other.

Char and Meri looked at each other in wonderment. "Mad?" asked Char.

"Why should we be mad?" Meri chimed in.

"Uh, isn't it obvious? Your father had an affair with my mother!"

"Among others," said Char, with a raised eyebrow.

Sake almost bored a hole through her. There'd been others?

"Ask Jeanne. She's been here in this house practically the whole time our parents lived here."

From the time Char had started down this road, Jeanne had sat mute and motionless save for her eyes, which flickered like bluebirds between the three siblings, assessing their reactions. Now, even at Char's invitation, she still kept her counsel.

"Besides," added Meri, "that was a long time ago. Our mother's been gone for over a decade."

Sake's voice went down an octave. "I did know that." Again, thanks to the Web.

Char said, "I can't believe you thought we were mad. You've been living here for over a month."

"What about Savvy? I barely said two words to her before she left for her honeymoon."

"Nobody's mad at you. *Trust me.*"

Sake felt as though a weight she'd been carrying for years had just been lifted off of her. Still inferior, but no longer wary of simply crossing paths with her sisters in the hallway for fear of feeling their resentment.

"And now you are at Mon Rêve," Jeanne finally spoke up.

"Now I'm at Mon Rêve, which is just like it sounds—a dream—even though all I'm qualified to do there is wait on customers. And studying online for my GED."

"Wow," said Meri. "You are amazing, to have survived all of that."

"It wasn't as awful as it sounds," Sake said, dialing back. The reluctance to paint an ugly picture of Haha was hardwired.

Above all, she didn't want their pity. Sake didn't do pity.

"If you don't mind my asking, where is Haha now?" asked Jeanne.

Sake shrugged. "I haven't seen her in almost a year. But my birthday's coming soon. I'm hoping she'll resurface for that, if not before."

Char said, "Well, I think it's great that you're getting your diploma."

"What else do you have to do to get into the CIA?"

"Six months' experience in non-fast food service, which I already have—assuming I can get my old boss to vouch for it—and a letter of recommendation."

"You could ask Mr. Volant for a recommendation," said Meri. "But what about your old boss? The one you said was 'no prince'?"

Char turned to Meri. "The financial records from her previous place of employment would prove that she'd worked there. Wage slips, taxes . . ."

Sake shook her head. "Teeny wasn't heavy into record-keeping. He paid us in cash."

"Once you're at Mon Rêve for six months, you won't need your old employer to vouch for you," said Jeanne.

"Whoa." Sake's palms went up in self-defense. Six months? She'd gradually been giving more thought to the CIA. But all this talk made the prospect seem frighteningly real. "One step at a time."

What if she failed?

Chapter 23

On his computer screen, Bill watched the credits from yet another movie roll by. He must have watched a dozen of them since the night he'd totaled his car trying to multitask.

He rested his head back against the recliner and pushed off the side table with his hand to swivel from side to side. Any movement, no matter how slight, was better than this constant sitting still. He was so over movies. So over computer games. So over being stuck in this chair.

His lung didn't hurt any more when he inhaled. And yesterday at his check-up, the doctor had said his broken ribs seemed to be healing on schedule.

He had to find some way to keep from going bananas while biding his time until he could drive again. He considered all the usual diversions: yet another movie, checking in with the office, texting with friends, reading the latest real estate journal a third time.

None of those things could cure the longing that was eating him up inside.

So when his phone rang, his spirits leapt . . . until he saw the name on the screen.

"Hi, Deb."

She had been back twice since that awkward day Sake had walked in on everyone sitting around his kitchen table.

By the second time, Deb's smarty-pants blathering had started to grate on him.

Hypocrite. Everyone knew Bill Diamond was as loquacious as a Fox News reporter on Red Bull. But you couldn't have two know-it-alls trying to hold forth at the same time. It just didn't work.

"Hey! Listen, I'm stopping by the deli for lunch and I wondered if I can bring you a Reuben or something."

"Uh, hold on . . ." He faked a yawn. "I just closed my eyes . . . was up all night finishing my book."

"Oh. Well, do you want me to just drop it off for you to eat later? I have to rush back for a staff meeting by one, anyway. The new computer system is giving everyone fits. Our administration is making the excuse that . . ."

"Deb?" he cut in. "I appreciate the thought, but I've got leftovers in the fridge, and it sounds like you're pretty busy. If it's all the same to you, I think I'll take a pass this time." He might be sorry as soon as he hung up, but he couldn't handle another dose of Deb right now.

He pressed end and the silence of his apartment descended around him again.

Only an hour had passed since he'd last gone to the door to holler for the dog, but he grabbed his crutch and struggled to his feet anyway.

"Taylor!" he yelled out the door.

Bill never lost track of how long The Beast had been gone. It was always the same number of days since his wreck. The odds of Taylor returning now were practically nonexistent. He looked down at her bowl, which Mom had refreshed just that morning when she'd come to check on Bill. The sad, neat pyramid of kibble was still intact.

But what did it matter how bad he felt? *Imagine how Sake feels. She lost her life in the city, then her dog, and then you dumped her, too.*

He limped back to his chair, remembering the last time she'd been *here*—in that spot on the floor right next to his chair. He'd spent the minutes after she'd flounced out in that short skirt fantasizing about what was under it and all the things he wanted to do with it.

Despite Deb's hourglass curves, he never had thoughts like that about her.

Maybe it was finally his heart talking, not his head.

He picked up his phone.

An hour later, Sake stuck her head in the door. "I'm here. Don't get up." She came in holding a cake-shaped container.

Bill had forgotten she still had keys. He rotated in his chair to see her, with a smile so wide it hurt his cheeks.

The sight of the books, newspapers, and sports magazines heaped around his La-Z-Boy stopped her in her tracks.

"Sorry about the mess. My parents brought me all this stuff to keep me busy while I'm under house arrest. Think I've read it all—twice."

"I brought you cake." She stepped over a magazine on her way to the kitchen.

"I suppose it's too much to hope that the guard didn't confiscate the file inside of it?"

She set the container down on the kitchen counter and walked into the living room, taking a seat across from him on his L-shaped couch.

"Is that dress new?"

She smoothed the skirt out on her thighs. "Jeanne got it for me."

"You look"—*sweeter than the morning and hotter than a fox in a forest fire*—"really pretty."

One eyebrow arched. "Don't get your hopes up. This ain't no conjugal visit."

He snapped his fingers. "Dang."

By now, Bill knew Sake's tough talk was all a put-on. She could slip in and out of it like—*well*. Best not to think about her slipping in and out of anything, in his condition.

"They take away your razor, too?"

His hand went to his jaw to rub his beard. "You don't like stubble? I'll shave it." Next to her, he felt like the shaggy, old mountain lion he'd once seen limping across Ridge Road. Still, his shit-eating grin refused to be tamed. She must think him a total fool.

"I didn't say that," she replied with a half smile, a sidelong glance.

"What kind of vehicle are you tooling around in? I forgot to ask the last time you were here."

"I think it's a Subaru. They got so many vehicles up at that winery they don't know what to do with them."

"Work still going well?"

She sat back and crossed her legs, swinging one bootie rhythmically.

Nice view. Don't move an inch.

"It's good. Coworkers are nice. Some ladies came in already knowing I worked there, somehow. They recognized me before I even opened my mouth. So weird."

"That can be a real problem, just so you know. Char and Meri both have been chased by paparazzi."

"They told me."

"What?" Bill started. "You mean to tell me the ice has broken up on Dry Creek Road? Now there's a story the media would love to get its hands on."

A smile blossomed on her face, the most serene smile Bill had ever seen on her.

"Thanks to Jeanne. She kind of corralled us together. Got us planning a baby shower for Sauvignon. Did you know Savvy was already knocked up when she got married?"

"Jeanne?" Bill had only heard half of what Sake said. He was too busy trying to pinpoint everything that was different about her since he'd last seen her.

"Papa calls her his cook, but she's way more than that. Practically runs everything at the house."

"Did she happen to be wearing a big pink hat at Savvy's wedding?"

Sake pulled a face. "Seriously? You think I can remember what color hat someone had on the day I almost died?" She leaned in, warming up to him. "Try to keep up! Did you know my sister was already preggers when she got hitched?"

"I thought everybody knew that."

Sake threw a hand up in the air. "See? That's what I'm talking about. Maybe you don't have to be perfect to be a St. Pierre, after all." She hopped up. "Want some cake?"

Bill didn't have the pistachios to tell Sake that she was the only one in the whole valley who thought of the St. Pierres as perfect. Her father, in particular.

Without waiting for an answer, she went to the kitchen. Bill turned his chair to follow her with his gaze. He couldn't believe he'd ever thought of Sake as a nuisance to be gotten rid of. Now every second of her presence was a gift.

She returned holding a plate and two forks.

"I could only find one saucer."

"The rest are probably in the dishwasher. Here." He grabbed his crutch and struggled to get up without looking too clumsy. "I'll sit next to you so we can share."

"Are you sure? That chair is probably your safest bet."

"I'm so sick of that chair I'm planning on burning it as soon as I get this cast off." He hobbled over and dropped onto the couch, muttering, "And this was going to be the season I finally broke eighty."

She sat down next to him and handed him a fork.

"This cake is fantastic. Did you get it at Mon Rêve?"

"I came up with this recipe years ago. You sure did make short work of that. Want some more?"

Another chance to watch her body sashay across his floor? *You bet.* "You made that yourself?"

"So yeah," she said, after they'd polished off the second slice. "Char and Meri aren't so bad, once you start talking to them, get inside their heads."

"What happened to you thinking you were Cinderella and Char and Meri were the wicked stepsisters?" Bill poked her in the side and she folded in half, giggling. When she sat up again, her shoulder landed against his. She didn't move away.

"I said we were talking. I didn't say we were besties. Things haven't gone *that* far."

"Maybe this Jeanne will help you all work through it, when the time is right."

Sake's leg lay next to his. The contrast of his baggy gray sweatpants only made her firm muscles, her bare skin appear sleeker. Damn the consequences—she was irresistible. He put his hand on her thigh.

Sake noted his hand on her leg as coolly as if she were contemplating signing a variable rate mortgage with a hefty balloon payment.

Where was that girl who thought so little of herself that she'd whisked her top off right here in this very room, offering her precious body as payback for driving lessons?

And what had happened to that man who'd turned his back on her for someone who supposedly suited him better?

"I missed you, Sake."

She looked up at him, clear-eyed. "Because you're that guy who always needs people around and you haven't had that lately?"

"I've had people around."

She raised her eyebrows. "Oh yeah? Who?"

"My parents. Keith, my golf buddy. John, another Realtor."

"Where's your doctor friend?" Sake's eyes circled the room, as if waiting for Deb to pop out of a closet. "Thought she was more your type. Got her life on lock . . . all 'pruhfeshnal.'" She made little air quotes. "Your mama's *so* in the car with her, in case you didn't know. How come you didn't call her if you're lonely?"

"*She* called *me* earlier today, I'll have you know."

"But?"

"I told her not to come."

Bill's pulse picked up. He reached his arm around Sake and drew her close. They stayed like that, nose to nose, for a moment, breathing in the scent of each other. And then he kissed her. Softly, at first, and then his long-suppressed desire regained traction. He tested her lips with his tongue . . . tentatively, then, when she reciprocated, harder until finally, he poured himself into her, leaning over her lithe body with his broken one.

All those evenings with her sitting inches away when she was learning to drive, it was like touching her would have broken some lame teacher–student taboo. And then, after he'd met Deb—his ideal match, on paper—he'd simply pretended his desire for Sake didn't exist. But he'd never been able to put her aside completely. And now here she was, in his arms, hot and sweet and firm and soft, all at the same time . . . and all those weeks of denial ran together, culminating in a need stronger than anything he'd ever felt before, for anyone.

He pulled back to catch his breath and to sweep his gaze down her fine-boned body.

"I thought we were played out."

"Sake," he breathed. "We're just getting started."

When she lifted her mouth for round two of kissing, the urgent tug of need in Bill was leaving his usual propriety in the dust. Impulsively, he slid his hand up under her skirt, his heart thrilling when she lifted her hips to grant him access. Single-mindedly he grasped at the strip of nothingness wrapped around her hips and tugged, first one side then the other, working her panties down until they were out of sight and out of mind.

When he brought his hand back to her, she coiled like a spring. He was exultant. Finally, he'd timed something right. Working around the impediment of his cast, he reached an arm around her waist, hauling her hips down so that they were under his. Now nothing stood between them but his sweats, and he could get them off in—

"Stop!"

"What?" *Please—not my parents stopping by unexpectedly.*

"Listen!"

And then he heard it, too: a scratching sound.

Sake pushed Bill away to scramble off the couch, tripping over a stack of books in her haste, and tore open the door.

"Taylor! My baby!"

Chapter 24

Against all odds, Taylor had made it through her ordeal unscathed.

"Oh, thank God. What that poor animal must have been through these past few weeks," said Bill's mom when he called to give her the vet's report.

Whatever Taylor had endured while she was gone, it would remain as mysterious to Bill as Sake's past in San Francisco.

Bill knew that Sake was no innocent. But she was also nothing like the defiant thug she tried so hard to convince everyone she was. Inside that rough exterior was a precious gem.

She showed up the next day with another box.

"What's this?" he teased, rubbing his stomach. "Not another whole cake, I hope."

"Fresh produce from the farmers market. You can't have your dessert until you eat a healthy lunch."

"Come here," he said, with an altogether different concept of dessert in mind. After losing out to a wire-haired terrier the previous afternoon, Bill's morning had lasted an eternity, waiting for Sake's shift to end. With every passing day, the stronger his body grew, the weaker his resistance to her charms.

He pulled her down to kiss her lips. "You're a godsend."

"I don't know about that. What I am is hungry. Let me go throw something together for us."

From his chair, he watched her work. She was familiar with his kitchen now. She didn't have to stop and think where to find the olive oil or the salt or the napkins. She moved smoothly back and forth between the fridge and the sink and the table.

"Come and get it."

"Be careful what you ask for."

Watching him drag himself over to the table to eat properly, she grinned. "I'm not very athletic, but I'm pretty sure I could outrun you."

After his meal, when Sake offered him a shoulder to hobble back to the living room on, he pretended that was easier than his crutch and took it, just to lean against her body.

Once Sake had got him situated again with his laptop and books and TV remote, Bill took her wrist. "Sit with me a minute."

He scooted around to face her, still holding on to her. "Have I told you how much I appreciate you?"

To say nothing of how much I want to read every inch of that fine body like a blind man reading braille? He touched her small but capable fingers, imagining the ways in which they could bring him pleasure.

"It's the least I can do. I figure by the time I leave, we'll be even."

By the time I leave... That was another thing that he'd thought about during his long, empty days.

"Is that all this is to you? Coming to see your dog? Paying off a debt?"

"You're *still* helping me. What else am I going to do with my time? My life is on hold, too. I can't go anywhere until my birthday."

"And what exactly happens then, assuming you stay out of trouble and get your GED?"

"Papa promised to set me up, same way he set up my sisters. You know. Paid for their college and everything."

She put her hands on the edge of the couch in preparation to get up again, to his regret.

"Anyway. Tossing a salad is nothing to brag about. I feel like there's so much more I could be doing for you. Wait till tomorrow. The chef at Mon Rêve is doing choux à la crème."

He kept talking to keep her there. "Salad is exactly what I need. If my mom were here, she'd be feeding me starch with a side of starch."

"Don't knock it. I wish my mo—"

Sake caught herself.

"Tell me."

She averted her eyes.

"Don't run away from me. Tell me about your mother."

"There's nothing to tell," she said curtly. But she sat back anyway, looking around at the walls of his living room, anywhere but at him.

Bill entwined his fingers with hers, giving them a squeeze of encouragement. "I don't believe you. You don't just fall out of the sky here one day, twenty-two years old, full of rage—"

Out of the blue, Sake turned on him full-throttle. "Tell me you wouldn't be angry if your fucked-up female parental dumped you with different 'friends' at the beginning of every month when the check came, left you for whatever man she's sprung on, and didn't come back for days. And then she was hungover, sick, and bruised, all the money gone! That's the way it was, month after month, year after year. For the longest time, I thought Papa quit visiting me because he didn't love me anymore. . . ."

Ping!

In the pocket of Sake's uniform, her phone rang.

"I know you're going to tell me to get that," she said, using Bill's penchant for doing the right thing against him.

Normally, he would have. But not this time. Right now, he wanted her all to himself, safe from past influences that might drag her down. Or back to the city, away from him.

Straightening out of his embrace, she raised her phone to eye level. When she saw who it was, she dropped her hand into her lap, then rose on a sigh and stepped outside his front door, effectively shutting him out.

"Hi. I want to talk."

Sake frowned at the phone. Was this really Rico? He sounded so . . . *sober.*

"Is it Haha? Did something happen to her?"

"I haven't seen your mother."

"Then what'd you want to talk about?"

"I went to see the D.A."

Sake's head swam with possibilities, none of them good. "What for?"

"I told him to drop the charges against you. Boom. End of problem."

"Rico. You can't 'tell' the D.A. to drop the charges. It doesn't work that way. It's up to him."

"I know. But I'm the victim—"

Technically.

"—and the victim's word counts for something. He said he'd take it under consideration."

Sake looked down at the tiny square of suburban green where she stood, outside Bill's building. She wondered where Rico was standing, what he was looking at as he talked to her. Random mental snapshots took Sake back to San Francisco. Suddenly she missed her home turf with a ferocity that rocked her like a ten on the Richter scale. She missed walking barefoot on hot concrete, like she had every other August of her life. The unexpected vista of the Pacific Ocean between the houses up on Tank Hill, a reminder that you lived on the edge of a huge land mass. The intriguing scents, the city folk in their mad celebration of individuality. Whatever else San Francisco was, it was a place where you could be yourself.

"Are you planning on going to the arraignment in September?" she asked. It would be the first time she and Rico would see each other since the day she left in such a hurry.

"If you want me to. And I'll tell them you didn't do anything wrong. It was all my fault."

Maybe he would, and maybe he wouldn't. At least it sounded like if he did show up, he wouldn't say anything against her.

"I miss you, Sake. I love you. Come back. You said you would."

Sake wasn't sure what she wanted anymore.

"I got a job," Rico said, sounding somehow both humble and proud. "Cut way back on my drinking, too. I'm getting my shit together—"

Behind her, Sake heard the creak of a hinge. She whirled around to see Bill there in the open doorway, leaning on his crutch.

She turned back toward the street in a vain attempt to protect him. Bill thought she was the innocent one. He had no idea.

"I'm glad."

"And—oh yeah, guess what else. I ran into Francine. Bunz got bought out by someone, and now she's the new manager. They're redoing the whole place. She told the new guy what happened and they want you back. She told them you'd be here on your birthday. They're going to get a hold of you."

"That's good for Francine."

"Come back, Sake. It'll be different this time. There could never be anyone but you for me."

"I can't talk right now."

"Don't hang up—"

"Good-bye, Rico."

Click. Sake whirled around to see the hurt in Bill's eyes.

"It was him again, wasn't it?"

Bill let her squeeze by him to go back in the apartment.

"Are you in some kind of trouble?" he asked, closing the door behind them.

"I don't want to bring you into all this."

"I want to be brought into it. What happened back in San Francisco? What made your father insist on making you stay here?"

Sake sighed. "The whole thing was blown way out of proportion. Rico was drinking—"

"Rico drinks *a lot.*"

"All I did was swat him with my sweater. One time. *He* was the one who'd gotten belligerent with *me* for not agreeing to buy him more beer when the bar refused to serve him . . . started yelling until the neighbors called the cops. The zipper caught him just right. Slashed a big welt down his cheek. But that's evidence. One swat was enough to get me arrested."

Bill started to steam like a rocket about to take off. He wanted to fly to San Francisco that very minute and put his fist through Rico's face.

"That's when Papa found me. His lawyer friend down in the city who had been looking for me recognized my name."

He ran his hand through his hair. "Why couldn't your papa find you before that? Were you . . . *hiding* from him?"

"Not hiding." She flopped back down on the couch. "It's so hard to explain. I just . . . didn't want to be found."

Bill came over and sat down next to her.

"Maybe if Haha had never stopped liking Papa and moved us out of that pretty, light-filled apartment on Eugenia Avenue he kept us at and took me to move in with that other man, Roberto. And then when that didn't work out, another man, and another, until I got the men's names and faces all mixed up."

"And then what happened?"

"I got tired of the insanity, man. So I rebelled. Quit following her on her knee-jerk whims."

"And then?"

"She couldn't stop herself. After a while, she quit coming home."

Bill clenched his teeth. So many things were coming together now. He wanted to press rewind and fix Sake's entire past. He had to settle for resting his hand on her leg.

"Left alone like that, you'd think you would have turned toward your father, instead of away from him."

"I thought he was ashamed of me." She brushed away a rogue tear.

Bill was appalled. "Why would any father be ashamed of his little girl? Especially you?"

"The city's the ideal place to hide a bastard."

There was nothing he could say to that.

"Haha has never missed my birthday. We have an unbroken tradition. We always meet at a certain shrine on September first."

"I'll be rid of this thing"—he nodded toward his cast—"by then. Let me take you."

Sake lifted her head. "It's all decided. Papa's taking me. He wants to see Haha, too. Plus, September first is also the date of my arraignment. That day's going to be mad busy. Rico said the place where I used to work is under new management. They want to talk to me about coming back."

They sat there in silence for moment, each thinking their own thoughts.

Finally, Bill was resolved.

"I want you to stay."

He dipped his head. Her mouth was a welcome distraction from his thoughts. If he couldn't fix the past, he could make her feel good in the present. She let him gently push her back until she was half-lying down against the back of the couch. Their kisses grew more and more ardent. He rolled onto his hip, taking her along with him onto their sides, facing him, his half-bent leg with its cast high wedged high between her V. Bill reveled in the warm, delicious scent of her. The rhythm of her breathing, the play of sunlight on his living room wall. If he could imprint this scene on his psyche hard enough, he could replay the memory after she was gone.

She slipped her hand under his shirt and slid it along the skin of his back.

He did the same, finding her bra clasp. He stopped kissing her, looking into her eyes as he snapped it free. It was the first time they'd both been on the same page. A breakthrough, a stepping stone.

She pulled him down to her again, and when his hand slid around to the front of her to cup her tiny breast, she shivered. He craved getting even closer.

"Come here." He lifted her from her waist, and next thing he knew she was astride him, her hair falling down in a curtain around his face, blocking out the rest of the world.

He pulled her shirt over her head, dispensed with her bra, and looked at her body. Then he drew her arms up over his head, bringing one nipple within reach of his worshipping mouth. After a while he set her back again and looked at her. Her eyes were pools of ebony. He touched her lower lip with his fingertip, tracing a lazy line down her creamy skin, along her windpipe, between her breasts, down to her navel.

"I want you to stay," he repeated, firmly. And then he lowered her body to his mouth again, to suckle her other breast.

Bill cupped Sake's rear end. In one, swift move, he hoisted her knees up over his shoulders. She gasped with surprise and fell forward, catching her weight on her hands well above his head. He felt the fabric of her skirt catch on the scruff on his chin. "I'm going to show you just how much."

After their breathing had returned to normal, they lay side by side, Sake's ear against Bill's chest, Bill watching his hand making long, slow strokes down her arm. He looked down at her tattoos. "What do these symbols mean? I've always wondered."

Sake looked too. She hesitated. "This one on the left says, 'Not seeing is a flower.'"

"Translation?"

"In other words, things will never be as you imagine, so you're better off not seeing them. Reality never measures up to expectations. Love, but don't trust."

He'd had to ask.

"And this one?"

"The right one says, 'Put not your trust in princes.'"

Chapter 25

Sake was rolling fondant into the shape of pea pods, to top the cupcakes she had baked the previous night, when she got a phone call from Bunz.

"Sake St. Pierre? This is Tom Latimer, new owner of the Bunz Bakery chain."

Sake couldn't let her icing get too warm or it wouldn't be workable, so she tucked her phone beneath her chin while she continued to work.

"Francine gave me your number. I understand you're now up in Napa working at Mon Rêve."

"That's right."

"We're instituting some sweeping changes. All our outlets are being completely gutted and remodeled. Francine has been promoted to take the place of your former manager.

"In going over the books, I understand there've been some . . . let's say, inconsistencies in the way the store has been run in the past. Some back pay that may be due to you."

Her two weeks' pay.

"I'll be glad to get a check out to you if you'll just tell me where to send it. In addition, Francine recommended we interview you to head up the Cole Valley store."

Cole Valley! Sake's dream neighborhood in San Francisco.

"I'm calling to see if you'd be interested in—"

"Why, that's enough cupcakes to feed the entire valley!"

Sake turned to see Jeanne peering over her shoulder.

"Excuse me," whispered Jeanne, her hand to her lips. "I didn't realize you were on the phone."

"I'm sorry to interrupt you, Mr. Latimer, but I'm up to my neck in fondant. Could I call you back later?"

She ended her call and then let Jeanne in on the secret that she was entering half her cupcakes in the contest to get into the CIA. "But, Jeanne, no one else can know about this. That way, I won't be embarrassed when I don't win."

"Nonsense! This pea pod theme you came up with is adorable." She kissed her bunched fingertips. "I have no doubt the CIA judges will think so, too."

"The shower should be over by three. That should give me just enough time to jump in the Subaru and drive up to St. Helena to deliver these by the four o'clock deadline."

The batch Sake had earmarked for the shower was already the centerpiece of the dessert table, artfully arranged by Meri. As Sake finished crafting each contest entry, she carefully set it into one of the special cake boxes she had purchased to get them safely through the ride up to St. Helena.

"Jeanne!"

Sake and Jeanne looked up.

"Look out the window!" cried Char. "There are all these cars coming already. And see that silver BMW? That's one of Papa's friends. What's he doing here? I didn't invite him!"

Sake followed Jeanne to the front room at a trot, peering out over her shoulder. Sure enough, a string of cars was already lined up down the drive.

"I didn't invite half those people!" said Char. "This event was going to be small and intimate, like Savvy and Esteban wanted!"

"What's going on?" Sauvignon floated into the room in a filmy dress that skimmed over her burgeoning figure.

"What else? Your papa is at it again," said Jeanne with a perturbed expression. Purposefully, she strode back to the heart of the house, followed by the others.

"What are we going to do? We don't have enough food!" cried Char.

"Don't stress. It's just a baby shower," Savvy said.

"Sauvignon is right, as usual," Jeanne said. "We will deal with your father later. In the meantime, I always order more food from the caterer than is needed, just in case."

"A little bit extra is not going to cut it!" said Char, pacing the tiles. "You saw all those cars!"

"Char, take a breath," said Savvy. "The control freak in you is winning."

"I am not a control freak!"

Jeanne and Sauvignon shared a skeptical look.

"I'm a control *enthusiast.*"

Sake heard Bill Diamond's words all over again: *"I'll bet if you look hard enough, you'll come across flaws in the others, too. They're only human."*

Ta-da.

Jeanne said, "What is a slightly more serious problem is that we are not quite prepared for our guests to arrive this early."

"Great!" Char threw her hands in the air. "Not only did Papa invite guests without telling me, he told them the wrong time!"

Jeanne dashed off her apron. "They're only a half hour early. The catered food is already in place and now—*voilà*—my salad is finished. Chardonnay, all you have to do is change your clothes."

Char glimpsed down at her forgotten shorts and racer-back tee. "Arg!" She sprinted from the room without waiting to hear Jeanne finish.

"We'll have the caterer open the wine while we wait for the others to arrive," she told Sauvignon and Sake. "That will make everyone happy."

Sake had never been at such a large party. To her chagrin, she found herself as much the object of scrutiny as her oldest sister's baby bump. At least today, unlike on the day she'd crashed into Sauvignon's wedding, she had something respectable she could converse about—her new job. Yet people still insisted on bringing up that long-ago catastrophe.

She was explaining to an inquisitive couple where she worked when she heard a familiar voice at her shoulder.

"Mon Rêve. Best pastry shop in the valley. Service isn't bad, either."

She whipped her head around. *Black coffee and two chocolate-chip croissants* . . . the man in the denim shirt from the patisserie!

He stuck out his hand. "Don't think I ever properly introduced myself. Name's Walter."

Clearly, Walter hadn't used the party as an excuse to dress up—or get a haircut. His thinning hair was still sticking out in all directions of the compass, as usual.

"You know Sauvignon?" asked Sake, dazed, her hand limp in his.

"Your father invited me here. We go way back. All he talks about are his daughters."

"Are you sure you're at the right house?"

"Why do you think he went and asked all these folks to come to his oldest girl's baby shower? I was invited to Sauvignon's wedding, too, but I couldn't make that affair. Now, I'm not saying he doesn't have his faults, just like anybody else, but no one can ever say Xavier St. Pierre doesn't love his girls. He's pleased as punch to have finally got you up here."

Sake blinked in astonishment.

"That said, I never put much stock in a person's relatives. Got some high-flyin' relations of my own. Nice enough folks, but they're the last people I'd want to be stuck in an elevator with. I prefer to judge people on merit."

Walter scooped up a handful of salted nuts from a silver dish as he looked around at all the pink and blue decorations. "I don't mind saying, I feel a little out of place. In my day, these shindigs were only for women."

"My sisters call this a coed shower."

"That so?" He looked around. "Well, if this is coed, where's your man? The one you left the city for?"

Was Bill her man? Truthfully, she wasn't sure what he was. "He's just a—friend. A really good friend."

"That so?"

"Bill insisted I go to the hospital after I was in a helicopter crash, took care of my dog when she couldn't stay here, and even taught me how to drive. If it weren't for Bill, I wouldn't have been able to accept my job at Mon Rêve because I'd have had no way to get to work.

"Now Bill's the one hurting. Broke his leg and demolished his car. He hasn't been able to work for weeks. Chardonnay invited him to come today, but he said he wasn't up to it."

"Leg not getting any better?"

"Not fast enough to suit him."

"What kind of work does he do?"

"Commercial real estate. He's really frustrated about not being able to get around. He's putting all this pressure on himself to sell this one listing so he can buy his dream house."

"Oh?" Walter might be a little rough around the edges, but his eyes shone with intelligence. "What listing is that?"

"Don't ask me about the specifics. All I know is it's off Twenty-nine on the way up to St. Helena—El Camino, yes, that's it—and it has a nice assortment of stores. A health clinic, an insurance office, wine shop, and a couple of little restaurants, yada yada. Bill says since it's all leased out already, whoever buys it won't have to look for tenants."

"This Bill—he have a last name?"

"Diamond. Bill Diamond."

"Well." Walter patted her arm. "I hope things work out for him—for both of you. You're a nice girl. Sassy, but I like a bit of sass in a woman. I should go mingle now, or whatever you're supposed to do at these things."

No sooner had Walter disappeared into the press of people than someone else stepped up to ask her for the hundredth time how she was faring since the helicopter accident.

As she steered the conversation yet again in a more positive direction, she realized that with every repetition, remnants of her old life—Rico, Bunz, and her arrest—were starting to fade into the past. But she couldn't let this extended wine country vacay make her forget about Haha. After all, that was the whole point of being here: obeying Papa's arbitrary demands so he would eventually give her the money to start over, once she and Haha were reunited.

As the noise level grew and the crowd pressed in tighter, Sake slipped through the throng, back to the kitchen, where she could breathe easier.

There she spotted Char and Jeanne huddled together. "These guests are like locusts, eating everything in sight," Char whispered. "What are we going to do?"

"The extra wine probably didn't help. It stimulates the appetite."

"How many do you figure there are?"

"I'd say at least a hundred," replied Meri, coming in from a different room.

Double the number they'd been counting on.

"Did you see the buffet table? It's decimated. And the cupcakes are going fast."

When Jeanne lifted her eyes to the wall clock, Sake did too. A little flutter of panic seized her. *Three-fifteen.* She had to get on the road to get those cupcakes to St. Helena *now,* or she'd miss the deadline.

Jeanne pinched her lower lip together. "If we started passing coffee and dessert, maybe then people would take the hint."

"But we don't have enough to go around," replied Char.

"Yes, we do."

All three women's heads jerked toward Sake.

"I made extra cupcakes."

Non, non, non, Jeanne mouthed, shaking her head from behind the other girls where only Sake could see her.

Sake went to an out-of-the way corner of the kitchen and returned with her stiff white cardboard boxes piled up to her chin.

"Here's an extra four dozen. Added to what Meri already put out, this should be just enough for everybody."

Char wasted no time reaching for the top box. "Thank heavens! How did you know?"

"You're a lifesaver, Sake," Meri said, diving into the next box, withdrawing Sake's painstakingly made contest entries to put them on a platter.

Jeanne caught Sake's eye again to make sure she saw her grateful smile.

Sake glowed with the warmth surrounding her.

Maybe she was never meant to get into the CIA, after all.

Wasn't that call from the new owner of Bunz earlier today a sign?

Chapter 26

Bill called Sake at the end of her shift the following Saturday to give her the good news. "I got my cast off!"

"How does it feel? Can you walk?"

"Aw, man, it's great. I still have to use my crutch, but I'll be rid of that in no time, wait and see. Dad and I are going car shopping this weekend. I've been studying the reviews, the mileage stats, options and stuff for weeks, and I got it narrowed down to three models. The salesmen are rubbing their hands together, waiting for me."

"Only Bill Diamond makes an appointment to look at a car. Probably even mapped out your route to the different dealerships."

"You say that like it's a bad thing."

She felt his smile through the phone.

"Dad and I will narrow it down today, then tomorrow I thought I'd load up The Beast and we'll come get you and take the top contender for a test drive."

"What do I know about cars?"

"I don't want to buy one without your thumbs-up. Case closed. Don't you want to come?"

"You know I do. Besides, I got some good news, too. . . ."

Sake had sat for the GED last Saturday. She'd been on pins and needles waiting to get her scores in the mail.

"I passed. I'm a high school graduate!" Bill felt Sake's euphoria through the phone line.

"Congratulations. I'm proud of you, Sake. You've come a long way."

Bill *was* proud. Except for the selfish little piece of his heart that broke off and spiraled like the first leaf of autumn, down . . . down . . . down to the darkest recesses of his soul. Sake's passing the GED meant she'd fulfilled her papa's mandate. In only two more days, she would be free to go back to San Francisco with a fat pocketbook, just in time for her annual birthday rendezvous with her mother.

But Bill had learned some things, too—about himself. What he needed, versus what he'd thought he was supposed to want. And he planned to spend every second of these next two days showing her.

"Bill?"

"Yeah." He snapped out of his thoughts. "Pick you up tomorrow morning." He wasn't asking. He was demanding. He had more to show Sake than just his potential new car.

The next day, Sake listened patiently while Bill ran down the list of his top candidate's bells and whistles. "So, how'd you like 'er so far?"

"For real? A car's a car. No matter which one you pick, give it a week and it's going to end up looking the same on the inside as your old one, all Bill Diamonded out with your color-coded Post-its and tissue boxes and pens with your logo stamped all over them.

"I'm just grateful you can finally get out of the house and back to doing what you like best—selling real estate."

Though he kept his eyes carefully trained on the road, he couldn't help but grin. But it was more than just being able to drive again.

How had he ever gotten the idea that the future mattered more than the present? *Now* was all anyone really had. Soaring down the highway with Sake by his side, The Beast in her lap, and that new-car smell in his nostrils, Bill realized something: he was happy right now, in this moment. Sake was right. What did it matter, the model of car he ended up with? In this present moment, Bill couldn't want for more . . .

. . . almost. Some habits were too deeply ingrained to let go of.

At the intersection of Elm Street, Bill turned.

"Don't tell me. You're still obsessed with that house?"

"The last time we were here, it was mid-summer, remember? The landscaping was at its peak." Bill inched closer. Now the first blooms were done, the jade-green lawns yellowed. Fall was just around the corner. Soon school busses would be crawling down this residential block.

"Still for sale," said Sake, when the sign came into view.

"How about that."

She smirked. "Like you haven't been checking online every blessed day."

The heading on the data sheet read, *Charm, Dignity, and Character.*

But this time, instead of just a drive-by, Bill had yet another surprise in store for Sake.

"You might think you know me, but you've still got a lot to learn."

As he pulled into the driveway, her expression changed.

"What are we doing?"

"Want to see what it looks like inside?"

"You got a key?"

"My friend John has it listed. He gave me the code to the lockbox. A little-known advantage among Realtors."

Bill grabbed his crutch from the back seat. He already knew what the bungalow's interior looked like. He'd been in it twice, before he'd ever met Sake. This walk-through was for her.

Front porch . . .

When Bill showed a property, it was only after carefully researching every aspect. Normally he used the client walk-through to deliver a persuasive argument, pointing out the highlights, hammering home the benefits. It wasn't merely a sales pitch if it was truly the best possible location for his buyer.

But this time, he wanted Sake to form her own opinion, without his influence. It went against everything he'd been taught about sales—to say nothing of his elaborate life plan—but this time he was determined to follow his instinct, not his training.

Gracious yet informal living room/dining room with polished hardwood floors and fireplace, the perfect setting for gathering with friends and family.

With Taylor in her arms, Sake gravitated toward the kitchen like a bee to honey.

And there is no telling what you'll cook up using your fully updated gas appliances.

Bill watched as Sake's keen eye honed in on the range, then traveled across the marble countertops and stainless sink and fridge. He had to force his feet to stay glued to the living room floor when she wandered down the hall. To let the house speak to her, just as it had spoken to him months ago.

Spacious yet intimate master bedroom, a private place for quiet times. 2 baths eliminate early morning traffic jams.

She stayed back there a long time. He was dying to know what she was doing. Gazing out at the big tree in the backyard, seeing a picnic table under it? Picturing where would be the best place for a dresser . . . *a bed?* And if so, did her thoughts stray further afield . . . to what pleasures nights in that bed, in that bedroom, in that house, might hold?

Finally he heard her footfalls returning, only to turn to go up the stairs.

Bedrooms upstairs are quaint with slanty roof and recessed dormers. Abundant closet space.

He searched her eyes when she came back down, but she could've been a professional poker player for all she gave away.

"Backyard's this way." Bill hobbled to the door.

She put Taylor down. "Don't open it till I put Taylor's leash on her. I don't want to lose her again."

Full-panel cedar fence with custom gate and trellis.

"Don't worry. She won't get lost here."

The second he opened the door, Taylor tore down the length of the yard and back, circled Sake, and scrambled away again before she could be caught.

While Taylor kept busy burning off excess energy, sniffing out secrets known only to the canine world, Sake ventured more cautiously.

Bill tried to see the property afresh, through her eyes. The elm in the far corner . . . the heavy-headed rhododendron blossoms nodding next to viburnum in the beds lining the fence.

From the heart of the yard, Sake stood still, framed by the leafy setting. Bound, yet still wild.

She destroyed him in that mini dress. Her black hair glistened in the sunlight. An image of a middle-aged Sake, face softened by time yet still beautiful, came to him, followed by a silver-haired version. This fantasy had nothing to do with what he *ought* to do. It was grounded in intuition.

He couldn't hold his tongue a second longer. "What do you think?"

Over her shoulder, she answered, "Out here it's free, yet protected."

"I'm not talking about Taylor."

"Neither am I."

She whirled around on a heel. "Bill, why are we here? Why torture yourself? You said the only way you could afford this house was if you sold the strip center."

He limped out to meet her, taking both of her hands in his. All the words he'd been holding back came rushing to the surface. "I always planned to buy a house only once I had a substantial enough down payment to get a short-term mortgage. You know me. Always thinking things through. But it doesn't have to be like that. You've made me see that when something feels right, you have to run with it, even if that sometimes means deviating from plan.

"I've been socking money away since I was a DJ in high school. I'm already in a better position than most people to buy this house. What I need to know is: do *you* like it?"

She pulled out of his reach and spun around in a circle with her arms out. "It's adorable for the right couple. A perfect little couple who's madly in love." Then she stopped, her eyes boring into his. "Why are you torturing *me*? What happened to 'I'm a lot older than you' and 'we're in different places in our lives'? What happened to Dr. Deb?"

"I was wrong." He pulled a reluctant Sake into his arms. "I thought I had it all figured out. Then you came along, and I realized that if my plans worked out—if I ended up with a 'Dr. Deb'—a few years down the road I'd be a miserable old fart married to an overbearing harpy."

Sake looked doubtful.

"Say something."

"This is some serious shit, Bill. You know I'm ill-suited for that."

There she went again with her street talk . . . her self-defense mechanism.

"I still got a lot of unfinished business. I can't just abandon my mother."

Like she abandoned you? Thank God he hadn't said that aloud. He couldn't bear the thought of adding to the burden Sake already shouldered. *Or, is it that Rico dude Sake's afraid of abandoning?*

His hands slid down her arms. "At least let me ride along with you and your father to the city on Monday. I want to be there, to help support you during your arraignment."

"No." She looked down. "I know you mean well, but this is between me and my mother."

And her and Rico. He pinched the bridge of his nose. Then, finally, he nodded. "If that's what you want." He started trudging toward the house, his bones heavy with rejection.

"Let's go, Taylor," called Sake behind him. Her voice had lost its energy, too.

At the back door, they turned as one to see The Beast planted flat on her stomach in the middle of the yard.

"Come on, girl."

Taylor looked content to stay there in that yard forever, even if it meant being disobedient.

"Stubborn dog," muttered Sake, stomping back to snap on her leash.

The dealership was expecting its car back. Bill was driving Sake up to Domaine St. Pierre to drop her off when she suddenly felt all the blood drain out of her head.

"What's wrong? You're pale as a ghost."

But Sake couldn't have answered if she'd tried. There, parked right in front of the staircase, was a murdered-out black hooptie. And leaning against it with his arms folded was a lean, shaggy-haired guy.

Bill pulled in behind the car. "Don't tell me." They sat there staring through the windshield for a moment, bracing themselves for a confrontation.

Then Rico dragged his body off his car to saunter toward them, full of swagger.

"I think you should maybe stay here," Sake said to Bill as she opened the door and put one foot on the ground.

"Think again," Bill said, clearly bent on following her.

Bill's limp had miraculously disappeared. The three met halfway between the two cars, Rico and Bill facing each other like gunslingers in an old western, sizing each other up.

Rico grinned at Sake. "Damn. You said your old man was rich. You didn't say he was *RICH.*"

"How'd you find me?"

"The App Queen. Who else?"

The woman in The Mission who was never not on her phone.

"When she showed me this palace on the map, I had to come up and see it for myself. No wonder you didn't want to come back. But now you got to. I got something to tell you."

Sake's breath stopped.

"Got a call from the D.A. yesterday. They dropped all the charges, just like I asked them to. We don't have to go to court."

She whooshed out a breath of relief. "Are you sure?"

He nodded. "But there's more. I found Haha."

"You did?! Where?"

"Black Orchid. Sitting there at the bar, like she never left."

"Omigod. Did you talk to her?"

"Nuh-uh."

"Why not? Why didn't you tell her I've been looking for her?"

"Well . . ." Rico looked askance at Bill. "I don't know how much you'd want me to say in front of—strangers."

Sake and Bill exchanged their first glance since Rico had started talking. Bill's expression was more serious than Sake had ever seen it.

"Dude. If there's a stranger around here, it's you," Bill told Rico.

Sake stepped between them, her body equidistant between them. "You can say anything in front of Bill."

Rico shrugged. "You say so. Your mom was pretty wasted. Even if I *had* said something, doubt if she'd remember."

"You lost her again!"

"Hold up. Bartender says she's there every Sunday till around one. That's why I'm here. To take you down there myself. Right now." Rico tossed his head back toward his car. "Let's roll."

Bill was the only one who wore a watch. "It's already close to noon."

That meant there was no time to waste. Bill still wore his concerned look, and Rico's body was already angled toward his car. There, in the middle, Sake felt like the prize in a tug of war.

At the top of the staircase, there was a noise and all three of them looked up to see Papa standing there framed in the double doorway, like some sort of god. Peering over his shoulders from behind were her sisters.

Regally, Papa descended the steps one by one, taking in the whole scene: ice-cool Rico and his black car with its opaque windows and matte paint where chrome used to be. Bill, chest puffed out. And Sake, torn between the two.

By the time Papa reached them, his eyes were full of fire. He pointed at Rico. "I know who you are. You're the *salaud* who had my

daughter put behind bars! Get off my property now, before I have you
forcibly removed!"

Rico held up his palms. "Get some chill, *bruh*. I forgave her—"

"*You,* forgave *her?* Why, you—"

"Papa, Rico came to tell me the D.A. dropped the charges. We
don't have to go to court tomorrow. It's over."

"You think I don't know that? My lawyer called me yesterday. I
don't care why this derelict is here. I want him off my property—
now."

"I said, chill. I'm going," said Rico, retreating. Just before he slid
into his car he leaned his arm on its roof. "Sake, baby. Last chance.
You comin'?"

"Are you mad?" yelled Papa. "My daughter is not going anywhere
with you."

Sake felt the pull of all three men, each willing her to decide in his
favor. To do what was right for *him.*

She turned to Bill. "I have to see my mother. You understand."

In her arms, Taylor wriggled with all her might. "Hush." What
had gotten into her? Why now?

"I forbid it!" said Papa, stepping toward her. "You stay right there,
mademoiselle."

"Rico found Haha. I have to go to her, Papa."

"Tell me where! I will have my people go. Or, if you insist, I will
take you there myself tomorrow, for your birthday, even if your court
date has been cancelled. There is absolutely no need for you to associate with this . . . this *vermin!*"

With a roar, Rico fired up his engine. Acrid-smelling blue smoke
billowed out the exhaust pipe.

"Please understand, Papa . . ." Sake started toward it.

"Sake—" Bill came after her. "Don't do it. Don't go with him. I'll
take you. We'll follow him in my car."

"I have to do this—on my own terms."

"Wait!" Papa strode toward her with his hand out. "You won't be
using my credit card to finance this wild duck chase."

Sake paused with one hand on the door handle. Without that card,
she had nothing.

She drew Papa's card from her bag and laid it on his palm.

"And don't forget, our agreement does not end until tomorrow. If you leave now, I am under no obligation to fulfill my part of the deal."

Only one day short.

In her arms, Taylor writhed again, catching Sake off guard. "Oh!" She watched helplessly as Taylor tumbled from her arms and scampered as fast as her short legs would carry her—back to Bill.

"I'm sorry, both of you . . ." Sake said, tearing a wistful gaze from Papa to Bill before turning her back on them.

She sent a pleading look to her sisters, still inside the front door with horrified expressions at what she was about to do.

They had accepted her without question. Now she was turning her back on them to salvage what was left of her past.

Then she jumped into Rico's car before she could change her mind.

Chapter 27

Rico floored it. "About time," he said, as the car fishtailed across the gravel. "I can't have the cops catch me without my Ls."

"You're seriously not serious." Sake fastened her seat belt, as Bill would have wanted her to. Then she got a bright idea. "Let me drive. I got my license now."

"No time," said Rico, eyeing her up and down, now that he had her within his grasp. "You look hot, by the way."

"I see your face is healed."

"You can still see it if you look close."

Rico exceeded the speed limit the whole way. Sake rode with one hand braced on the door handle and the other on the console, conflicted between begging him to slow down and hoping against hope to catch Haha before she left the Orchid and blended once more into the crazy quilt of the San Francisco subculture.

At last, they entered the city limits.

"Finally," said Sake, looking at the clock on the dash. "We still have ten minutes until one."

"Relax." Rico's head lolled on his shoulders. "Your mother isn't at the Orchid."

Sake turned to him in horror. Then again, why should she be so surprised? This was Rico. "You brought me all the way down here under false pretenses?"

"Oh, I know where she is. But it's not there."

"Then where?"

"Cole Valley. The App Queen found her for me. Just like she found you."

Sake's brow knit in confusion. Cole Valley was quaint and community-oriented. The opposite of the area she'd feared Haha was staying at.

"So, tomorrow's September first."

He'd remembered her birthday? Even if he had, why bring that up now?

"The day the rent's due."

Sake felt a slow burn creep up her face. Just when she thought he couldn't stoop any lower.

"I don't get paid at my new job till the fifteenth. You think you could help me out?"

Sake huffed in disbelief. When she found her tongue, she said, "First of all, I haven't lived there since the middle of the summer. Second, I don't have any—"

"Do you seriously expect me to believe you're broke? After where I just picked you up from?"

"My father's rich! I'm not!"

"You never paid a dime in rent the whole nine months we were living together."

"You never asked me to. It's *your* apartment. You invited random people to stay there all the time, free of charge, and without my input. I'm not on the lease. All I had was a corner of the bedroom—"

"You think those couple times you put out was enough to earn you room and board?"

A wave of nausea washed over her.

He shrugged. "But then, like mother, like daughter."

Sake had once fretted out loud, wondering if Haha got paid for being with so many men. She had vastly underestimated Rico's memory—and his craftiness. To lay bare her soft spots and grind them into the ground with his heel . . .

"Now. You want to see your mom, or not?"

Part of her just wanted to jump out of Rico's car and run as fast and as far away from him as she possibly could. But if she did that, she might never find Haha. As much as she'd hoped her mother would simply show up at the birthday shrine tomorrow, if she was brutally honest, the chances were more like fifty-fifty. At best.

And then she remembered: her earrings.

She'd always known the day would come when she might have to sacrifice them. She felt to make sure they were still there.

"You know where there's a pawn shop?"

"Three blocks over."

Minutes later, Rico pulled up to Pawn-It-Off.

"Wait here."

"What, so you can hold out on me? Naw, I think I'll come in with you."

Sake walked up to the counter like a zombie, Rico close behind.

"How much?" she asked, taking out one earring, laying it on the counter. If the one stud covered Rico's rent, maybe she could hold on to the other one.

Rico rested a forearm on the counter, one sharp eye on her precious diamond. She couldn't bear to watch while the guy turned it over in his dirty fingers, ogling it with some kind of special lens.

"Fifty cent."

"Excuse me?" she asked, blinking.

"Kidding."

She slumped over with a sigh of relief. "Please don't do that to me. Not today."

"No, I mean this ain't even worth that. It's fake," he said, handing it back.

"No it's not! I got it from my father when I was sixteen years old! It's real!"

"Sorry."

Furtively, she took out the other one. "Here. Look at this one."

Sighing as if he were doing her a monumental favor, the man rolled it between grubby fingers. "Fake."

He dropped them into her hand and went back to rearranging his merchandise, while Rico glared at Sake—as if she'd done this on purpose.

"Papa would never buy me fake diamonds and say they were real. It makes no sense."

Rico peeled his body weight off the counter and loped toward the door.

There was nothing she could do but follow. "I've never had them out of my ears since I've been on my own," she uttered, mostly to herself.

"Welp," said Rico from the side of his mouth, "that only leaves the time when you lived with Haha."

She stopped in the center of the sidewalk so abruptly that a couple of pedestrians had to detour to avoid bumping into her to peer down at the studs still in her palm.

Haha did it. Haha pawned her diamonds and replaced them with fakes, a long time ago.

Somehow Sake staggered the rest of the way to the car.

Rico pulled away from the curb.

"Where are we going." Her monotone flattened the question into a statement.

"Where do you think?"

Without attachment, Sake watched the sun-drenched, boho streets of The Haight unfold into the tree-lined, gentrified Cole Valley. It was like watching a documentary. This world she couldn't wait to get back to now seemed totally alien.

Rico braked in front of a Victorian with bay windows that jutted out over the sidewalk. "This is it."

Sake stepped out onto the street and slammed Rico's car door, already peering up at the three-story house's peaked roof. She didn't bother to turn when she heard Rico drive away. Somehow, she knew she'd never see his face again.

All good to the gracious.

Still on autopilot, her feet carried her up to the door, painted a cheery magenta color.

"Mommy," hollered the little boy who answered the bell. He stared at Sake with unabashed curiosity. In the dim interior, Sake made out a brass lamp, an Oriental rug.

A protruding stomach preceded the woman who came. She looked ready to burst with the weight of her full-term pregnancy.

That isn't Haha. This time the App Queen got it wrong.

When the woman saw Sake, her smile disappeared. "Go back inside," she told the boy. She stepped out onto the stoop, pulling the door closed behind her without latching it.

Lowering her voice, she asked, "Why did you come here?"

"Haha?"

"How did you find me?"

"Haha? *What are you doing?*" Sake couldn't take her eyes off her bulging mid-section. A woman of her age, pregnant again?

"You shouldn't have come. Go now."

"But . . ."

"I said, go."

"I can't go! I've been worried sick about you!"

"I have a new life now. Everything's different."

Sake's eyes brushed over her mother, from her hooded eyes, over her demure sundress, down to sandals revealing a professional pedicure. Aside from looking tired, she was a far sight from what Sake had feared she'd find—a drug-addled, broken-down street person.

A sudden burst of rage displaced endless months of anxiety. *"Didn't you ever think of calling me? It would've at least been nice to hear that you're still alive!"*

Behind Haha, the crack in the door slowly widened, the boy's black crown reappearing, his thumb in his mouth.

"Who is it, Emma?" called a man's voice from somewhere deep inside.

Haha gave the boy a gentle shove. "Run and tell Daddy I'll be right in."

"Daddy?" Sake's eyes flew to the gold band glinting off Haha's left hand that curled atop her belly. "Are you married?"

From around the edge of the door, the boy's dark eyes came back to stare at Sake yet again. He looked perplexed, as if looking in a mirror.

"Is he yours, too?" Sake pointed. "Is that my half brother?"

"Sake. You have to go. Please."

"You could have called me anytime in the past nine months! You have my number! I never changed it, for that very reason!"

Haha looked past Sake's shoulder. "Take her. I can't talk here . . . now."

With that, her mother turned and once again shooed the boy, slipping inside behind him, shutting Sake out of her life with a soft click.

"Wait!" Sake lunged forward, stopped by a firm hand on her shoulder.

"Sweetheart. Stop."

Sake yanked out of the phantom hand's grasp, falling onto her hands and knees on the concrete steps leading up to the stoop.

"Haha!" she wailed, ignoring the pain of her skinned palms to get up and lunge toward the door again.

A pair of strong arms grabbed her around the waist, folding her in half just before her fingertips at the end of her outstretched arms clawed down the painted wood.

She fought against the force, but it easily lifted her body up and turned it in the opposite direction.

"Sake. Come with me now. You can count on me. I won't leave your side."

When Bill Diamond's voice at last registered, somehow all the fight drained out of her. She let him set her feet back down on the concrete, put his arm around her, and lead her away from Haha's pretty, suburban house, a short walk down the shadow-dappled sidewalk to his car, where Taylor stood panting with her front paws on the window ledge.

"How—?"

"I couldn't let you run off with that degenerate alone."

"But, this car. It isn't even yours. . . ."

"It is now."

Chapter 28

B ill took Sake home to his apartment, brewed her some tea, and put her to bed, holding her close for a long while until at last she fell asleep with a face still tear-stained. Now he stood over her, marveling at the blackness of her hair strewn across his white pillowcase. He'd fantasized having her in his bed countless times, but not like this.

He didn't feel a smidgeon of guilt over stealing her phone from her bag. He needed to look up Xavier's cell phone number to fill him in on what he'd witnessed in the city and assure him his daughter was home safe, here in Napa. But when Xavier demanded Bill bring Sake back to Domaine St. Pierre immediately, Bill was prepared with a response.

"With all due respect, sir, Sake said she wants to stay here tonight. She'll be home tomorrow."

They'd talked it out the night before. All Sake's hopes of a mother-daughter reunion had been shattered to bits. And with Rico nothing but a bad memory and the court hearing cancelled, the Bunz interview wasn't nearly enough to coax her into returning to the city on her birthday.

Xavier considered Bill's words. "You are a fine, decent man, Bill Diamond."

A regular mensch. That's what he wanted to be for Sake. Someone safe. Someone steady. Someone trustworthy.

And Bill knew exactly how he was going to prove it to her.

Sake was used to waking up in strange places. She took her time, letting her eyes adjust to her surroundings . . . past the nightstand where a long, thick white envelope leaned against the lamp, she saw

184 · *Heather Heyford*

an upholstered chair with an oxford shirt neatly draped over it. Through the slats of venetian blinds, leaves shimmered green and silver. She heard muted kitchen sounds. Then her nostrils caught the scents of cedar and bergamot, and she knew.

She stretched on a massive yawn, and sat up, rubbing the sleep from her eyes.

From the kitchen, she heard the workaday call of "Taylor! Breakfast!" A small smile tugged at the corners of her mouth. So this was Bill and Taylor's morning routine. Though it had been going on for six weeks, she had yet to be there at that time of day, to witness it.

There was something she needed to do, first thing—alone. She looked up the number of the local sheriff.

She finished her call just in time to see a bare-chested Bill Diamond watching her, holding a coffee mug in one hand and in the other, an amateur-looking cupcake with a single, glowing candle stuck into it.

"Is what you just said true? You saw your father fill out his logbook the day of the helicopter crash?"

"Have you ever known me to lie?"

Bill gave her a sly, complicit look, then came and lowered himself beside her on the bed.

Smiling, she said, "You've got icing in your hair." Her eyes skimmed over Bill's toned torso, from his nicely-formed shoulders to his taut abs to where a line of tawny hair disappeared into his flannel pajama bottoms.

"Happy birthday to you, happy birthday to you, happy birthday dear Sake, happy birthday to you. Make a wish."

She knew *exactly* what she wished for. She took a breath, then blew out the flame. Wasting no time, she bit into his feeble but honest attempt at baking.

"What's it taste like?"

"Diabetes," she replied around a mouthful of cake.

Bill rocked back, laughing. "So, better than it looks, then."

With a second bite, she asked, "When did you . . . ?"

"Last night, after you went to sleep. Found a recipe online. Here." He doubled up the pillows behind her. "You don't have to get up yet. It's your birthday. You can sleep in if you want."

Sinking back into them, licking her lips, she eyed his coffee cup. "Got any more of that?"

"Sure do. Want some?"

"I'm ill-suited for sleeping in."

"Be right back."

He returned with a matching mug and crawled back under the covers next to her.

"I must've been hungry."

"You went to bed without your supper." Their eyes met in unspoken acknowledgement of all that had gone down the day before.

"Let's not think about that today. It's your birthday. Today you get anything you want." When he took another drink of coffee, Sake noticed yet more icing along the edge of his palm.

"I can't imagine what the kitchen looks like," she mused. "You got this stuff all over you." She brought his hand up to her mouth.

Bill watched, mesmerized, while she slowly, deliberately licked the icing off his hand. His well-intended smile ebbed away.

When her job was finished she transferred her attention to the center of Bill's palm, planting in it a lingering, wet, kiss, ending with a swirl of her tongue.

Then she lay down on her side next to him and slipped her bare leg between his flannel-clad ones, hooking a foot around his ankle.

"Thanks." She cupped his cheek, putting her thumb over his dimple. "Thanks for everything."

His breath caught when she slid her hand down his side, running her finger around the inside of the elastic on his PJs.

"You don't owe me anything, you know." His voice came out strangled.

"This isn't about that." She kissed his mouth.

After that, there were no more words. Skin to skin, from the most tentative caress to the boldest thrust, tapering off only to crown again and yet again, their bodies choreographed what words couldn't say.

When Sake woke again, the room looked somehow the same, yet different. From the shade of the walls, it must be midday. But that wasn't the only weird thing. Then she realized: she was upside down in the bed.

From the direction of her feet she heard a deeply satisfied male voice croak, "You're crazy."

"Where are you?" She giggled.

"Up here."

She fought her way back through the impossible tangle of sheets, once again breathless. "Are you complaining?"

"No, ma'am." He cupped her head and kissed her swollen lips. "Are you going to open your present now?"

"I thought you just gave me my present."

He propped an elbow on his pillow and laughed, showing his straight white teeth. "And here I thought *I* was the recipient. I meant this one." He reached across her to the nightstand for the envelope.

"Open it."

She pulled out what looked like an official document.

"The rest of the world has gone digital. All except real estate. We're still up to our eyeballs in paperwork."

"Offer to Purchase?" she read out loud.

Then she read the address aloud. "Three Elm Street." A thought occurred to her. "In Japan, odd numbers are lucky."

"And today you turn twenty-three. The seller gave me a verbal acceptance. There're just the formalities to go through, and I should be moved in by fall."

Sake sensed Bill's satisfaction as concretely as the walls and the floor that surrounded them.

Ping!

"That'll be your father. I called him last night. He's probably wondering why you haven't come home yet."

Home. The word conjured up a collage of unrelated images. What did a real home feel like? All Sake knew was what it *didn't* feel like. She'd lived in so many places she couldn't even list them all. She envied Bill, who knew without a doubt that he wanted to live at 3 Elm Street, and her sisters. Even during their time away at school, the winery had always been their North Star. And on top of all that, she felt guilty for being envious.

She peered up at him from her pillow. "It sounds so thankless, but the winery doesn't feel like home to me."

"Maybe home isn't a building," said Bill, playing with a strand of her hair. "Maybe it's finding your place in the world. Not just where you lay your head at night, but everything. Who you're with, what you're doing . . . all those things coming together in the right place and time."

She slipped the idea on, and it fit perfectly, like a cozy sweater in her favorite color. Without her mind knowing why, her body relaxed deeper into the mattress. A restlessness that had agitated her insides for as long as she could remember stilled.

"You don't sound like no Realtor."

Grinning, he kissed the tip of her nose. "I know. Keep that advice to yourself, or my reputation'll be toast."

Ping!

"I told your papa everything. I hope I didn't overstep."

"Hardly," she huffed. "You spared me the agony."

"Hey." He looked around. "You seen Taylor?"

"I thought I heard you feeding her breakfast."

"I called, but I don't think she ever came."

Sake got out of bed and started looking around, calling Taylor's name.

"This place isn't big enough for her to have gone far." Bill went to the living room, Sake the bathroom.

There, atop one of Bill's good bath towels in the tub, lay Taylor . . . and that wasn't all.

Sake squealed. "Bill! Come in here! Quick!"

Chapter 29

When they got to the winery later that day, it was crawling with more workers and trucks than Sake had ever seen. "What's going on?"

"Looks like the crush has started," said Bill. "They say everything else in a grower's life gets put on hold when they're bringing in the grapes. Once they're picked, they have to be processed right away, no matter what time of the day or night."

When Sake and Bill walked into the kitchen, her sisters stopped talking midsentence. Then they each uttered some lame excuse, got up from their chairs, and left the room.

Sake sniffed. "Welp, it's official. I suck at being a sister."

"They'll get over it." Bill's deliberately blank expression didn't fool Sake. That was only to keep her from getting upset all over again.

But what did Sake expect? The first time she'd shown up here, for the wedding, her sisters had let bygones be bygones, not blaming Sake for her mother's sins. Expecting them to welcome her back into the fold a second time, after she'd turned her back on them and all they represented to go back to San Francisco with an epic loser like Rico? That was beyond the pale.

Jeanne bustled in from the direction in which her sisters had gone. "Sake." She took her by the shoulders, kissing each cheek in turn. "Thank God you came home."

"You're not . . . mad?"

"Angry? Of course not. Your papa told me what happened in San Francisco. We were both worried sick about you. We are only relieved to have you back."

"Where is Papa?"

"Outside with his vineyard manager. They began picking sauvignon blanc before dawn. But I assure you, he will be in as soon as he can get away to wish you a happy birthday."

She took Sake's arm in hers. "Come into the dining room. I have something to show you."

Bill followed behind them.

"Surprise!"

Sake's hand flew to her mouth. There, toasting her with champagne flutes and wide grins, stood Char, Meri, Savvy, their men, and her new friends from Mon Rêve.

"Happy birthday! Happy birthday!" Everyone descended on Sake with hugs and wishes.

"I hope you're not too overwhelmed," said Meri. "But we couldn't let your special day pass without a celebration . . . just us family and a few friends."

Char joined in. "Nice timing, being born on September first. With the crush starting, Papa didn't have time to rally his friends for this little celebration."

"The desserts are all from Mon Rêve," said Sauvignon, showing her the spread on the buffet table. "Your coworkers made sure to bring all your favorites."

Jeanne poured her a cup of tea, which Sake almost spilled on the carpet when Bill squeezed her opposite side in his one-armed hug.

"You knew," she said accusingly, feeling her eyes dancing.

"Dude. Only since last night, after you were asleep."

She sampled the amazing food created by Jeanne and the bakers at Mon Rêve while she listened to the simultaneous chatter of her sisters and the others that filled the room with a joyful noise. And then Meri brought her a small box tied up in a silk ribbon.

Sake smiled apologetically. "I think I know what this is."

Of course, it was the bracelet Sake had returned in her fit of pique, months ago, when she was still resentful of Papa bringing her here. But that wasn't all. There was also another bracelet, custom made for Sake.

"See this? It has a Japanese character charm, copied from that tattoo on your right arm. I'm thinking of doing a whole line based on these. I think they'd be real conversation starters. Maybe you could help?"

Then, Char gave her—*a chef's kit?*

"Um, this is great. . . ." Sake said, perplexed, unzipping the canvas bag.

"See?" said Char, reaching into the bag. "You've got all these different sizes and shapes of knives—don't ask me—and whatever this thingy is—"

"I think that's a melon baller," laughed Sake.

"Right! Who doesn't know that? A tool to ball melons. And this doodad . . ."

"Lemon zester," supplied Sake.

"Of course! Lemon zester."

"How did you know I like shiny things?" But Sake wasn't sure when she'd actually *use* those tools . . . until Sauvignon handed her an envelope.

"This kind of goes along with Char's gift," she explained. "I heard you were interested in applying to the CIA. When Char told me what a rat your old employer was, that he wouldn't even write a letter verifying that you'd worked there six months, I made a phone call. This ought to take care of it."

The letter was signed by Tom Latimer, the new owner of Bunz.

Savvy winked. "Having a sister who's a lawyer can come in handy. Keep that in mind."

Mr. Volant, who had been watching, stepped up. "And I'll be happy give you that letter of recommendation. With hopes, of course, that you'll stay on at Mon Rêve. At least until you become a famous pastry chef."

At the word "famous," Sake pulled a face.

Jeanne presented Sake with three heavy white aprons, monogrammed with her name.

"Now you have everything that you need." Char glowed.

"Not quite," said a voice.

Sake turned to see Papa's assistant, Bruno. From behind his back he flourished a piece of hard-sided luggage in a screaming print: yellow with red and orange and blue hearts scribbled all over it.

Sake held it out. "This is a masterpiece of funk!"

Gravely, he pronounced, "It is my responsibility to see that any daughter of my employer is equipped with the necessary *accoutrements* to travel in style."

"I'm glad you take your job seriously," joked one of the men.

They heard footsteps and everyone looked up to see Papa in the doorway. He was decked out in cowboy boots and a bandana, his eyes white holes where his aviators had been on a sunburnt face. Dusty and dirty, he looked like a man in his element. He spread his arms when he saw them sitting there.

"Here you are, all of my girls, in one place."

Without knowing how she did it, Sake found herself running to him.

"Papa."

He folded her into his arms *"Ma chérie,"* he said into her hair. *"Joyeux anniversaire.* Come out to the patio with me. I can only stay a moment before I must go back to work. The grapes, they will not wait, not even for birthdays."

Outside by the pool, Papa turned to face her. "My lawyer told me what you said to the authorities about the logbook."

She looked down at her own boots and shook her head. "All this time, I've been blaming you for hiding me." Peering up again, she asked, "Why didn't you tell me it was Haha who kept us apart?"

He cupped her head against his chest so that his voice was a rumble against her ear when he replied, "I would never say anything to turn my daughters against their mothers."

Is Haha really the only one who had behaved badly? Sake wondered as she basked in the comfort of her father's embrace.

"I remember well the day you were born. I held you in my arms; it was I who named you Sake. Everything was good for a while."

Sake pulled back from him. "But . . ." She didn't know how to sugarcoat it. "You were married to someone else. How was I 'good'?"

On a sigh, he looked across the pool, out toward the distant mountains. "There are many different kinds of marriages, *ma chérie.* I hope you will only ever know about the good kind." When he returned his gaze to hers, his eyes were filled with a fathomless sadness.

Then he broke into a smile. "Do you recall the house on Eugenia Avenue?"

"Yes! My favorite house! Back when everything was still normal . . ."

"I found that place for you and Haha. But eventually, things changed. I would come to visit, and you weren't there. And one day, I came only to find that Haha had moved out, and taken you with her."

"But why didn't you do something?"

"Go through the courts? And have you taken from your mother? I considered it. Perhaps if you had been a boy. But I couldn't take a girl from her mother. I saw what it did to the others."

When her sisters' mom died.

"And so I simply waited . . . all the while, trying to keep up with your whereabouts. Always hoping the day would come when you could draw your own conclusions."

He held her at arm's length, looking at her with fondness. "And now that day is finally here. Now you are home, where you belong."

Suddenly he frowned, tilting his head from side to side. "Where are your earrings?"

"It doesn't matter. It's all good, now."

"Almost. You have fulfilled your part of our arrangement, and now, as promised, I will fulfill mine."

In all that had happened, Sake had almost forgotten all about their pact.

"There is an account in your name at my bank. My finance man, Thomas, will be texting you with the information."

Chapter 30

Later that fall

Sake and Bill, their hands full, breezed past each other at the screen door. Bill was bringing in Papa's gift of a bottle of wine and Jeanne's bouquet of the last sunflowers of the season, and Sake was taking another tray of warm brioche and strawberry jam out to the backyard.

"Nice buns," said Bill, holding the door open with his back, eyes aimed somewhat south of Sake's tray. "I'll be right behind you with the drinks."

She flushed with pleasure at his compliment and her stress—the *good* kind of stress that came from having your very first party at your very first house turn out to be a raging success.

Sake's sisters and their men had come and gone at the beginning of the afternoon and Bill's parents were just leaving as Papa and Jeanne arrived. Now Bill and Sake had given the last house tour of the day—all except for the one upstairs bedroom.

Sake should have been exhausted, but she was giddy.

"See that woman with the short blond hair in the red sweater? Her name's Carly and we're the same age! And she's a food blogger and she just moved three doors down from here last month! We're practically *twins!* Wouldn't that be cool if you hit it off with her husband?"

"I met another golfer. *Score.* Maybe I'll get a match in yet this year."

"And the other one, over by the hydrangea bush—oh, I forget her name—the redhead? We saw each other walking our dogs the other morning but we were both too shy to introduce ourselves. We'll probably be seeing each other every day!"

"Hey, do we have any vases?" asked Bill from over at the sink, looking lost with his armful of flowers.

"You poor man. Just use a pitcher. You can run upstairs and check on"—she glanced furtively out toward where Papa and Jeanne waited beneath the big elm—"*you know.*"

"I've got it covered. Remember the code word?"

"Shhh! When you say *golf.*"

Sake wove through the yard full of smiling faces, hands plucking brioche off her tray as she went.

"Word of your baking skills is spreading," Jeanne told Sake. "I'd better sample this while there's still some left."

"I got the recipe at CIA," Sake said, the reference to her college popping out of her mouth before she knew it. She'd managed to get into the fall semester by the skin of her teeth.

Papa smiled an *I-told-you-so* smile. "School is going well?"

She rolled her eyes. "You were right. Is that what you've been waiting to hear? Best. Idea. Ever." She grinned sheepishly.

Papa took a tiny pink box out of his pants pocket and deposited it in her palm. "Do you know? You have made me very happy," he said, enclosing her hand in both of his for a moment.

"What is this?"

He kissed both her cheeks. "Something for you to open later. To replace what was rightfully yours."

Her earrings.

"It's important that my daughters know they are all loved equally."

Bill appeared, carrying the drinks tray. He set it on the picnic table, then handed Papa and Jeanne their wineglasses and Sake her steaming mug of tea.

Papa raised his glass to Bill. "I understand congratulations are due to you. You sold Russ Cross's strip center to Cornerstone Properties."

"Yes, sir. Thanks to Sake, here." Bill tossed an arm around Sake's shoulder.

"All I did was mention how hard you work and that you'd had a bad break," said Sake. "Who knew Walter was the owner of Cornerstone?"

"*And*, described the property to a T, even down to the location," added Bill. "Now he has me looking for other, similar properties for him. I'm going to be so busy, I'll have this mortgage paid off in no time."

"Well," Papa said, "cheers to both of you."

Sake clinked her mug along with the others, then held it in both hands to ward off the autumn chill.

Looking up through crispy gold and orange leaves to the sapphire northern California sky, Jeanne said, "The colors of these leaves are stunning."

"Bill's actually looking forward to breaking in his new rake."

"The leg, she doesn't trouble you?" asked Papa.

"It's good as new. But between being laid up over the summer and now having a yard to take care of, who knows when I'll ever play *golf* again."

Sake lit up. "Hold on. I got something to show you."

Moments later, she returned holding a wriggling, white ball of fur.

"What do you have there?" asked Papa. He set down his glass and came toward her.

Carefully, Sake transferred the squirming puppy to Papa's arms.

"Ha. Well, well," he said, scratching the dog on the head. "Look at this. What is his name?"

"He doesn't have one yet," said Sake.

"But where did he come from?"

"Taylor was lost for a couple of weeks in the middle of the summer. Must've had a thing with some hot dog."

"More like a fling with a Vienna sausage. There is only one?"

"She probably was really stressed, not getting enough to eat, sleeping wherever she could find a quiet spot. She may have miscarried others, or maybe this one was all there ever was."

"But—" Jeanne looked around warily. "His mother? She's not—"

"She's fine. I know how you feel about dogs, Jeanne. Taylor's up in the extra bedroom."

"Sake took Taylor to the vet as soon as she came home," said Bill. "The only thing we can figure is if she had just been impregnated, the vet wouldn't have been able to feel the puppy—or puppies—in there."

Though she remained on the fringe, Jeanne seemed to be growing more and more intrigued with the bundle Papa cuddled against his jacket.

Suddenly the puppy surprised Papa with an unexpected flip, nearly leaping out of his arms.

"Oh!" Jeanne lunged forward, hands reaching out to break his fall. "Attention, Xavier! You almost dropped him!"

Papa chuckled calmly. "Our little friend here is a *beau cabot*. A shameless actor who likes the attention. Honey, maybe you should show me the right way to hold him."

Honey?

"No, I—"

Papa gently pressed the pup to Jeanne's breast, leaving her no choice. The pup immediately snuggled up under her chin.

"You see?" Papa said. *"Un beau cabot* if ever there was one."

Jeanne turned away to hide her smile and walk slowly across the yellow grass to the other edge of the yard where she couldn't be over-heard whispering into the puppy's ear. But try hiding a cute baby animal. She was stopped at least twice by other partiers, oohing and ahhing over him.

Behind her back, Bill and Sake grinned conspiratorially.

Finally Jeanne circled back, one hand cupping the puppy's bottom and the other protecting his body like a shield.

Papa said, "It looks like you have made a new friend."

"Cabot is not like other dogs. What will you do with him?" she asked Sake.

"Whoa, whoa, whoa," Sake exclaimed, waving her hands in protest. Her idea was working even better than she'd hoped. "I can't take—'Cabot'—away from his mother. Bill and I are keeping both of them. But, hey, thanks for giving him a name. You can visit whenever you want. Do you want me to take him now?"

But Cabot's eyes had drifted shut.

"Shhh! Not now!" Jeanne said softly. "He's just gotten warm and comfortable." She turned to do another circuit of the garden perimeter.

"Well played." Papa nodded with a twinkle, after she was gone. "Well played."

"Dude. Got any more of this Lite?"

Sake turned to see her new acquaintance, Carly, clinging to the arm of a guy wearing a wrinkled patchwork blazer and loafers with no socks. The guy held his can upside down to indicate to Bill it was empty.

Sake, barely able to contain her grin, locked eyes with Bill.

He lit up. "Sure do! BRB."

* * *

Bill regarded the horde trampling his grass as he hefted yet another case of brewskis out to the big tin ice bucket on the patio. The whole lawn was going to need to be aerated, and as soon as that job was done, it would probably be time to rake the leaves. Finding time for that golf match was looking more and more improbable.

All the way back at the end of the yard, under the elm tree, Sake caught his eye. There, cupping her mug of tea, bootie'd feet planted in the garden, she positively bloomed.

Hole in one, Bill Diamond. Hole. In. One.

Rapid Fire Q&A with Heather Heyford

What author had a profound effect on you?

LaVyrle Spencer

What do you wish you'd known from the beginning?

Do what feels right, not what others tell you to do.

What is the best compliment you ever received?

Someone once told me I'm the kindest person she knows.

Do you believe in writer's block?

Writing from the heart is the best antidote.

What is your favorite wine?

Kim Crawford Sauvignon Blanc from Marlborough, New Zealand

Did you always want to be a writer?

My dad's side of the family values education and books, while my mom's people are creative types. I've always painted and had a knack for fiber art, and I think I was born knowing how to read, LOL. After teaching art for a while and getting my work into a gallery, there was a story in my head, banging to get out. For me, happiness is a balance of writing and making beautiful things.

Recipe for Crème Brulee

Thanks to Chef Elizabeth at Harrisburg Area Community College for allowing me to observe her class on making custard desserts. The most fun part of preparing this easy yet impressive dish is using the kitchen torch to caramelize the sugar on top. The prep doesn't take long, but plan ahead. This dish requires 4 hours to chill and a half hour to return to room temperature before caramelizing.

1 vanilla bean
2 cups heavy whipping cream
6 egg yolks
⅓ cup sugar plus 8 teaspoons for caramelizing
Boiling water

Once you are familiar with the safe use of the kitchen torch, pre-heat oven to 350°F. Split and scrape the vanilla bean. Place the cream and the vanilla bean and its pulp into a saucepan and bring just to a boil. Remove from the heat, cover, and allow to sit for 15 minutes. Discard the bean pod or save for another use.

Set 4 (6 oz.) ceramic (not glass) ramekins into a 13x9-inch baking pan. In a large bowl, lightly whisk egg yolks. Add 1/3 cup sugar and mix well. Stir in the vanilla cream a little at a time, until blended. Divide mixture among ramekins.

Place pan with ramekins on an oven rack. Pour boiling water into the pan to two-thirds of the height of the ramekins.

Bake 35 minutes, or until top is golden.

Using oven mitts, carefully remove ramekins from water bath. Cool to room temperature, then cover with plastic wrap and chill 4 hours in the fridge, until set.

Remove from fridge and let sit for 30 minutes. Sprinkle 2 teaspoons sugar over each ramekin. Holding a ramekin in your non-dominant hand, caramelize the top by holding a kitchen torch 3 to 4 inches from custard, moving it in a circular motion until a light golden-brown crust forms.

Makes 4 servings.

Want to spend more time in Napa?

Keep reading for teasers from

the first three books in the

Napa Wine Heiresses series:

A TASTE OF CHARDONNAY

A TASTE OF MERLOT

and

A TASTE OF SAUVIGNON

HEATHER HEYFORD

A Taste of Chardonnay

THE NAPA WINE HEIRESSES

A TASTE OF CHARDONNAY

"Are you my Realtor?"

Chardonnay St. Pierre tried to hide her wariness as she approached the man who'd just stepped out of his retro pickup truck. This wasn't the best section of Napa city.

Their vehicles sat skewed at odd angles in the lot of the concrete building with the AVAILABLE banner sagging along one side. Around the back, gorse and thistles grew waist-high through the cracks in the pavement.

A startlingly white grin spread below the man's aviators.

"Realtor? You waiting for one?"

For the past half hour. "He's late." Char went up on her tiptoes, craning her neck to peer down the street for the tenth time, but the avenue was still empty. She tsked under her breath. She should've taken time after her run to change out of her skimpy running shorts, she thought, reaching discreetly around to give the hems a yank down over her butt. And her Mercedes looked more than a little conspicuous in this neighborhood.

Where was he? She pulled her cell out of her bag to call the Realtor back. But something about the imposing stranger was distracting her, demanding another look. "Have we met?" She squinted, lowering her own shades an inch.

He turned sideways without answering and examined the nondescript building, and when he did, his profile gave him dead away.

Oh my god. Char's breath caught, but he didn't notice. His whole focus was on the real estate. She'd just seen that face smiling out from the People magazine at the market over on Solano when she'd picked up some last-minute items for tonight's party.

"What have you got planned for the place?" he asked, totally un-self-consciously.

Then she recovered. To the rest of the world, he was Hollywood's latest It Man. But to Char, he was just another actor. Who happened to have a really great dentist.

"I could ask you the same thing."

"I asked first."

Though she wasn't at all fond of actors, her shoulders relaxed a little. Obviously, she wasn't going to get raped out here in broad daylight by the star of First Responder. It was still in theaters, for heaven's sake. He couldn't afford the press.

Still. This building was perfect. And it'd been sitting here empty for the past three years. Just her luck that another party would be interested, right when Char was finally in a position to inquire about it.

To Char's relief, a compact car with a real estate logo plastered from headlights to tailpipe pulled up and a guy in his early thirties bounded out with an abundance of nervous energy.

"This business is insane," he said by way of introduction. "Dude calls me from a drive-by and wants me to show it to him, like, now, right? So I drop everything, even though I'm swamped with this new development all the way over on Industrial Drive. And then he doesn't show up till quarter of—"

He caught himself, pasted on a proper smile, and extended his hand toward It Man.

"Bill Diamond. And you're Mister . . . ?"

"McBride." The actor shook his hand, then turned and sauntered back to the building with his hands on his hips and his eyes scrutinizing its roofline.

"Ryder McBride?" asked Diamond. "The Ryder McBride? Oh!" A smile overspread his face. "Cool! Very cool. Nice to meet you, man." He nodded once for emphasis.

Char stepped up, removing her sunglasses and slipping them over the deep V of her racer-back tee.

"Hi." She thrust out her arm. "I'm—"

The Realtor's eyes grew even wider, as his hand reached for hers.

"I know who you are. . . . Chardonnay St. Pierre."

He was still holding on when Char's phone vibrated in her other palm. One glance at the screen and she sighed.

"Excuse me."

But Diamond didn't let go.

"I've got to take this," she repeated, pronouncing each syllable slow and clear. She gave a little tug, and he came to, his fingers relaxing. "It's my little sister."

She ducked her chin and pressed answer.

"Where are you?" Meri's voice sounded tense.

"Downtown."

"You've got to come meet Savvy and me. Papa's in jail."

Bill Diamond was still gaping when Char dropped her phone into her shoulder bag.

"I'm so sorry. Something important's come up and I have to run."

Like a guy who'd come to expect disappointment at every turn, his face fell. "Oh."

Char felt a stab of empathy.

"Did you want to reschedule?" His brows shot up hopefully.

It was a given. But right now concern for her family eclipsed everything else. "I'll have to call you."

As she turned to go, Ryder spoke up.

"I'm staying. Mind showing me around?"

Char stopped in her tracks halfway to her car and glared back at him. She thought he'd barely noticed her. But she'd swear his broad grin was designed purely to tease.

"Excuse me? This is my Realtor."

"Ah, actually . . ." Bill cleared his throat, looked at the ground, and then back up at her. "I work for the seller."

"But I'm the one who called you to meet me here," she insisted.

He looked from Char to Ryder and back as he juggled his options, then shrugged. "But you're leaving."

Char's thoughts raced. She hated to leave those two here together, to cook up some deal to steal the building out from under her, but she had no choice. "Fine. Bill, I'll be in touch," she called, climbing into her car, then pulling out of the lot a little too fast.

She loved Papa. Truly, she did. But at times like these, she'd give anything for an ordinary, run-of-the-mill dad, in place of the notorious Xavier St. Pierre.

HEATHER HEYFORD

A Taste of Merlot

THE NAPA WINE HEIRESSES

A TASTE OF MERLOT

Grinning so hard her cheeks might burst, Merlot St. Pierre wove through the tightly packed crowd to the front of the art gallery, the jingling of her trademark stack of bracelets obscured by polite applause.

When she finally reached the podium, she clutched its clear acrylic edges and paused to commit the scene to memory, her gaze bouncing from face to familiar face. A rare sense of belonging washed over her, satisfying—if only for the moment—a cavernous emptiness inside.

Chardonnay and Sauvignon had even driven down from Napa for the annual exhibit—though not Papa, of course. He was perpetually busy, tied up in the never-ending cycle of planting, picking, and pressing grapes. Savvy smiled maternally, and Char brushed away a proud tear. Though they tried to blend in by hugging the wall at the back of the room, her sisters' expensive clothes and skyscraper heels elevated them to another class altogether. From a casual glance, nobody would've tagged Meri, in her scuffed flats and faded jeans, as their sister.

Just as well.

Meri waited for the clapping to taper off, then leaned into the mic. "To the Gates faculty, thank you from the bottom of my heart for this award. And to my fellow students, our shared appreciation for the craft I hope to spend the rest of my life perfecting fuses us together like one big, extended family."

The kind Meri had always wanted.

And in less time than it had taken to walk to the podium, her speech—and with it, the reception—was over.

Ten minutes later, still basking in the glow of her achievement, Meri excused herself from a small circle of well-wishers for a quick trip to the ladies' room. Hidden behind the stall door, she heard footsteps, followed by a voice.

"Did you see her up there?"

Meri's hand froze at the lock. She knew who that was. Her portfolio storage slot adjoined Meri's. They came in contact almost daily.

"The wine princess? I know. Made me want to gag. But you know how it is: 'Them that has, gets.' " Chelsey. Meri had known her since freshman year. "Still, it's not fair! She doesn't need the accolades. The rest of us are going to have to eke out a living, for real. How does she get the Purchase Prize?"

With shocked dismay, Meri flattened her palms against the door, cocked an ear, and held her breath, straining to hear through the sound of water running in the sink and paper towels being ripped from the dispenser. That first voice belonged to Rainn—like Meri, a jewelry major, except that she was a graduating senior and Meri still had another year to go.

"How do you think? Her old man donated a gazillion bucks to the college."

"Hmph," came another, mocking snort. "Should've guessed."

"Art is her hobby," said Rainn. It was the ultimate insider insult. "Everybody knows she'll never be a real jeweler. Just go back to Daddy's mansion and become a professional shopper."

"Have you seen it?" Chelsey asked.

"The winery? Only in pictures."

"She invited me up one time, over winter break. The pictures don't do it justice. Even if she does keep making jewelry after graduation, she'll never have to make a living at it. It's not fair. She's taking up space here that could've been given to a real artist. No wonder she calls her line 'Gilty.' "

Derisive laughter rang off the lavatory tiles. Still hidden, Meri cringed and squeezed her eyes closed, desperate for it to be over.

"C'mon, you look fine. It's the last Thirsty Thursday at O'Brien's. Everyone'll be there."

Everyone? Meri had spent last Thursday night hunched over her bench hook, buffing her final project. She'd been invited to O'Brien's once—back in the fall, after her twenty-first birthday—about the same time she'd developed a fascination with the historical uses of gemstones. She'd declined the offer in order to do research. She'd never been invited again.

A door creaked, and blessedly, the voices receded.

In a fog, Meri sank slowly onto the toilet seat and stared down at her cracked, work-stained fingertips until they all blurred together in her tears.

It was Mark Newman's idea to troll end-of-year student shows for fresh blood. While his boss at Harrington's was at least willing to humor him, if she'd had her druthers he'd be sticking with the stale, tried-and-true vendors.

After finding a parking spot, he walked all the way across the Gates College of Art and Design campus, only to find he was at the wrong building and had to cut back. He'd probably miss the speeches, but that was of no consequence. Receptions were for friends, family, and colleagues. Mark was there solely to see the work.

He'd scouted art schools in Chicago, Miami, and New York that spring, and so far, nothing had grabbed him. Where was all the new talent? Maybe Gloria was right, these excursions weren't worth the trouble.

He browsed through the two-dimensional art, the video installations, the ceramics and sculpture, saving the best for last. A leisurely, methodical sweep of the gallery was his way of pinpointing the location of the jewelry display cases, and as usual, he made a game out of it, letting the anticipation build, deciding which case he'd examine first and which he'd save for last.

When he finally got to the fixture in the center of the room, his roving eye came to an abrupt halt at five strands of flat braid connected by a perpendicular clasp. The alternating metals—yellow, white, and rose gold—lent fresh appeal to the simple design. Next to it, a royal-blue card with the words PURCHASE PRIZE sat slightly askew, a last-minute addition to the carefully arranged display. The piece begged to be touched, stroked—always a sign of good art. No wonder Gates had elected to buy it for its permanent collection over all the other projects created that year.

Mark looked up, his enthusiasm building by the second. Only a few people remained in the gallery, congregating quietly on the opposite side of the room. Deftly, he tried slipping his fingers into the crack between the lid and the side of the case. Locked, of course.

Pulling out his jeweler's magnifying loupe, he bent close, straining to examine the piece as best he could through the layer of glass, to read the name on the hand-drawn tag attached by a silken cord.

GILTY. That was aggravating. He wanted a real name. On the other hand, the craftsmanship was outstanding. He'd never get over what could be achieved with simple tools in talented hands. Retail was his business, but design was his passion. Design, food, and football, in that order.

He let his loupe fall from the black leather thong around his neck and draped his hands possessively around the corners of the wide case, pulse quickening with the thrill of discovery. There had to be someone in authority here, someone with a key.

The reception was really winding down now; there was a growing trickle toward the exit. Mark didn't see anyone wearing a name tag. He went up behind two women who might be students.

"Excuse me." His voice sounded surprisingly calm, given how hard his heart thrummed. "Quick question."

The young women half-turned, their blank faces sizing him up with mild annoyance. Simultaneously, their eyes widened as they turned fully and broke out in cat-like smiles.

"Anything," the shorter, sultry-looking one purred, giving Mark a glimpse of the shiny barbell puncturing the center of her tongue.

Down, girl. Damn. He'd have to wear this old shirt more often.

"There's a mixed-metal bracelet over there with a tag that says 'Gilty.' The Purchase Prize winner. Know whose work it is?"

Their smiles went sour. The one with blue hair and a sleeve tattoo opened her mouth to speak but was interrupted by Barbell Girl.

"No idea," she interjected, eyeing Mark's loupe. "But hey, do you have a card or something? I can ask around. . . ."

"I'd appreciate it," he said, reaching into his back pocket.

"I'm Rainn, and this is Chelsey." Rainn lowered her lids while she drew a lengthy lock of raven-colored hair through stubby fingers, then tossed it back.

"Mark Newman." He peeled off a few cards and held them out.

"Harrington's?" Her smile morphed from merely seductive to blatantly opportunistic, displaying beautiful, white teeth. Individually they were perfect little pearls, but strung together they formed a wolfish grin that was downright unsettling.

"Nice meeting you. If you run into Gilty, have her—or him—give me a call."

He returned to the case, snapped some photos through the glass, and left the building.

He'd already forgotten the two students when he noticed them again across the street from the gallery, heads still bowed over his card like it was the key to the Grail.

He couldn't help smiling to himself. For an aspiring jeweler, it was.

As he walked back to his car, he pulled out his phone and scrolled for Gilty online, but nothing showed up.

So he'd call the school, first thing tomorrow morning.

He brightened with anticipation. Purchase Prize? He'd show them a purchase prize.

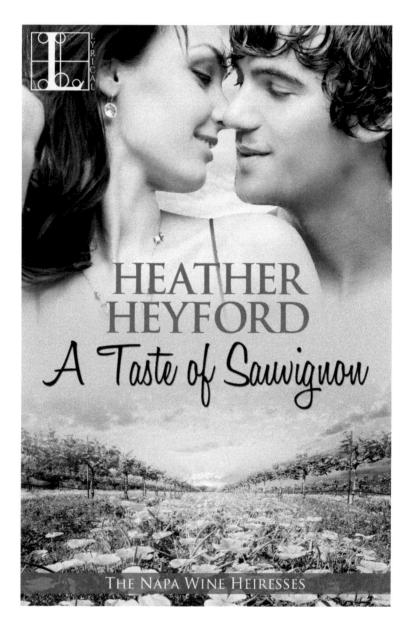

HEATHER HEYFORD

A Taste of Sauvignon

THE NAPA WINE HEIRESSES

A TASTE OF SAUVIGNON

Sauvignon St. Pierre pulled the first little black dress from the left side of the rod in her precision-tuned walk-in closet. Later that evening, she would replace it on its padded hanger and hang it to the far right. And so on for the next two months, until today's dress came back into rotation.

From neat rows of acrylic boxes, each with a photo of its contents taped onto the end, she picked out a pair of two-and-a-half-inch black pumps.

The only aspect of her workday routine that couldn't be pre-arranged was which of her myriad fragrances to wear. Not even *she* could plan her mood ahead of time.

This morning, her hand hovered over flagons of every shape and pastel hue before landing on Maman's special rose perfume . . . for luck.

Savvy had made a calculated decision to become a lawyer when she was only thirteen. Fourteen years, three hundred thousand dollars in tuition, and two progressively thicker lenses later, she'd been offered a junior position with a small firm in her Napa hometown—either *because* her last name was St. Pierre, or in spite of it. And today, at the weekly meeting, she was finally being assigned her own case.

At precisely eight-thirty-five, one porcelain cup of chamomile tea, one bowl of Greek yogurt, and half a banana later, she slid into her black Mercedes to make it to her law office in time for the crucial nine o'clock meeting.

She looked both ways before steering the sleek sedan out of the long gravel drive of Domaine St. Pierre onto Dry Creek Road. Her car cut a perpendicular path between rows of yellow-green mustard flower buds alternating with what appeared to be dead sticks wedged upright in the soil. It was only March, though. The sap was rising. By summer, the mustard would be over and those "sticks," laden with leaves and berries, would steal the show, drawing thousands upon thousands of tourists to Napa Valley—doubling her drive time to and from work. But this morning, there was no other vehicle in sight.

She double-checked her reflection in the rearview to make sure the gold clasp on her pearls lay on her collarbone, just so. Then she pinched an earlobe to secure a diamond ear stud, brushed a microscopic speck of lint from her shoulder, and cupped the chignon at the base of her neck.

Satisfied that all was in order, she began a mental preview of the day. She fast-forwarded, picturing herself seated side by side with the firm's partners around the long conference table, eager for the chance to finally prove herself worthy of someday becoming the first female partner at Witmer, Robinson and Scott.

"Diana! Susanna! *¡Vuelve!* Come back!"

Esteban leaned on the handle of his pitchfork, grinning as he watched his mother toddle after a clutch of her errant Ameracaunas. Expertly, she snatched up a hen into the crook of her arm and brandished a threatening finger in her face. *"¡Chica traviesa!* You naughty girl. How many times do I have to tell you do not go down the lane, eh?" Beneath her long strokes, the chicken's feathers flickered iridescent gold, green, and orange in the morning light. She softened her tone to a tender purr. "My beautiful little *chica*."

Esteban shook his head. Madre was as fond of those stupid birds as she was of him and his sister. If possible, her attachment to her "girls" seemed to have only deepened, now that Esmerelda was married and living in Santa Rosa.

"Esteban! Can you look at the fence again? My *chicas* must have poked another hole somewhere," his mother pleaded, gently setting Marlena down with the others to shoo them back toward the paddock.

"Sí, Madre," he said, lapsing briefly into his native tongue.

Away from the farm, Esteban prided himself on his command of English. Mr. Bloomquist at Vintage High had even offered to write him a college recommendation.

"Your chem teacher said she'd write one, too," he'd coaxed. "We agree it would be a waste of your verbal and analytical skills not to continue your education. You could start out at NVCC and transfer to a four-year school later. . . ."

Esteban had been helping out on the family farm ever since he could lift a spade, but he'd never questioned why it was that plants were green. When he'd learned that what made them that way was a substance called chlorophyll that captured the sun's energy to make sugar out of air and water, he'd been fascinated. From then on, he'd been somewhat of a science geek.

After Mr. Bloomquist's offer, he'd imagined himself for a minute in a white lab coat, peering through a microscope at chloroplasts and ribosomes. The thought had made his scalp tingle.

But Esteban Morales was born to be a farmer. What would Padre do without him?

"This afternoon," he responded to Madre. First he needed to check on the effect of last night's rain on his tender lavender plants. The worst thing for lavender was mold.

Another stray—Natalia?—ran helter-skelter into Esteban's field of vision, down the muddy lane from where Padre had already thinned celery seedlings in the truck gardens earlier in the morning, past the paddock and the house toward Dry Creek Road. *¡Mierda!* Was he actually beginning to distinguish one of the flighty creatures from another?

"No this afternoon—now!" Madre scolded. She grabbed her broom from the porch and used it to sweep Natalia back toward the paddock. "You see this?" She gestured animatedly. "Before they all run onto the road and get hit by a car, and I have no chickens, no eggs, no money to pay the bills!"

Esteban chuckled under his breath. The Morales family would never be rich, yet they were hardly in dire straits. Losing a random eight-dollar chicken here and there wouldn't break the bank.

"Okay, okay."

Madre's appreciative grin was a reminder of her unconditional love, no matter how stern she pretended to be.

He continued in the direction of the shed. "I'll go get my tools."

Seconds later, he cringed at the squeal of rubber on asphalt and a sickening, avian screech.

Savvy slammed on the brakes the moment the chicken darted into view, but too late. She felt a thump, heard a squawk, and cringed. *I can't be late for work! Not today!* Yet something about the stricken expression on the face of the farm woman toddling toward her stabbed at her heart.

Mrs. Morales. She'd seen her stout silhouette a hundred times from a distance as she drove past the modest ranch house on Dry Creek Road, but she'd never met her next-door neighbor face-to-face. Still, thanks to Jeanne, the St. Pierre cook, she knew all about the Moraleses. Jeanne bought vegetables from their stand at the Napa farmers market. As far back as grade school, Jeanne had been rattling on about the Moraleses, their daughter, Esmerelda, and son, what's-his-name. But while Jeanne had only good things to say about the family, Papa always said Mr. Morales was nothing but a big pain in the *derriere.*

Savvy threw the gearshift into park, got out, and strode around to the right front tire, bracing for what she might find.

Directly behind the front passenger-side tire lay the deceased—intact, thankfully, but motionless, its beak frozen open in its final squawk.

"Marlena!" The older woman stopped short at the edge of the lane. Her chest heaved with effort. Calloused palms flung in helplessness toward the dead animal. "*Marlena!*" she sobbed.

Savvy looked from Mrs. Morales's furrowed brow to the chicken—er, Marlena—and back.

Lips pressed into a tight line, she swallowed her squeamishness, squatting down for a better look. The last time she'd been this close to a chicken it had been covered in a delicate morel sauce.

What was she supposed to do? She glanced back up at Mrs. Morales to see her cross herself, then back down at Marlena. *Don't birds carry all kinds of diseases? Bird flu? Salmonella? Mites?*

She took a resigned breath, the farm odors of wet earth mingled with manure assaulting her senses, and steeled herself. This was all her fault. It was her responsibility to fix it.

Gingerly, she slid her bare hands under the hen's body. The unfamiliar feel of stiff feathers atop warm jelly—apparently Marlena had been neither smart nor athletic—brought up the taste of bile. Somehow she found the strength to swallow it back.

Slowly, she turned and gently deposited the animal into its owner's outstretched arms.

"*Dios mío.*" Mrs. Morales hugged the hen to a bosom that threatened to ooze from between the buttons of her shirt and rocked the bird, all the while chanting something that sounded like, *sana, sana, colita de rana*—whatever that meant. Obviously, the chicken had been a well-loved pet.

"I'm so sorry!" Savvy cried, torn between the urge to embrace the grieving woman and the longing for a hazmat shower.

And then from out of nowhere, an agrilicious, king-sized man in faded jeans, snug plaid shirt, and silver belt buckle the size of a turkey platter jogged up to them, and in a flash, Savvy forgot all about death and God and germs. She even forgot about work.

Heather Heyford learned to walk and talk in Texas, then moved to England. *("Ya'll want some scones?")*

While in Europe, Heather was forced by her cruel parents to spend Saturdays in the leopard vinyl back seat of their Peugeot, motoring from one medieval pile to the next for the lame purpose of "learning something." What she soon learned was how to allay the boredom by stashing a *Cosmo* under the seat.

Now a recovering teacher, Heather writes romance, feeds hard-boiled eggs to suburban foxes, and makes art in the Mid-Atlantic. She is represented by the Nancy Yost Literary Agency.

CPSIA information can be obtained
at www.ICGtesting.com
Printed in the USA
LVHW01s1134230918
591102LV00001B/145/P